GHOSTS AND EAGLES

THE FUTURE IS CERTAIN

PART 3

D. J. SAWYER

Copyright © 2024 by D.J. Sawyer

All rights reserved. No part of this publication may be reproduced, stored in any form of retrieval system or transmitted in any form or by any means without prior permission in writing by the publishers except for the use of brief quotations in a book review.

ISBN:

Paperback: 9798301628610

www.vexillumpublishing.com

To Karen, Trinity, Daisy and Tig.

Contents

PART 1

I.	A Stabbing	3
II.	Latrine Duties	13
III.	The Miracle of Mithras	29
IV.	Julia	39
V.	Macro's Return	47
VI.	A Brush With The Future	51
VII.	Centurions' Reunion	61
VIII.	Return to The Mansio	77
IX.	Trapped	85
X.	Macro and Julia	95
XI.	A Final Journey	111
XII.	Place of The Yew Trees	123
XIII.	Silent Enemy, Deadly Killer	143
XIV.	The Attacotti	169

PART 2

XV.	Face Masks and Old Bones	181
XVI.	Spades, Shovels, Trowels, and Brushes	199
XVII.	The Jigsaw Pieces of Time	213
XVIII.	A Familiar Face	231
XIX.	Epilogue	245
XX.	A Final Word	249

PART 1

I

A Stabbing

"Same shit, different day," thought the man climbing the stairs leading up to the Staffroom. His slow, banister clutching ascent suggested a weariness with the drudgery of day-to-day routine in running a school for the last twenty-eight years. Gone were the Halcyon days of steering your school as captain of the ship where your word was law, was gospel. His slow laboured ascent gave him a couple of minutes for the hundredth time to look forward to his retirement as well as review with regret those changes he had seen from his early days as a green classroom teacher back in the 1970s, to his rapid rise to a Headship he had once coveted more than life itself. But then came the changes. Time changes everything, nothing stays still. It may sporadically and unaccountably slow to a pace akin to his laboured steps up stairs to the Staffroom, but time is inexorable. You never know what it offers around the corners of days, weeks, years, decades, even centuries ahead. Headmaster Bill Shortland could have no idea what the 'gift-curse' time held for him and his school and the local community in a few hours' time…

Climbing the time worn concrete stairs was slow work these days, much slower than his meteoric rise up the ladder to his Headship. He paused to gather his breath at the top of the staircase where the landing took a sharp left and led to the Staffroom.

"Just over thirty years in this one school," he thought as he took the last step, right hand down and resting on his arthritic knee. He chuckled as he recalled those days as a twenty something year old teacher who could bound up here taking two steps at a time. And that was often well after school hours when he had already completed a ten-mile jog around the local streets and park!

"Oh well, time passes, we age, sometimes almost imperceptibly, but nevertheless, we age."

At the end of the corridor leading to the Staff room, Mr Shortland paused, hand on door handle, to glance through the small window set in the middle of the door. He smiled with relief, spotting the teacher whose help he needed. After school gate duty was now a regular feature in recent years. The Caledonian Road was no longer safe for homeward bound students. Gangs were rife in the area, as was the peddling of drugs right outside the school gates themselves. There had been occasions when Mr Shortland walked to the end of the long school drive down to the Caledonian Road and questioned dubious individuals waiting, ready to prey on pupils as young as Year 7. Kiddie 'sweeties' offered to pupils leaving to go home, free sweets spiked with God knows what substances to hook unwary and innocent children. The Caledonian Road was known to locals as 'The Cally.' Mr Shortland considered himself a local these days.

"Why don't the school cleaners clean properly," he thought noticing the ingrained dirt around the worn brass door knob. Decades of sweaty handed nervous young teachers returning from a particularly challenging lesson with class 'bottom of the pile' in room wherever. Everything was changing in his later years of being in charge. The lady cleaners of previous years, employed by the local council used to do a wonderful job, very thorough. Every square inch of the school cleaned with pride in their work. Even the classroom indoor potted plants were watered throughout the long summer break. These days, left to the tender mercies of the cleaners employed by the private company contracted to replace the council cleaners, the potted plants wilted and died, brown and brittle husks sitting pointlessly in the dust dry soil of plastic flower pots. Nowadays school cleaning was more of a quick hoover and cursory flick of a duster. Everything was changing.

Mr Shortland opened the door and headed over to the teacher sitting at the computer desk at the far end of the staffroom. The thread bare faded grey carpet led the way to where Mr MacRonald sat poring over a pile of mock GCSE Year 10 History papers. He sat back and removed his pince-nez glasses perched on the end of his nose and laid them neatly beside the pile of papers stacked before him.

"Ah, Bill." He smiled up as Mr Shortland leaned forward to rest his hands on the edge of the desk. He was always tired now at the end of these school days which seemed to grow ever longer by the year. He sighed his tiredness in Mr MacRonald's direction.

"Cornelius," he nodded at the pile of exam papers. "Doubtless there are more than a few grade 'A' stars in there after a year studying under your auspices, the inspiration that you are. Mr Legend himself."

"I'm more than hopeful, Bill. We have some very sound prospects here." Mr MacRonald laid his hand palm down on the pile of mock exam papers and patted them.

"Gate duty calls, I guess?"

Bill nodded. "Sorry, Cornelius, I wouldn't ask but.." he turned to look around the Staffroom at the few teachers there during the last period of the day. Mostly young teachers and inexperienced, they could prove more than a liability if asked to stay after school hours to help 'police' the school gates. Anyway, the younger generation of teachers weren't keen on doing more than coming into school, teaching, and going home as soon as possible. Different breed, contrasting times, different attitudes. Gate duty was monotonous, standing at the end of the school drive saying goodbye to hundreds of pupils, the younger ones hurrying, the older students strolling out onto the notorious Caledonian Road. 'The Cally,' was considered one of the most dangerous parts of Islington these days, even by the police who were not too keen to even patrol the area outside the school at the end of the day. Equally, bus drivers often passed the stop just outside the school gates when they saw the gathered hordes of milling kids waiting to board the bus like a rampaging army, little barbarians. Bill glanced at his watch, habit rather than seeking confirmation of the time.

"Half three, then?"

"Half three," replied Cornelius.

Bill turned and walked back out of the Staffroom.

It was quite natural, understandable that Mr MacRonald, a keen historian, knew all there was to know about the history of the Caledonian Road. Dissecting the path of the earlier Holloway Road it was built in the 1800s. Holloway Road took its widely used name from the term 'hollow way', the ghost line of an ancient, usually Saxon trackway which successive generations of travellers' feet wore away until the track ended up lower than the surrounding landscape. The Caledonian Road was named for its Scottish roots and heritage. Caledonia, the region of the British Isles we know as Scotland. Caledonia, the wild unconquerable land of the Caledonians and Picts. That thought made him reach down to his left calf, an instinctive reaction to the throbbing ache which plagued him since that Parthian arrow head ripped into the muscle, leaving a festering poison threatening his life. Thank Mithras the Greek legionary surgeon carried out his butchery with skill enough to remove the arrow head and treat the raging infection. But the pain never went away completely. It stayed with him all the way to the northern frontier of the Empire and retirement from the Sixth Valeria Victrix Legion to the vicus, the civilian settlement outside Vercovicium fort on Hadrian's Wall.

A glance at the Staffroom clock told Mr MacRonald it was time to join the Head down at the school gate. Popping the cap back onto his red biro, he moved the pile of mock exam papers to one side and placed the red biro exactly central on the top of the papers. Everything neat and tidy, an almost military precision proclaimed its presence here. The corridor landing to the Staffroom had one or two downcast, sullen looking miscreants waiting for teachers they had been summoned to see after school. Mr MacRonald smiled at them as he passed by, hoping the walk down to the school gate would ease the nagging pain in his left calf. A little walk often did the trick, like oil lubricating a rusty joint. The trickle of pupils hurrying out of classrooms turned into a tumultuous flood coursing down the central corridor of the school leading to the foyer and reception area where the main entrance to the building opened out onto the school drive leading down to the Caledonian Road. Conscious of the need to hurry, he quickened his pace to keep up with the tide of adolescent uniformed humanity as it called, shouted, and jostled its way down the main drive to where the Headteacher was already waiting.

"Damn." Mr MacRonald hated being late, very unmilitary of him. He was ahead of the tide of pupils behind him, like followers of an ancient biblical prophet. He arrived at the gate to join Mr Shortland, a little breathless and offering a placatory smile.

"Don't worry, Cornelius. No need to apologise. I'm always grateful for your support on gate duty. After all, it's not in your job description," Mr Shortland chortled.

They rubbed their hands together at the same time, although it wasn't cold for the time of year, just an unusually dull, grey July day. The pupil tide swept around the two teachers, turning right, and left onto the Caledonian Road. An untidy, chattering queue milled around the nearby bus stop, at which buses rarely stopped this time of day.

The Scottish heritage of the area first stamped itself on the landscape in the form of the Royal Caledonian Asylum built in 1828 for orphans of Scottish soldiers killed in the Napoleonic Wars. The institution brought with it a sizeable Scottish presence until the building was demolished in 1903. Sadly, that local Scottish community, blighted by poverty and unemployment, had seen the growth of 'post code' wars in recent years. The threat of gang violence along with the local drug problem, meant that school gate duty was a sad fact these days. In keeping with the area, the most notorious local gang went by the name of 'The Cally Brothers.' Their ages ranged from ten years to early twenties. Scum, Scottish scum from an extensive line of warring gangs plaguing the Gorbals slums, dating back to parents, grandparents, great grandparents and beyond, lost in the mists of time. Mr MacRonald recalled history, the gangs of Ancient Rome, wielding influence as much as the ruling classes themselves, Knights, Senators and even Emperors.

The real world broke into his musings. A bus roared past, in its wake howls of disappointment and indignation from the untidy queue of pupils. Mr MacRonald watched as the bus sped off along the Caledonian Road, coming to an untimely halt behind the last vehicle in an unexpected traffic jam barely two hundred yards down the road. With yells of triumph edged with hope, the ragged bus stop gaggle broke up and chased after the stranded bus. The pupils ran with no thought of safety for themselves or consideration of other road users, piling into, across and along the Caledonian Road, zigzagging between the traffic, coats flapping, school bags clutched tight. Perhaps they would catch the bus, perhaps not. One thing was certain, the bus driver would not be opening the doors however much the 'little savages' hammered at them and howled their demands for entry. He would stare ahead stoically, ignoring the 'barbarians at the gates.'

Something caught the eye of Mr Shortland. He nodded at Mr MacRonald, followed by further nod down the road to their right.

"Interesting, Cornelius. Looks much like the lot who turned up a couple of weeks ago, if I'm not mistaken." He was shielding his eyes now and peering at the approaching group of youths. They walked in a tight huddle, indistinguishable the one from the other. Standard uniform, hoodie, 'trackie' bottoms, a calculated impersonal, generic mix of blacks and greys.

"Pick that up now, boy!" The miscreant scooped up the sweet wrapper before it took flight on a gust of wind.

"Sorry Mr Shortland, sir." Rubbish retrieved the boy hurried away to merge with the army of his compatriots streaming down Caledonian Road.

Mr Shortland returned his gaze to the group of nondescript youths approaching the school gates. They halted twenty metres away, looking for all the world like a harmless bunch, with no other than their laughter and horseplay. And yet, there was something about that laughter. It sounded unreal and menacing, more like an icy tinkle than a normal teenage laugh. The 'Cally Brothers' knew nothing of laughter unless it was as a result of someone else's pain or loss. One or two of them now cast thin, rat faced glances towards where the two teachers stood.

The earlier tsunami to leave the school at the end of the day, now subsided into a trickle of upper school students who liked to keep their dignity by strolling down the school drive, chatting casually, and conducting themselves in an adult fashion.

"Should've brought the umbrella." Mr Shortland looked up at the grey heavens from where a fine mist of drizzle was falling, beading his and Mr MacRonald's jackets.

"Shit weather for early July."

"Mmm." Mr MacRonald agreed and squinted up into the drizzle. A quick glance at his watch told him it was four fifteen. He wiped away the drizzle beading the watch face with the ball of his thumb to confirm the time, pulled the jacket sleeve down before thrusting both hands into his coat pockets. There was a chill in the air despite the time of year. This damp weather would not make a good weekend for the re-enactment society. They were due to pursue their past time camping in a field in West Sussex, two contuburnium, sixteen men of like-minded ancient warfare enthusiasts living, dressing, and equipped as Roman legionaries from the VI Valeria Victrix legion. He always felt a mixture of, he never knew quite what really; re-enacting today a life you had lived two thousand years ago brought its own problems and certainly not ones you talked to your companions in arms about. Especially when they commented on his beautiful gladius, just how realistic it was and 'where could they buy such an authentic looking replica?' Mr MacRonald smiled to himself at the recent memory of retrieving his two-thousand-year-old gladius from the sniffy journalist at The Northumberland County News.

"Sorry, Bill, I didn't quite catch that."

"I was saying that as soon as these lads have passed us, I think we'll stop for the day. I'll get us sorted with a cup of coffee in my office." The Headteacher squinted up into the now more insistent drizzle and pulled his jacket collar up. "Turning even chillier now."

They say that the sensation of being stabbed with a knife is akin to being punched. You don't realise at first what has happened. You think it's just a punch, then the blood flows, seeping through your clothes. You put your hand on where the pain is. It feels warm and damp, then you see the crimson and you know. Shock and horror, realisation, panic, if you don't faint first. And so it was with Mr MacRonald. His attempt to intervene in a 'beef' between a member of the 'Cally Brothers' gang and one of his older school pupils, resulted in a stab wound under the teacher's armpit. He fell, even as the realisation hit him. The chill in the late afternoon air matched the chill creeping through Mr MacRonald's body as he lay wheezing and gasping for breath on the damp pavement. The sound of a distant siren was the last thing the teacher heard before darkness and an even greater chill swept over him.

II

Latrine Duties

It was mid-morning on a grey autumn day. A watery sun struggled to break through the northern mist cloaking Vercovicium fort, lying dense and still in the valleys either side of Hadrian's Wall. A handful of wraith-like figures moved between barrack blocks and granaries which were either partly demolished or being repaired. The mist muted sounds of hammers and wood saws rasping rhythmically drifted around the fort. Down in the damp gloom of the latrine, Lucius Verus leant forward from the bench where he was sitting to reach for a clump of damp moss to wipe his backside. The choice of moss available didn't amount to much today. Not that you could see clearly in this dimly lit latrine. Many clumps had already been used, whilst others weren't large enough to do justice to the job of cleaning oneself. What you didn't want to do was pick up a previously used and carelessly discarded wad of moss. Auxiliary Lucius Verus sighed, screwed his eyes up and decided on the best of a bad clump, wiped himself and reached further back, feeling for something. It was a 'something' which wasn't there, a 'something' which would not appear for centuries to come; handle to flush toilet waste away. Lucius wrinkled his nose at the foul smell of human waste and frowned at his strange behaviour, and yet somewhere deep in the recesses of his memory, he thought… that he needed to pull down on a handle to complete his business? Shaking his head to clear his confusion, he stood and was about to pull his twenty first century linen boxer shorts up, when fellow Auxiliary, Clodius Brennus ducked through the doorway and into the gloomy latrine. He was followed closely by a pale faced companion.

Brennus smiled without humour and pointed at Lucius' boxer shorts. "Get those off, Verus!" The two newcomers stood framed in the open doorway. Lucius stared at them, while his memory scrabbled at the fleeting glimpse of this moment at a different time in his past or was it his future? If that's possible…

♦ ♦ ♦

Centurion Drusus was not a happy man. The wooden chair was uncomfortably close to collapse and here he was having to deal yet again with Lucius Verus and his persistent presence in Drusus' life since that fateful night last month. Drusus glanced around the chaotic wreckage which was the fort commandant's headquarters office. The northern frontier with its great Wall of Hadrian had been breached by barbarians and the world of Roman Britain plunged into dark chaos. There had been deaths, many deaths, most notably that of his former commander, Tribune Caius Metellus along with the surviving members of the Tribune's body guard, whose corpses lay in the courtyard of the crumbling villa, fifteen miles north of the Wall. Drusus pushed the thought away. Duty called. He would have to organise a party to recover the bodies of his Commander and his bodyguard. Burial rites would need to be performed, for Christian and pagan trooper alike. So much to think about and organise now he was the surviving senior officer. Life had been a great deal easier as a centurion. Others made the big decisions, others like the aristocrat Tribune Caius Metellus.

"That accursed villa." The words escaped his lips in a barely audible mumble.

"Sir?" Balbinus interrupted Drusus' thoughts.

Centurion Drusus looked up at the three youths standing the other side of the fire scorched desk. He scratched at the dark stubble shadowing his face. It irritated him. It was more beard than stubble, and Centurion Drusus favoured a clean-shaven look rather than the barbarian beard so prevalent amongst the upper echelons of male society in these later days of the Roman Empire. Not that Drusus would have looked at history of the time he inhabited as such, the later days. He was a citizen of Rome, and his job was to serve the Emperor and the Empire. The last few weeks, the escape from Vercovicium in the face of barbarian invasion and treachery of the garrison, the desperate search for the Tribune's daughter, Julia's story, the battle at the villa and the escape back to Vercovicium, meant he'd had no time to address his toilet and personal hygiene. A glance around the room told him the same story, the story he had lived with, and been part of, for the past month. Chaos and destruction in this room, chaos, and destruction in the fort, all along the Wall from east coast to west coast, and to the north and the south. The civilised world overwhelmed.

"Perhaps as far south as Londinium itself," Drusus thought as he stared vacantly at the miscreants standing before him. Unsure of what was to come, the young boys stood downcast, their gazes fixed on the floor. Drusus continued to stroke his irritating beard. The sound of men at work, rasping saws, thumping hammer blows drifted into the silence of the room. Distraction whispered in his ear yet again. Drusus remembered Londinium. He'd passed through the province's capital the previous year when he had travelled up from Richborough with his Commander and the bodyguard. A decent sized city, comparable with Nimes in southern Gaul from where he and Tribune Caius Metellus had travelled to assume the Tribune's new command at Vercovicium fort on Hadrian's Wall. That was a lifetime ago, or so it seemed to Drusus.

"Sir?" Balbinus's voice pulled Drusus from his pointless reminiscing. Comfortable days, back then. Centurion Drusus resisted the temptation to lean back in the rickety chair he inherited from his former Commander who now lay dead at the mysterious villa, north of the Wall. A corpse which, along with the others of the Commander's bodyguard, would need to be recovered. The funerary rights have to be followed, for both Christian and pagan soldiers of Tribune Caius' bodyguard. If, that was, there were any remains to be found after the Picts had finished with the prized Roman corpses. Drusus shuddered and looked up at Balbinus. Did the man ever stop chewing garlic? And besides, where did he get his endless supply of garlic bulbs from…? Certainly not wild garlic cloves which were far too small to provide Balbinus with hours of contented chewing. One of life's mysteries, Drusus decided and pulled his wandering mind back to the matter in hand.

"Latrine duty would seem to fit the crime, centurion," Balbinus ventured, assuming his centurion's long silence meant uncertainty over the nature of punishment to be handed out. Drusus moved his gaze from Balbinus's garlic clove munching jaw to the boys standing alongside him. He eyed the three of them up and down. Lucius and Clodius both sported a black eye each as they raised their heads to look at Drusus.

"Lucius Verus, Clodius Brennus and…?" Drusus waved at the third boy.

"Albus, sir." The third boy was a pale ghost, his pallid face matching his name. His timid demeanour belied any bully.

"What am I going to do with you?"

As he spoke, Drusus nodded Balbinus in the direction of the shuttered window. A stuffy, smoky smell hung in the room. The early morning gloom in the office retreated into the corners of the room as Balbinus threw the shutters wide with a resounding bang. Light and faint warmth of the morning sun seeped into the praetorium office, along with the sound of men's voices chiming above the insistent, urgent rasping of wood saws and the short, rhythmic clatter of iron hammer heads driving in iron nails. Barracks were the priority, shelter from the elements. On the Wall, weather could change completely from one hour to the next and it was now autumn. Granaries and store rooms could wait, after all, there was unlikely to be any grain to store this year due to the invasion, and as for stores…? Fresh air cleared much of the smokiness from the room.

It had been only three weeks since Centurion Drusus escaped from the villa of death beyond the Wall at the command of Tribune Caius. In Drusus' charge were the Lady Calpurnia and the Commander's daughter, Julia.

Tribune Caius sacrificed himself and his few bodyguards to save his wife and daughter, entrusting them to the safety of Drusus and trooper Balbinus. The boy, Lucius, had tagged along as they made their way back to the relative, but precarious safety of Vercovicium fort. Back to the present, the past was the past and the future, whatever that might hold, needed attending to.

"Trooper Balbinus, what strength are we currently at?"

"Forty-two, sir. Including these and a few other boys."

Since they had returned to Vercovicium from the carnage at the mysterious villa, the fort had served as a magnet to the few soldiers still loyal to Rome and seeking safety in numbers. Stragglers drifted in from the surrounding countryside, now still and quiet after the eruption of the barbarian invasion. Here and there across valleys, hills, woodland, farm and field, faint traces of smoke trails drifted heavenward as the last fires of burned-out homesteads and farms bore testament to the destruction wrought by the invaders on their way south to richer pickings.

Balbinus lowered his head to spit out a spent, tasteless garlic clove. Drusus frowned and Balbinus paused mid spit. A tight smile creased between Balbinus' red, puffy cheeks. Spitting could wait, Drusus' worried thoughts couldn't. What did the future hold for the province, for its people, for himself and his new command? Balbinus gave words to Drusus' thoughts. He mistook Drusus' steady gaze in his direction as an invitation to speak.

"What will happen next, centurion?"

"To..?"

"Well, to us, to the province? Will the Emperor Valen..tinian," he stumbled over the name, "will he come to our rescue, or will Rome abandon us, finally?"

Drusus stood and stretched wearily, the creaking of the damaged and disjointed wooden chair accompanied by the fainter creaking of his leather armour. He held up his hand to signal an end to any speculation about either their future, or that of Roman Britain. He was about to issue orders for the punishment of the three young boys standing before him, when Lucius spoke.

"Rome will return, Emperor Valentinian will reclaim his province. All is not lost. The relief army will arrive early next year in Spring, under the command of General Severus." Lucius wore a puzzled frown at his own words. Who was General Severus and how on earth did he, Lucius know of such a being?

Drusus sat down and smiled up at Lucius without humour.

"More of your dark magic, boy? What are you now, a sage, able to look into the seeds of time and make predictions about which seed will grow and which not?"

Lucius shifted uneasily at his own unbidden announcement. At his side, Balbinus belched and farted in the same moment, smiling to himself at such a marvellous feat of synchronicity. His was a simple world. Chew garlic cloves whenever you can, eat, sleep, belch, obey orders and escape death at the hands of the barbarian enemies.

Lucius cleared his throat. The puzzled fog clouding his mind cleared and his frown turned to a smile.

"Centurion Macro told me, sir. That is when, well when he was a teacher, I think." The fog of forgetfulness settled again over Lucius' flow of half grasped memories which melted away on the instant they surfaced, like breath on the wind. A darkened classroom, a shaft of bright light, whirring noises and.. the smell of burning pine cones.

"Your centurion was a brave man. He would have died well. Hopefully in the battle and not later as a captive of the Picts. His sacrifice, along with the others, allowed our escape. A teacher you say?" Drusus shook his head, as if clearing his mind. This was a ridiculous conversation, a distraction. He sat back in his chair.

"Trooper Balbinus," Drusus' tone of voice returned to the business in hand, that of disciplining the miscreants waiting before him. He spoke in that flat, matter-of-fact military way. "Balbinus, issue these…boy soldiers with wooden shovels and set them to work clearing the sewer outlet down at the latrine. It's backing up and it stinks down there. The outlet flow at the southwest corner of the fort wall needs to be cleared. As these three like causing shit, then it seems proper that they can shovel shit. Dismissed." Drusus made to stand but refrained from doing so. Better to remain seated and dignified until the others had left the room. The damaged chair might collapse at any moment and send him tumbling to the floor. As Balbinus and the three boys filed out of the headquarters office, Drusus stared at Lucius Verus' strange shoes, the battered, dirty pair of Nike trainers which looked so alien and out of place in Centurion Drusus' world of leather footwear like boots and sandals. A strange boy indeed. Strange and dangerous in Drusus' opinion. There was something other worldly about him. Had the boy not saved Lady Calpurnia's life with a mysterious laying on of hands when she choked on a hazel nut? For the second time in a month, Centurion Drusus sighed under the demands of his role, that of the man in charge with the weight of military responsibility on his shoulders. He stopped short of cursing his dead commander, Tribune Caius, for being inconsiderate enough to die. The list of his new responsibilities worried their way impatiently into Drusus' mind. Secure Vercovicium fort as best as possible, recover Roman bodies from the accursed villa to the north and check the mansio, the 'Plenum Amphoras' down in the south valley. Visit local farms and homesteads if he had time enough and sufficient number of troops. He smiled grimly at the word 'troops.'

His recently inherited duty pushed a little more insistently, and Drusus rose wearily from behind the desk, one hand steadying the back of the rickety chair. The huge oak desk in front of him had held little attraction to the barbarians pillaging and ransacking of Vercovicium fort. They were in search of gold and silver, of coins, wine goblets, jewellery, anything of value easy to carry away. That would not include a Roman military wooden chair, and a huge solid oak desk, barely moveable under normal circumstance and of no value. Centurion Drusus traced a forefinger up and down one of the scores of raw gashes on the table top. Deep scars, scored into the surface from axe and sword blade wielded by frenzied barbarians, hate filled for anything Roman. Charcoal black scorch marks told of a pointless attempt at setting fire the top of the desk. Wanton, aimless damage.

"A garrison of forty-two. Forty-two what? And who? Old men and boys? Loyal soldiers, farmers, traitors returning to the scene of their betrayal?" These were questions Centurion Drusus would have to wrestle with as commander of Vercovicium fort. And then there was the Lady Julia. He allowed himself a smile at the thought of her name. Enough for now. Too much time wasted in idle thoughts and recollections, he needed to focus, to assume 'gravitas.' The smile vanished. Drusus reached for his gladius resting in its scabbard hanging from the baldric. In one accustomed movement he picked up the weapon and flipped the baldric strap over his left shoulder. A brief adjustment and Drusus opened the door to step out into the organised chaos that was Vercovicium frontier fort. He looked in the direction of the latrine and cupped his hands to his mouth. The garlic chewer had had enough time.

"Balbinus! To me, now!"

Drusus' bark carried above the clattering, rasping, and hammering of repair work filling the interior of the fort and caught the attention of Balbinus just as he unceremoniously thrust wooden shovels into Lucius' and Clodius' hands. No third shovel for Albus. The morning mist still lingered around this damp, low lying corner of the fort, like an unwelcome watery ghost. Two thousand years later, this same autumn mist is inclined to linger in the same spot as tourists take their obligatory walked around the outside perimeter of Vercovicium fort, these days in the tender care of English Heritage rather than the thousand strong Third Tungrian Cohort. A mist, nature's thin membrane you can't feel, tough or grasp, linking past, present and future, a half world if you stare at it long enough.

"You, ghost face, you can use your hands to shovel shit." Balbinus smiled his garlic bulb chewing smile, turned, and pointed to the opening at the bottom of the fort wall behind which stood the latrine. There was the overpowering stench of human waste, which grew stronger with the pale morning sun. Here was the lowest point of the fort, facing southeast and downhill. The Roman military engineers who had built Vercovicium three hundred and fifty years ago during the heyday of the Empire, had placed the fort latrine in the ideal place. The lowest corner of the fort, ensuring good drainage and sanitation, as was the case with Roman forts across the Empire.

Balbinus knew truly little, if anything at all about events three and a half centuries before his life, nor would have been the slightest bit interested in them. A shrug of his shoulders would dismiss any tutelage about the glories of Rome and its Pax Romana during the golden age of the Empire. Thirty years from now, Balbinus would be long dead, and Vercovicium would be abandoned to wolves, robber bands and time.

Balbinus hawked and spat into the sea of human waste clogging the sewer outlet, turned on his heel and made his way in the direction of Drusus' bark. As soon as he was out of sight, Clodius hefted his wooden shovel menacingly.

"Right, Lucius Verus of the fancy underwear and exotic shoes, you can shovel the turds while I supervise."

Albus' giggle was met with a cold stare as Clodius informed him of his part in the proceedings.

"Take this." Clodius' hurled the heavy wooden shovel, catching Albus squarely across the bridge of his nose. Albus yelped like a puppy and clutched at his injured face as the shovel landed at his feet. Clodius smirked. Flies rose and buzzed from the trail of slime extending down the slope, past the remains of the vicus and down into the wide valley to the south where lazy smoke trails told of still smouldering farms and settlements beyond the vallum, the great ditch to the south of the frontier.

Clodius Brennus folded his arms and leaned back against the fort wall.

"Apart from those fancy linen underpants and footwear, Lucius Verus, how did you come by that black stone? The one you keep under your bed. Exceptionally smooth and polished. Looks expensive." A derisive finger jabbed at the leather pouch hanging around Lucius' neck.

"And what's in there?" Clodius made to lunge forward and grab the pouch holding the Great Red Bloodstone of Mithras. Lucius stepped back, careful not to slip in the slime beneath his feet. Clodius grasped at thin air and cursed under his breath.

Lucius turned his back on Clodius and, shovel in hand began to scrape away at the foul-smelling human waste blocking the exit drain at the bottom of the fort wall. Flies buzzed angrily at this disturbance and the three boys waved their hands to keep them at bay. The dried crust covering the thick swathe of waste, gave way under the wooden shovel blades, releasing a noisome stench. It was enough to make you vomit.

Somewhere at the back of Lucius' brain, a pin point stab of pain announced its arrival. The pale blue vein on his temple pulsed, echoing the throb of pain. Lucius stopped shovelling and leaning on the handle he pinched the top of his nose between forefinger and thumb, much as we do to try and ease the first signs of a headache.

"I didn't tell you stop, Verus!" Clodius yelled. "Get shovelling! And before you do, give me that pouch thing hanging from your neck. I want to know what is in it."

Lucius continued to lean on the shovel and pinch the bridge of his nose. Stars and flashing lights exploded behind closed eyelids as he tried to block out the troubling morning sunshine. The throb of pain moved from the back of Lucius' brain and spread across his forehead. He felt dizzy. Clodius' voice sounded distant, echoing, as though coming from the far end of a tunnel, The Dartford Tunnel came to mind, 'whatever that might be,' Lucius thought.

Albus looked up from where he was kneeling, trying to unblock the sewer exit hole at the base of the fort wall, hands covered in shit, the bridge of his nose a vivid red, trickling blood from one nostril. A drama was about to unfold, and Albus was not going to miss it, but a well-aimed hefty boot to the side of his head delivered with a bully's accustomed precision, sent Albus sprawling face first into the muck. So much for the friendship of a bully. Clodius turned his attention back to Lucius and pointed at the leather pouch holding the Great Red Bloodstone of Mithras.

"Now!" It was more a scream than a yell. Lucius gripped the pouch and closed his eyes. The thrum of rubber tyres on tarmac filled his head, engines roared and bright lights winked intermittently. Lucius opened his eyes just in time to see Clodius' grasping hand lunge towards him to tear the pouch from around his neck. He took a step back, and Clodius stumbled forward to land with a splat face down in the greenish tinged, brown mire, like those dry crusted summer cow pats our feet dodge through fields, Nature's land mines. Cursing, Clodius raised himself onto his hands and knees and turned his head up to face Lucius.

"You'll pay for that, Verus," he threatened, spitting stale shit from his mouth. Lucius looked from Clodius to Albus and back at Clodius. This was the moment. In one swift movement, Lucius hefted the wooden shovel and brought the flat of the blade crashing across Clodius' face, catching him square on the cheek bone which shattered. Clodius shrieked, clutched at his broken cheek bone, and collapsed back to the ground. The strange thrumming in

Lucius' head increased to a roar as he stood in disbelief at what he had just done. Albus was whimpering like a dog, holding his hand up in supplication and a feeble attempt at self-defence, fearing the worst. Lucius in turn, raised his hand to his temple where the distended vein throbbed. Clodius was struggling to get onto all fours, a brutish snarl ripping across the undamaged half of his shattered face. One of his teeth was hanging loose, a thread of blood trickled down his chin. When he spat, his spit was rose tinged. He threatened, his words muffled by a swollen tongue.

"Thust you wait, Verush," The hanging tooth parted company with the gum. Clodius spat it out.

The inside of Lucius' head was roaring with a mix of distorted sounds, a deep insistent thrumming, the noise of traffic racing by, Mr MacRonald's classroom voice, spectral, Lucius' own asthmatic coughing. The battle clash and clatter of weapons surged and smothered all the other sounds battering away at the inside of his head. He needed to go. Centurion Drusus would not take kindly to this act of rebellion, striking a fellow soldier. He dropped the wooden spade and made for the south gateway of the fort to his left. As he ran along the berm, the open space between the fort wall to his right and the weed choked defensive ditch to his left, the Great Red Bloodstone of Mithras bumped against his bare chest, and with each bump, it grew warmer.

At the south gate, Lucius turned right and made his way through the towering, barrel roofed gateway and into the fort. He could hear the sounds of men busy repairing the damaged barracks. With no one in sight to notice him, he made his way to the latrine. He paused for a moment.

"What about my mobile phone?" Whatever a 'mobile phone' was. Never mind, the possibility of escape from Clodius' furious revenge was the priority. Centurion Drusus would not be a happy man. Lucius Verus wasn't exactly a favourite of the centurion, even less so than Clodius Brennus and Albus… whatever his name. Lucius hurried to the latrine and pushed against the wooden door which had been mended and remounted on its hinges. Once inside, he closed the door and stepped up onto the toilet bench running the length of the wall. He glanced up into the dark recesses of the timber framed roof. Spiders lived their comfortable lives hidden amongst the hanging grey and black webs festooning the gaps between the rafters. Their unhurried if short lives, continued, unaffected by barbarian invasions and other such disasters afflicting humans. A question nagged. Wasn't there something to pull down from the rafters, from amongst those black hanging cobwebs? A jacket, a school folder, a mobile phone? Lucius Mabutt was pushing Lucius Verus to one side, back into the past where he belonged. Questions and thoughts careered through his aching head. Each thought, each question, clamoured and fought to be heard and answered. Some questions were simpler than others to ask, like 'who exactly am I?' but impossible to answer.

The shouts outside the latrine block were coming closer. Clodius Brennus had recovered his wits after the blow from the wooden shovel, and now he was on the trail of Lucius with Albus in tow. The Great Red Bloodstone of Mithras glowed hot through the leather pouch and was on the verge of burning Lucius' chest. He sat down on the toilet bench and grasped the hot pouch. The rasping cough caught him by surprise and tore through his chest like a ripsaw. Dizziness flooded all his senses. He let go of the leather pouch, both hands gripped the edge of the wooden toilet seat with whitened knuckles. The world swam before him, even though his eyes were shut tight against the onslaught of sensations, feelings. The wheezing from his lungs piped shrill and high pitched, like a musical parody as Lucius fought for breath. He sucked air into his lungs, exhaled in the same gasping moment and battled for the next breath. He'd been here once before, and the fight for breath focused his memory. Same struggle, same place, same time. The heat emanating from the Great Red Bloodstone of Mithras seemed to bring comfort and discomfort in equal measure. He needed his asthma inhaler and felt for a non-existent pocket in his Roman tunic.

The cough when it came, burst from his wheezing lungs with such force it shook his whole body and threatened to crack a rib. Phlegm and sinus snot flew across the latrine to land on the toilet bench opposite. Lucius slumped forward, hands gripping his knees, struggling to open his eyes, drowning in their own tears. His world imploded and he threw his head backwards, banging it on the wall. His head slumped sideways onto his shoulder, mouth open, eyes staring, body limp enough for him to slide slowly onto his side. The wheeze of a long-drawn-out breath escaped from his blue lips, his legs trembled and were still.

III

The Miracle of Mithras

Mr Fiennes, leading trauma surgeon in his field, nodded to his assistant who dutifully dabbed at the surgeon's sweaty brow with the wad of cotton wool clasped in the tongs of a long-handled pair of forceps. Mr Fiennes nodded brief thanks and squeezed his eyelids shut as was his custom at the end of any lengthy and challenging operation. No one in theatre saw his pursed lips puff a sigh of relief behind his mask.

"Thank you, everyone. Wonderful team work, as ever. Looks like our patient will pull through. Nasty wound, very nasty, touch and go."

No one replied. There was the accustomed understated judgement on the results of another lifesaving operation. Familiarity with the renowned and great man was not what you sought. Instead, the relief around the operating theatre was palpable as the clitter-clatter of surgical instruments being tidied away for sterilisation, echoed around the hard and sterile operating theatre. The super bright lights over the operating table lost their other worldly glare as loud clicks announced the end of their job for today. Operating gowns rustled and surgical gloves snapped back with a 'thwack' as they were peeled away from tired hands, fingers were flexed relieving cramp. Caps were removed and tousled hair shaken free, apart from Mr Fiennes who remained fully clad in his theatre gown, cap, and gloves. It had been a six-hour long operation to save this knife attack victim's life. He was lucky that the point of the knife blade had not reached deep enough into his chest to puncture his heart.

Mr Fiennes turned away and strode out of theatre, a quick scrub down and a cup of strong coffee called. Double espresso would do the trick today. A sad case really, the operation today, he thought as he freed himself from cap, gown, and gloves. The water ran noisily from the taps in the sluice room, a welcoming feel as he thrust his hands into the warm flow.

"What is the world coming to when a teacher is stabbed whilst on after school gate duty?" he pondered, washing his hands. He was accustomed by now to the steady flow of young knife attack victims, as steady as the flow of water now running over his hands and rinsing the soap away. But teachers now? He thanked God that his profession, his salary, and his gated community kept such a world at bay, and that his children attended private school.

Mr Fiennes dried his hands under the warm air dryer, checked his hair in the mirror, a quick pat here and there to flatten rogue strands, and left the room. He would check on the teacher, Mr MacRonald, tomorrow morning on daily his rounds. He was more than satisfied with the stitches closing the near fatal wound under the teacher's armpit.

GHOSTS AND EAGLES

♦ ♦ ♦

Centurion Macro Cornelius Verus, one time Primus Pilus of the Sixth Valeria Victrix Legion was in a bad way. The pounding headache and painful gouge on the back of his neck weren't the worst of his pain wracked woes though. He was aware that he had suffered a serious wound from a sword thrust into his armpit. He had seen this moment countless times before on the battlefield, gravely wounded soldiers who recovered briefly, to be granted just enough time to realise they were facing their end. Those moments of wonder in their eyes as death waited patiently, a dark shadow looming over the shoulder of the dying soldier. Whispered prayers from comrades, pointless, yet somehow comforting seemed to help the dying on their journey to meet Charon, the Ferryman.

Macro groaned and rolled onto his back. He looked up. The sky was dark with the shapes of black crows circling above the dead bodies scattered across the villa courtyard. The braver birds were already about their grim task of pecking eyeballs from sightless eyes and dipping cruel beaks into gaping wounds. Macro prayed they'd leave his eyes. He would need them in the afterlife. Who wants to spend eternity wandering amongst the shades of the dead in blindness? His throat felt tight and he was thirstier than he could ever remember being. The puddles in the cobblestone courtyard glistened under the sun, bringing further torture to his fierce thirst. He licked his lips. The sudden downpour had thrown extra confusion into the brief battle for the villa which Centurion Macro and his fellow Romans had lost, but at least his enemy, the Tribune Caius Metellus had died too, not from any Pictish hand, but under Macro's own gladius blade. Mithras was avenged.

The Christian desecrator of his temple at Brocolitia on Hadrian's Wall, had been sent to Hades. Hell was too good for him.

Macro winced as a series of needle like pricks traced a jagged line under his armpit and stopped as abruptly as they had begun. Keeping a watchful eye on the circling carrion birds, Macro raised his right arm, wincing at the pain as he did so. His left hand found the space between the top of his bronze breastplate and his armpit. Fingertips ran along a line of neatly sewn stitches.

"What...?" His fingertips traced back and forth along the line of stitches as he marvelled at the perfect neatness of the stitching, which belied the customary crude, if efficient, work of a Roman army surgeon. The arrow head wound on his left calf from all those years ago paid testament to the basic skill of the Greek surgeon who'd put him back together in the Syrian campaign. If you escaped infection in a wound, you lived.

Macro ceased his delicate examination of the stitches; how in the name of Mithras, had he come by these stitches?

"Mithras be praised," was the only contribution his troubled mind could make to this strange situation. Saved by his god.

More crows were setting about their grim and ghastly task of banqueting on Roman and barbarian corpses littering the villa courtyard. Macro needed to escape this place of death. He knew that the rain-washed bodies would soon be lying under a burning sun, and then the smell of putrefaction and decay would be unbearable. A fly buzzed close by and Macro swatted at it, wincing in pain as he did so. But he was alive. How? A gift, a miracle from Mithras? Gratitude from the god for Macro's killing of the Christian Tribune, Caius Metellus? At that thought, Macro twisted his head to his left, wincing in pain from the wound to his neck. The face of the corpse lying alongside him was a lifeless grey, blood drained, a look of shock and surprise frozen in the glassy eyes in that instant when Macro had avenged his god, the Lord Mithras. Tribune Caius' gaze was fixed, staring into the eyes of his killer. Macro took little pleasure in the manner in which he'd despatched the Tribune. A gladius thrust, from behind. Cowardly. Not honourable, not worthy of a soldier of Rome.

Macro tried to recall events from the battle in this courtyard against the Picts. He was puzzled by the fact that, not only was he alive, but that the Tribune's head was still attached to his body. Something had stopped the Picts from severing the heads of himself and the Tribune, as prized battle trophies. There again…he felt for the wound on the back of his neck, a raw gouge, sticky with blood. It felt as if someone had tried to sever his head and stopped midway through the gruesome task. And then there was that neat row of stitches under his armpit. Lord Mithras be praised, a miracle.

A voice spoke close by. Instinctively and painfully, Centurion Macro reached for his sword, in that same instant sensing it was not there. He turned to his left, where the voice had come from. No one there, not soul. Just corpses and their black feathered carrion crows seeking dead eyes or open wounds. Despite the triumphant cawing of the birds, Macro heard the softly spoken disembodied voice, a voice from another time, but a time he knew, a time he had moved, breathed, and lived in.

"How are we this morning, Mr MacRonald? Comfortable I trust? Any pain?"

"Pain? Of course, damn you!"

"How is your memory? Can you recall the events which put you into hospital, into our care?"

The disembodied voice was soothing. Who was the owner? Centurion Macro craned his neck in all directions, which wasn't easy with his helmet impeding his efforts as it struggled against the uneven cobbled ground.

Macro licked his parched lips and spoke to the crows hopping busily from dead body to dead body. It was a good question too. What exactly had happened to him? He wrestled with his stubborn memory. He must have taken a blow to the head, helmeted as it was, during the battle. It wasn't unusual, a helmet had its drawbacks.

"I was on gate duty, outside the school." It was a flat statement. It didn't make sense. There was no gate in the villa courtyard wall and the villa wasn't, isn't a school. Macro squeezed his eyes tight shut. He needed to shake off this battle damage. Any severe blow to the head could result in memory loss and confusion, despite the protection of a helmet. He'd seen it a thousand times before, back in his days serving in the Legions for Rome.

But it was a school. He had joined the Headteacher on daily gate duty outside the school…on, that was it, on the Caledonian Road. He had a jumbled recollection of sorts, a half world of being and at the same time, not being.

The disembodied voice was back.

"Well, Mr MacRonald, I can assure you that your memory is fine. You were the victim of a knife attack outside the school gates. A gang member with a grudge, against one of your pupils? You simply got in the way, tried to intervene, and protect your pupil. A scuffle, an altercation of sorts ensued and you were caught in the middle. The perpetrators were a local gang, self-styled as the 'Cally Boys,' named for the Caledonian Road. Anyway, you get some rest and I'll return tomorrow morning to check your progress towards a full recovery."

Macro spoke above the growing din of cawing carrion feasting on Roman and Pictish corpses.

"I am recovered, thank you, doctor." A determination coursed through him, and he rose unsteadily to his feet. The helmet needed to come off. The neck guard rubbed at the open wound where the Pict barbarian had tried to part his head from his body. The swooping intervention of Hispana the Eagle of the Ninth, had put paid to the barbarian's attempts and Macro kept his head.

Centurion Macro swayed slightly as he took stock of his situation. At his feet lay the bloodied corpse of Tribune Caius Metellus. Beyond and all around lay the bodies of a pitifully few Romans and a vast number of barbarians. The black crows continued to complain loudly as they vied with their fellow carrion to gorge themselves on this glut of bodies. Eyes and exposed flesh wounds were easy targets but frustrated shrill cries from the crows told of armour and clothing covering too much flesh on the bodies. Hispana, Eagle of the Ninth had gone, else the carrion birds would not be feasting across the battlefield.

Macro scratched absent mindedly at the Scorpion tattoo on his right forearm, spat dust from his mouth and swallowed hard to wet his dry throat. The Scorpion insisted.

"Centurion, the man is dead, killed by your hand. The god, Mithras is avenged, he is satisfied. Your work is done, but what about the boy, Lucius?"

Macro's head snapped up at the mention of Lucius. Of course, that's why they were here! He for revenge, and Lucius Mabutt, his erstwhile student, to save a Roman girl. A mist as thick and dark as that which rides the River Styx, was torn away by a gust of wind bringing with it memories, clear and focused. Picking up his helmet, Macro stepped over the body of Tribune Caius, reaching again for the sword at his left hip, in the same moment knowing it would not be there. Muddled thinking, battle induced confusion.

"Damn!" He cast around for his weapon, despite being certain that it was gone, no doubt carried away triumphantly by a Pict as a worthy trophy. Macro's sudden movements disturbed the crows, deep in their grisly task. Yellow, cruel stabbing beaks, pecking and tearing with the practised ease of scavengers. Centurion Macro, still a little unsteady on his feet, took stock of his situation. Behind him stood the villa, all its wooden doors open and hanging askew at different crazy angles. Various worthless items were scattered randomly along the portico and out into the courtyard where the tide of ransacked items stopped as if at a high-water mark on a beach. Amongst the wreckage lay two bodies, Talorc the Pict warlord and his killer, the slave girl Rhiannon. The corpses went unnoticed by Macro, they held no significance or meaning for him. A trail of grey smoke drifted up from behind the villa building. Beyond that, a hill climbed away into the near distance. Macro hoped that Lucius had made good his escape before the villa was overrun by the Pict warband. Perhaps he had caught up with Centurion Drusus and the Tribune's daughter, Julia.

Macro needed to go. As he stepped over the bodies littering the villa courtyard, he recalled the last moments of the battle between the few brave Roman soldiers and the barbarian warband. The spirit eagle of the Ninth, Hispana and her heavenly intervention; Jupiter's thunderbolts ripping through the barbarian host as it tried to storm the villa defences, lightning bolts from Hispana's talons cutting a searing path through them, scattering Picts everywhere and delaying their assault on the villa for a short while. It was time enough for Lucius to escape the death and destruction being visited on the Romans. Enough time for the Tribune to send his daughter and his wife to safety accompanied by Centurion Drusus and a trooper, on the remaining two horses.

As the crowd of crows hopped and flapped away before him, Macro trod between the corpses littering the ground and made his way towards the gateway in the courtyard wall. The shattered remains of a farm cart lay to one side of the gap, a vain attempt by the defenders to slow the advance of the warband. Discarded weapons lay scattered everywhere, swords, axes, spears, on the ground next to their last owners, or in the vice like grip of lifeless Pict and Roman. The presence of weapons told Macro that no one had come to the villa since the battle, otherwise the weapons would have been collected for further use. The age-old custom of recycling anything of use from ancient battlefields. As that observation crossed Macro's mind, one word jumped into focus. 'Recycled.' The word pushed and nagged at him. That was it! Of course. Mr MacRonald knew all about recycling! Bins for this, bins for that, green, blue, or black. Not the thoughts of Centurion Macro, but of Mr MacRonald, History teacher. With his brain kick started, thoughts and questions flew around inside his head, like a cage of shrill wild birds beating their wings uselessly against their prison bars. He looked back to where the hill rose behind the villa. No point in going that way. Lucius would be long gone. But where? He might as well address that question to the mouldering severed head lying close to where he stood, a severed head with empty eye sockets. Naevius had been the first to die in the attack on the villa, his eyes providing the carrion crows with a taste to come. Macro thought it better to retrace his steps to Vercovicium fort. Decision made, he began the grim business of prising a gladius from the stiff dead hand of a dead Roman lying a few feet away. He would need a weapon, and on this recent battlefield, he was spoilt for choice.

At first the lifeless fingers would not yield their prize as Macro, lips pursed in effort and concentration, worked to release the sword handle. In what seemed like a belated funeral dirge, the melancholy cries of displaced crows filled the sky above the villa. Macro reached for his pugio, his military dagger, and a few swift cuts shortened the grim task of removing the gladius from the dead man's grasp.

The worn ivory hilt had the familiarity of a long-lost friend, and it took less than a second for the balance of the weapon in his hand to confirm his suspicion. Macro tore a strip of cloth from the dead man's tunic and wiped the blade of the gladius clean of dried blood. No need to read the legend incised on the blade. This was the gladius of 'Macro Cornelius Varus Primus Pilus of the Sixth Valeria Victrix Legion.' Mithras truly was with Macro this day. Armed once more, Centurion Macro sheathed his gladius and pugio, put on his helmet, stiffened his resolve, and marched out of the courtyard back down the trackway littered with corpses of Picts, leading up to the villa. Yes, the deep wound under his armpit was sore as Hades, but Centurion Macro was himself once more… Mr MacRonald, the Roman known as Centurion Macro Cornelius Varus.

IV

Julia

Julia Metellus awoke that morning just as Rhiannon's blood streaked, dead face floated into her waking dream, her friend's eyes as lifeless as cold glass. The rough horsehair stuffed mattress rustled as Julia stretched out her long legs and yawned. Rhiannon's bloodied ghost face faded. Julia's bedroom at Vercovicium fort, was cold and the smell of burning hung in the air, in every corner of the room. And now, her mattress lay on the floor, that same mosaic floor which only five weeks ago felt warm under her bare feet as she rose from her bed and hurried in slippered feet to breakfast with her mother and father in a different world, a different time.

The wooden bedframe on which the army issue mattress had once lain, was gone, smashed to pieces, dragged away for kindling to set fire to buildings in the fort. No cheerful hum from the underfloor heating system this morning, no warmth from the box flues in the walls running from floor to ceiling. The world had been turned on its head, as Roman Britain buckled and crumbled under the latest barbarian onslaught, caught in the grip of a huge barbarian conspiracy from beyond her frontiers. An unholy confederation of seaborne and land-based tribes had swept through Rome's northernmost province in search of plunder. From Hadrian's Wall to Londinium, from the mountain fastness of Wales across to the freezing flat lands of the east coast of the Saxon Shore, the province was in flames.

Julia groaned as she stretched battered and bruised limbs. There was no part of her body, her head which didn't ache, bruised, and battered from her gladiatorial fight with Rhiannon. A spectacle of parody and deadly intent. The loser to die on the point of a friend's sword, the winner to be burned alive. Death was all around Julia's life now. Her dead father, Tribune Caius Metellus and her dead friend, Rhiannon. She propped herself up on her elbow. The mattress crackled at her movement. A melancholy gloom hung in the room. The noise from the mattress subsided and was replaced by her mother's hushed voice.

"Are you awake, daughter?" Her mother's mattress crackled as she too propped herself up on an elbow.

"Yes, mother. How did you sleep?" A pointless question given the recent death of Lady Calpurnia's husband and the destruction of her aristocratic world.

"I dozed, rather than slept." There was a long, drawn-out sigh which did nothing to dispel the melancholy gloom.

"Your father's body." It was a barely audible whisper. "I can't bear to think of what might have happened to it. He must have a Christian burial, if that is, he is truly dead. I think they lied when they told me he is dead." The last few words were barely audible as her voice faded. Outside, one of the soldiers laughed loudly and his companions joined in.

There was silence between mother and daughter. Julia rose stiffly from her mattress and made her way over to the shuttered window. A faint draught through the wooden slatted shutters reminded her that the glass which once civilised the window, was gone now. An act of wanton destruction by the marauding Picts had left it shattered, the edges now ragged and sharp toothed lining the window frame, like an open-mouthed mythical creature baring its fangs. Julia reached through the gaping hole in the broken window and pushed the shutters open, a slave's job which Rhiannon had done in another time, another world. A world and a time lost under a deluge of memories, a mix of blood, dust, and pain. A world of loss, a world of death. The world in its present moment drifted in as the wooden shutters banged open against the outside wall, like the banging of sword on shield; gladiators pitted against one another, soldiers battling barbarians. Julia shuddered, as much at her memories as at the chill morning air. Her aching body reminded her of her recent ordeals, physical and mental.

She cast around the chaos and detritus of her former bedroom and picked up the rough woollen army issue cloak which Centurion Drusus had given her when they arrived back at Vercovicium after fleeing the carnage at the villa. The russet cloak and army issue linen tunic she was wearing, were her only items of clothing. Arranging the oversized cloak about her shoulders to cover as much of the ill-fitting tunic as possible, Julia made her way from the bedroom and down the dark corridor running between the commandant's house and the headquarters building adjoining it. A dark corridor full of even darker memories, a dark corridor with ash underfoot and the smell of smoke in the air, barbarian Picts hammering furiously at the wooden door.

♦ ♦ ♦

Centurion Drusus pointed at Clodius' swollen, reddened cheek bone which had puffed up under the black eye Lucius had exchanged with him earlier. The eye was pig like, heavy lidded. He tried to nurse the injury by every now and then raising tentative fingertips to his cheek.

"And Lucius attacked you, you claim?"

Clodius offered a mumbled, thick tongued painful reply through a lopsided mouth. Albus was paler than ever, watching proceedings, eyes wide.

"He did. No reathon at all. I wath bending down, clearing the thewer outlet, when he hit me acroth the thide of my head with hith wooden shovel." Pain and discomfort from his injury combined to lend Clodius' voice a comically lisping quality.

"Where is Lucius now? Do you know?"

"No, thenturion, I did run after him, back into the fort. I heard coughing coming from the latrine. It thounded like Verush wath hiding in there."

"And?" Drusus prompted.

"And I went to the latrine. The coughing stopped ath I opened the door, and.."

"Go on," Drusus prompted again. Clodius wasn't sure of what he should say next. The words, the sentence sounded preposterous unspoken, in his aching head.

"And Verush wasn't in there, in the latrine, I mean."

"Wasn't in there? What do you mean by that, Brennus?"

Clodius Brennus shifted uneasily, the soles of his boots scuffing on the floor.

"The latrine wath empty. He had definitely been in there, thenturion. I heard him coughing."

"Mmm.." Drusus was becoming impatient with this whole issue of quarrelling boy soldiers under his command. He was a centurion after all and not a school teacher.

"Magic once again, I have no doubt." Drusus spoke more to himself than anyone else. "Balbinus."

"Sir?"

"I want you to search for Lucius yourself. If he has left the fort, that makes him a deserter. If you catch him, bring him straight to me for punishment. I will sentence him to death, in accordance with Roman army law."

"Yes, centurion." Balbinus raised his arm in a tentative salute. He was shocked at his centurion's decision. He hoped Drusus hadn't caught his slight intake of breath.

"And search any of his belongings, his blankets and bedroll. I need evidence of his necromancy, his magic. I have seen enough with my own eyes. You recall how he saved Lady Calpurnia by making her breathe again, brought her back from the edge of death?"

Balbinus nodded, despite feeling uneasy at the threat of a death sentence being carried out on a young soldier. Lucius was odd, strange no doubt, but Balbinus felt there were more important matters to address than punishing this quirky youth.

The wooden door behind Drusus rasped open, grating against the floor. Everyone looked towards the door as it opened fully to reveal Julia, holding her army cloak tightly around herself.

"Lady Julia, the morning's greetings to you and your mother." Drusus looked over Julia's shoulder half expecting to see Lady Calpurnia.

"My mother is still sleeping. Greetings to you Centurion Drusus." She looked around the room. She sensed that she had interrupted something of import. Blank, dumb faces stared back at her.

"Has anyone seen Lucius?" Her question dropped into the silence. Outside the open window, hammers continued to hammer and saws continued to saw. Men shouted about the repairs being carried out.

"Well?"

Drusus coughed slightly and spoke in tones far gentler than those he used with his soldiers.

"He appears to have disappeared, according to these dolts. Last seen in the latrine, or so this fool claims." He gestured his disdain in the direction of Clodius, who was still trying to nurse his swollen cheek. The redness was slowly being replaced by a flowering bruise. A wound? Julia remembered with a shudder how the Pict warlord, Talorc, with his knife to her throat, had abducted her while Lucius hid in the latrine. Another world, a lifetime ago. She stopped herself revisiting the arena of death and the carnage at the villa. It was her turn to be dumb.

"Balbinus, the latrine, now. I will follow, shortly." Balbinus nodded in reply to his centurion's order and turned towards the door to lead the way. He motioned for Clodius and Albus to follow. Drusus turned to Julia.

"You're welcome to come too, Lady Julia." A shake of her head told Drusus enough. Julia didn't want to be an item of curiosity, walking through the fort in such a dishevelled state, wrapped in an oversized army cloak.

"Very well. I'll be back soon."

Drusus left the room and followed Balbinus, Clodius and Albus down the main gravelled road through the ruined fort to the southern gateway and the latrine.

V

Macro's Return

The lone guard atop the north gateway of Vercovicium fort shivered and pulled his cloak closer around his young shoulders which slumped under the unaccustomed weight of recently gotten ill-fitting armour. He stared north, into the distant, brooding wasteland of Caledonia. He shouldn't be here, well not yet anyway, not even a hint of a beard to declare his imminent manhood. He was always going to join the Third Tungrian Cohort at some time in the future, no doubt about that, but the time was not meant to be now. Every son of every garrison frontier soldier would automatically be enlisted into the militia along Hadrian's Wall, generation after generation for the last two hundred odd years. 'Tungrian,' the name of the garrison at Vercovicium, so his father had told him. A garrison named for the first cohort to be based there when the Emperor Hadrian ordered the Wall to be built, a thousand men, a mix of cavalry and infantry. The men were Tungrians, drawn from a tribe across the sea in what Romans called Germania, tough men, hard men. No

Tungrians here now. Over the decades the foreign soldiers married local Celtic women, their children and grandchildren becoming Celtic British, local folk who were 'Roman' in name only, Roman citizens, British farmer soldiers. His father, one of those farmer soldiers, divided his time between the family homestead just south of here, a couple of miles beyond the mansio serving the important travellers on the Military Way which ran parallel to, and at a distance behind the Wall from east coast to west coast. That mansio, along with his family farm had gone up in flames.

The gangly youth sighed and leant heavily against the spear he'd been issued with, along with the ill-fitting armour, while his brown eyes scanned the horizon from east to west and back again. Behind him, to the south, lay his world, his life. A life which had seen in its thirteen years, nothing of what lay beyond the family farm and the occasional trip up to Vercovicium fort to deliver grain, vegetables, or other farm produce. He rubbed at the blush of a birthmark which covered his left cheek. It was an accustomed action to reach for a blemish he knew was there but which he had never seen. No civilised luxury of a polished bronze mirror for the likes of him. If you were lucky, you might see a wavy, undetailed image of your face in the still water of a bucket or a pond.

His eye caught the movement of a figure in the distance. The blemished young face screwed up as he squinted into the distance. Yes, there! A figure making its way towards the north gate, zigzagging its way through the dense brush and undergrowth. As the boy guard watched, the figure disappeared now and then behind the low growing, wind swept and stunted clumps of trees fiercely determined to survive in this harsh landscape. The boy tightened his grip on the spear haft and bit at his lower lip. He felt his legs tremble. This was his first taste of being a soldier. He would need to call someone and inform them of the stranger's approach, especially as there were no gates in the northern gateway. Those now lay some distance away down the steep slope leading up to the fort. The boy felt a relieved as he caught sight of the transverse plumed helmet atop the approaching figure's head. The man limped heavily on his left leg and was near enough now to look up at the boy and raise his right arm, not so much in greeting, but more in weary acknowledgement. The boy raised his arm in return and made his way down the steep stone steps leading down to open gateway, his oversized spear trailing behind him, the wooden butt bumping rhythmically as he descended each step.

"Stranger at the north gate." His adolescent voice, however, didn't have the depth to carry above the din of repairs overlaying the fort. Anyway, the garrison of men and boys was spread thinly over an area which once housed one thousand men. There was no one in sight despite the racket of human activity. Arriving at the foot of the stairs, he grasped his spear more firmly and stepped into the open gateway. The man was making his way up the slope leading to the fort, hand cupping his left knee cap in what looked like an effort to ease the pain of the uphill walk. The youth summoned his courage, despite the fact that the stranger was dressed as a Roman centurion. He lowered his spear point in the direction of the man who was now close enough to abandon supporting his left leg, straighten his back and untie the chinstrap of his helmet and ease it from his head. The boy hoped the stranger would not notice the nervous tremble of the spear tip

"Halt, stranger." The boy's voice sounded ridiculous to his ears as the man removed his helmet completely, cradling it in the crook of his arm, then repeated the action to remove his sweat stained felt skull cap.

"Relax, lad. I'm Centurion Macro. I used to live in the vicus here outside Vercovicium, below the south gate." He removed his grubby neckcloth and, shaking it free, wiped it round the inside rim of his helmet.

The young recruit wasn't sure what he should do. Stand to attention? Challenge the centurion further, salute, or what? He opted for the best course of action and announced in as deep a voice as he could manage, "follow me," and then the afterthought, "sir."

VI

A Brush With The Future

Lucius' nostrils twitched and flared as the awful smell made him recoil. It was a unique smell, the smell of the past mixed with the smell of the present, old leather, dead mice, decaying vegetation with a waft of wood burner smoke, a curious smell of between worlds, between times. The dusty, musty smell of days long past. Lucius sat, legs shaking, breath racing and a pounding headache spearing through his sinuses. The smell of the 'now world' was cleaner, sharper, grass, vegetation and even the faint smell of heather, perhaps even traffic fumes. Or was he imagining it? He opened and closed his eyes, trying to make sense of what lay before him, trying to focus all of his senses. He drifted the palm of his hand across the harsh surface of the granite toilet bench. No smooth wooden seat, no clumps of dark green moss, no running water in the channel at his feet.

The southern wall of the latrine was gone, levelled to three or four courses of rough grey granite blocks. Lucius knew the answer before he looked around, he knew this trick of time, he'd been here before, or there before, depending on how you view time.

The latrine was gone, and that meant he was back. His heart raced and knocked against his ribs as he took in the scene around him. Yes! He was back, back in his own time, although for the life of him he couldn't latch onto precisely what 'his own time' was. Getting to his feet, he looked southwards down the slope towards the car park. It was half full, of wonderful, plain, and simple, straightforward cars. He was back, having escaped from the chaos and nightmare that was Roman Britain in its end of days. He sniffed the air. That smell of the past, the smell so many of us try hard to imagine, still lingered. To 'see' the past is easy and perhaps we can hear it if we coax notes from an ancient musical instrument, but the smells?... they are the most evocative, some people will claim. The smell of the London Underground during World War Two, a Tudor house, a Medieval village, Queen Elizabeth the 1st' gloves, King Charles 11's shoes, the wooden flooring under the cotton spinning machines in a Victorian factory. That type of thing.

Back to the present. Lucius thought he'd never been happier at any time of his life as he was right now. He stood. Feelings surged around, ebbing, and flowing like a manic tide lapping the shores of calm and reasoned thought. He needed to get a grip. He was back, yes but...he ran his hands down the front of his Roman linen tunic. He would have to find suitable clothing. And then there was his mobile phone, or more correctly there 'wasn't' his mobile phone. Lucius swallowed hard at the memory of Mr MacRonald's warning about taking his mobile phone back into the past. Shit! Couldn't be helped. Too late now. Now, or should it be then, his mobile phone was resting under his bedroll two thousand years ago…he looked across levelled fort of Vercovicium…just there. He pinpointed his gaze in the direction of the foundation stones of a nearby barrack block in which he had slept. A slow-moving group of sightseers was studying the layout of that same barrack block in the neatly mown English Heritage grass. No doubt they were wondering how the building had appeared two thousand years ago. One or two of them were quite expansive in bringing their imaginations into play, gesturing, and pointing knowledgeably as they filled in the details for their fellow sight seers. Lucius was sufficiently recovered by now to allow himself a chuckle at the groups' earnest efforts in trying to recreate the past of fifteen centuries ago. The past which Lucius had left only minutes ago after delivering a bone crunching swipe of the wooden shovel to that boy's face. The boy's name escaped Lucius. A name from, what?...He turned back and looked over the low remains of the fort walls to where he had been tasked with clearing the latrine sewer drain this same morning. Where were the latrine work party? There was not a single soul, Romano -Briton or otherwise. No brown slurry snaking down the southeastern slope and away from the fort. Just a gentle breeze stirring the expanse of rough grassland falling away into the valley below and towards the distant car park. That way lay great aunt Livia's guesthouse, the Cosy Kettle and safety. Lucius knew he would get strange looks from visitors and hikers alike as he made his way back down to the Cosy Kettle, back to his world, the real world. Re-enactors were a common enough sight up and down and along Hadrian's Wall, a wonderful way of bringing history to life, or so popular opinion said. It helped to 'bring the past to life' was the claim. In his two-thousand-year-old linen tunic, people would take him for someone bringing the Romans to life here on the northern frontier. The grubbiness of the tunic added authenticity to his appearance. No worries then. Saunter back to the Cosy Kettle as nonchalant as you like, even if the gathering breeze proved a tad chilly around the hemline of the tunic, offering an uncomfortable walk down to great aunt Livia's guesthouse. At least he was home now, safe. Just as he indulged himself in such positive thoughts of a safe return, a small group of visitors, led by a guide, sauntered over from the relic of a Roman granary, in the direction of the latrine. The world-famous latrine at Housesteads Roman fort was the 'piece de resistance,' left until last to be savoured by visitors, a stunning finale to any tour of Housesteads fort. Lucius brushed his hands once more down his tunic front and prepared to play the role of a re-enactor, adding that touch of Hollywood style authenticity to visitors of the 'Roman experience.' The short, stout woman acting as guide and font of knowledge in all matters relating to Housesteads fort, was waving a hand of encouragement, and judging by her short quick steps, enthusiasm for her subject, her visitor group following like sheep. As they reached the latrine, Lucius drew himself up, and folding his hands before him, prepared to address the visitor party. A quick head count told him there were eight persons, including the guide. The plump guide waddled to a halt and raised an imperious hand. The sheep dutifully gathered around the shepherd, shifting, and searching for a secure foothold on the uneven ground. The chatter died away as the guide introduced the remains of the latrine.

"And here, ladies and gentlemen," she pointed at the information board posted just outside the doorway, "you see one of the best surviving remains of a Roman toilet to be found anywhere in the empire."

Necks craned, fingers pointed, heads nodded and hushed voices expressed amazement.

"A wooden bench ran along the top of each side of the latrine, the long bench cut at regular intervals with suitable openings over which the soldiers sat to do their business. They would have faced one another across the granite flagstone floor. There is a surviving section of wooden toilet bench in Vindolanda museum." Faces paid fascinated attention and heads continued to nod in understanding." The guide warmed to her subject.

"In front of where the men were seated on the wooden benches, run two channels the length of the latrine. These would have supplied water for the men to clean their…well, you know, clean themselves after their ablutions. The square and the circular granite basins held water for hand washing purposes."

"I heard that the Romans used sponges to clean, to wipe themselves with. Is that true?" asked a tall gentlemen from the back of the group.

"Yes, and no. The wealthier Romans living say in Italy itself, or around the fringes of the Mediterranean might well have the luxury of sponges for hygiene purposes, but up here on the northernmost frontier of the Roman Empire, it is highly unlikely that soldiers had that luxury. Moss, dock leaves and rags would be the best for which they could hope."

The tall gentlemen nodded his thanks, as the rest of the visitor group reflected on the fascinating topic of toilet habits of our ancestors. Lucius was bursting to speak. He wanted to tell the visitors that he had indeed employed the services of a clump of moss earlier that same morning, right here, sitting just there. His hand made an involuntary movement to point out the seat he used. It was too much to hold back and he blurted out, "there, right there! I was seated there!" An insistent forefinger stabbed at where he had sat earlier. "And I used moss, the guide is correct." His excitement engulfed him. Here he was, fresh from the late fourth century AD, able to explain life fifteen hundred years ago on this very spot; a living witness to history. But would they believe him? They would think him mad, or so wrapped in his re-enactor role that he appeared to be living it! He felt a brief moment of awkwardness, which the listeners had noticed. Despite the slight chill in the air, his cheeks flushed a little. The guide's voice broke in.

"If you'd like to take time now to revisit any of the remains which we've seen this morning, please do so. I suggest we meet in, say twenty minutes, down at the shop and café, where I can answer any last questions while we all enjoy a cuppa. And don't forget the wonderful little museum, it's a real gem."

"No, wait!"

The group ignored Lucius' plea and one by one turned away to go about the business of taking one more look around Vercovicium. Only the guide remained, staring intently at Lucius, or more correctly at the spot where Lucius stood. She looked through him, not at him. Her dark eyebrows narrowed and for a moment she felt the cold brush of a spirit from the past in the present moment. A moment which, later on, she would recount to others, about the time she had been a guide at Vercovicium fort. That story which so many of us have, the story of what we think was a touch from the spirit world, an encounter with a ghost. The guide shrugged the moment away and turned to make her way down to the café for a well-earned cup of hot coffee and a blueberry muffin. And as Lucius watched her walk away, he heard faint, but growing sounds of hammering and sawing, punctuated by the shouts of men at work. One more try, before his sanity gave way.

"Wait!" He shouted, but his ears were deaf to his own raised voice. The hammering and sawing grew louder. Above the low the occasional calls of men at work came a more insistent voice, Balbinus' rumbling tones coming ever closer. A veil of gloom settled itself over and around Lucius. He pinched his closed eyes between forefinger and thumb, squeezing gently, and hoping to dispel this strange mix of worlds. Which was the shadow world? With his eyes open and focusing once more, the plump guide and her visitors had vanished and he was back in the latrine, complete with its walls and roof. Balbinus spoke from behind the closed door now blocking Lucius' view of the outside world of then, and the world of now. Now was the reality. His face fixed in a grimace of frustration and he bit his lower lip to hold back the threatening tears. A single tear welled up and trickled down his cheek.

"Shit!" his go to expletive, then for good measure, as he brushed the tear away, "shit, shit, shit!" He grasped at the Great Red Bloodstone of Mithras in its pouch hanging from around his neck.

Balbinus was still speaking from the other side of the door. Lucius leant forward and dropped the wooden latch into place.

"I know you're in there, boy. I just heard you. You need to come out now. No more games." Two hefty knocks on the door concluded Balbinus' instruction.

Lucius' tortured mind wrestled with the unbelievable, which had to be believed. Believed because it was happening to him right now.

A thick, muffled voice joined in, heavy with pain and the threat of revenge.

"You heard him, Luthius. Thenturion Druthus wanths you! You'll pay for thith." Unseen by Lucius, Clodius raised a hand to his ruined and throbbing cheek which glowed as red as his burning need for revenge. The bottom of the door shuddered as Clodius delivered two hefty kicks to it.

Lucius knew he was trapped, stuck in this 'here and now,' having just left the other 'here and now' of tourists, coffee, and blueberry muffins. Another world yet the same world. No point in waiting to be dragged out of the latrine. He rose unsteadily to his feet, took a couple of steps, lifted the latch, and opened the door. Clodius grinned his triumph as Lucius appeared from the latrine; a short-lived grin, as pain shot across his swollen cheek. Clodius winced and raised a tentative hand. Lucius Verus would pay, and Clodius couldn't wait to see the punishment. He hoped fervently it meant a fatal beating with cudgels by your comrades, and he himself would deliver the first blow. Not that Clodius Brennus had seen any kind of punishment of that severity in his brief time as a frontier guard on Hadrian's Wall. A Romano-Britons' knowledge of the past consisted of half-truths and folk memories handed down from centuries ago in imperial Rome's heyday. These days, what was left of imperial Rome clung on to its northernmost province by its fingertips.

Lucius was coughing loudly and repeatedly, holding his hand up to his mouth. Unmoved by his obvious discomfort, Balbinus pushed past Clodius and Albus, grabbed Lucius by the arm pulling him in the direction of Centurion Drusus who stood hands on hips. A sharp blow across the back of Lucius' head was followed by an equally sharp word from Balbinus.

"Cease your noise, Lucius. Your centurion needs to speak to you."

Balbinus spat out a tasteless, chewed husk of a garlic clove. A stony-faced Centurion Drusus said nothing, turned on his heel and made his way up in the direction of the headquarters building. The others followed, Lucius, his heart racing, his arm in the grip of Balbinus, coughed his way up to the headquarters. Frowning, he knew he was in big trouble for taking a shovel to the side of Clodius Brennus' head. The frown didn't last long though, as he caught sight of Clodius' injury, continuing to balloon around the slit of his black eye. Strange that Lucius' smile was returned by Clodius. Lucius frowned once more. Clodius knew something which he, Lucius, didn't. That cold smile foreshadowed more than a sharp reprimand from Centurion Drusus for Lucius' crime of striking a comrade.

VII

Centurions' Reunion

The soldier farmers conducting repairs on the barrack block nearest to the headquarters, paid scant attention to the small party making their way up the main north south road towards the centre of the fort. They were too intent on refurbishing the barracks. Winter was coming and they had spent too many chilly nights huddled under their cloaks beneath the cold Caledonian stars since the barbarians had struck. The rasping and hammering, the calls and shouts carried an urgency to complete the task as soon as possible. Doors replaced, windows with fresh wooden shutters, proper beds to sleep in and braziers to warm the ever-colder nights, would bring a semblance of a civilised Roman world back into their lives. Added to that was the bonus of a less odorous and foul-smelling latrine, which the men assumed had been cleared, cleaned, and made usable by the party of boy soldiers now following centurion Drusus up to headquarters.

As Drusus approached the building, he frowned and narrowed his eyes at the two figures waiting by the door. A man and a boy. He recollected the boy in his ill-fitting, oversized armour, mulberry coloured mark on his face and with recognition furrowing his brow further, Drusus recalled the stocky figure alongside the boy soldier.

"Centurion Macro. Shouldn't you be dead, up at the villa beyond the Wall?"

Macro raised a hand in acknowledgement.

"Centurion Drusus. Greetings and congratulations on your escape. The Tribune would be relieved to know you made it back to Vercovicium. The girl, Julia, and her mother are with you?"

Drusus stopped in front of Macro and nodded.

"I take it they are all dead…the Tribune and his bodyguard?" It was Macro's turn to nod.

"And you escaped, survived? That was fortunate Centurion Macro." Drusus smiled without humour.

Macro ignored the question. He was looking over Drusus' shoulder to where Lucius appeared with Clodius, Albus and Balbinus. Macro moved to step round Drusus and greet Lucius, but found his way blocked by the other centurion who moved his hand to rest on his sword handle. Macro threw him a quizzical look.

"Lucius! It's good to see you are safe, and that you made it back to Vercovicium under the protection of Centurion Drusus." Macro smiled. "If the girl Julia made it back too, then our work here is done. You have accomplished what you set out to do, as have I. We need to go, now." He gave Drusus an empty smile and took a sidestep. Like a chess move, Drusus matched him.

"He's going nowhere, I'm afraid. Lucius Verus is under arrest."

Macro frowned, and stepping further to the side of Drusus, he found his way blocked again, and this time there was a menacing rasp of swiftly drawn steel as Centurion Drusus drew his gladius and raised the point to Macro's throat.

"That's far enough, Centurion Macro. Lucius Verus will be going with me into headquarters where he will be judged and sentenced accordingly."

"For…what crime, exactly?" Macro lifted his right hand to guide the point of the deadly blade away from his throat, but Drusus tightened his grip and stiffened his sword arm against Macro's attempt.

"For the crime of assaulting a fellow soldier. That soldier, the idiot with the swollen brutish looking face." Drusus nodded over his shoulder to where Clodius stood, a parody of a lopsided smile playing across his bruised and misshapen face.

"And furthermore, Centurion Macro, there is Lucius Verus's strange magic to consider. His…tricks, his possessions which don't seem to be of this world. Like those shoes with the strange markings."

The moment hung in the air and was only interrupted when a soldier appeared, holding something in his hand. A shiny, black object resting in his open palm, holding his attention, even as he walked up to the group standing by the door of the headquarters.

His gaze still fixed on the thing in his hand, the soldier stopped short when he looked up to take in the scene of one centurion's sword point close to the throat of another centurion.

"Sir. Trooper Balbinus ordered me to search Lucius' bedroll. I found this, sir." Holding out his hand, the soldier presented Lucius' mobile phone to Drusus.

With his sword point still close to Macro's throat, Drusus glanced down at the mobile phone.

"Under his bedroll in the barrack block?"

"Yes, sir."

"And did you find anything else?" Drusus was peering at the mobile phone now and had lowered his gladius, but not sheathed it.

"No, sir."

The insistent clatter of repair work hanging over Vercovicium had died away as the soldiers opted for a break from their sweaty work. Here, at the very centre of the fort, the late morning sun's warmth was reflected off the stone buildings. Drusus felt an uncomfortable trickle of sweat trail down from his armpit.

"Inside, everyone." Slipping his gladius back into its scabbard, he pushed past Macro and made for the open door and the welcoming cool inside. Autumn it was, but after the long and scorching summer, this autumn hung onto the heat during the daytime in a thoroughly unseasonal way.

The rest of the party followed Drusus indoors, squinting into the gloom of the headquarters' office. Drusus took the mobile phone from the soldier who had brought it to him and dismissed the man. The centurion made his way to his desk and planted himself as firmly in the rickety chair, as he dared. Balbinus pushed Lucius forward to stand before Drusus, who laid the mobile phone on the desk with exaggerated care.

"Before I deal with your unprovoked assault on Clodius Brennus here, I want to know exactly who you are, Lucius Verus and what this object is." He pointed at the phone before him.

"It was given to me by my father, sir."

"Like your shoes, Lucius? I recall you telling us that your father had been some kind of merchant before he settled into farming. You claimed that your exotic footwear came from Persia, or even India. Is that right?"

"Yes, centurion."

"Yes, what?"

"The…well, the…stone," Lucius pointed at the mobile phone, "the stone came from the east too. I can't recall exactly where from, but…"

"And does this black stone give you dark powers? I remember how you saved Lady Calpurnia from choking. Bit of a miracle that, a dark miracle. You seem to come and go, but no one recalls ever seeing you in the fort or the vicus, or any of the surrounding farms or villages at any time before the invasion by the Picts. Where exactly are you from, Lucius?"

Lucius thought he knew where he was from, but memories were hazy. He stared at Drusus as though the centurion might answer his own question and save Lucius the trouble. Macro spoke into the silence crowding in on the room.

"He's with me, centurion. The lad suffered a blow to his head months ago, long before the invasion. I knew his father, a veteran soldier turned farmer. A farming accident. It has affected Lucius' memory."

Centurion Drusus took a hard look at each of Macro's bare forearms in turn.

"As I have noted before, you have upon you the marks of Mithras, Macro. The Serpent and the Scorpion. Why should I trust you? You know the Imperial Edict calls for the end to the worship of pagan gods. You must know too that the late Tribune Caius Metellus was sent here, to Vercovicium on the Wall, along with me and his bodyguard, to enforce the Emperor's wishes in matters of religious worship? We are all Christians now." Drusus smiled without humour. In these times you could be any mix of religions and beliefs to suit the moment you found yourself in. Well, that was Drusus' position on religious matters.

Macro bit his lip as he recalled how he had despatched that same Tribune Caius Metellus during the battle at the villa to the north of the frontier. The man who had desecrated the Mithraeum at Brocolitia.

"You are an unusual pair of friends, to say the least, Centurion Macro. I don't trust either of you." No one in the room moved or spoke. Drusus' slight nod to Balbinus was the only sign that this wasn't a tableau frozen in a moment of time. Balbinus turned on his heel and left the room. He'd barely gone for a second before returning with three soldiers, not boys, but men, and fully armed. They ranged themselves behind Drusus and drew their swords with a series of rasps. Drusus let out a sigh, of relief, however, the next few moments might prove difficult.

"Lucius Verus, whatever the mystery of your dark arts, this is a military tribunal and you will be sentenced for the crime of striking a fellow comrade in arms, this one here, Clodius Brennus, garrison soldier at Vercovicium fort." A fly buzzed and stopped abruptly as it settled out of sight. Somewhere in the shadowed world of the roof timbers, a timeless spider's web quivered, and eight legs twitched.

The door into the headquarters' office behind Drusus and his three soldiers creaked on its protesting hinges, opening as Julia stepped into the room, oversized cloak clutched about her. She stopped in her tracks at the scene before her. The three soldiers, swords drawn, standing behind Drusus, seated at the huge desk, told her something wasn't right. Looking between them, she saw Lucius standing alongside the centurion she recalled from the villa. Behind them stood two boys and the soldier, Balbinus. Tension hung in the room. The fly buzzed noisily again, trying to free itself from the cobweb hanging in the rafters. Julia ran her fingers through the tufts of auburn hair spiking her head. A regular self-conscious movement since the barbarians had shorn Julia's locks after her capture. Centurion Drusus was summoning up the gravitas he felt befitted the moment. He turned in his chair to glance at Julia, then he turned back to Lucius and spoke in a flat tone.

"Lucius Verus, frontier soldier at Vercovicium fort, I sentence you to death for striking a fellow soldier, one Clodius Brennus." The trapped fly buzzed frantically and stopped. Macro reached down to his sword handle. Balbinus had the temerity to speak.

"But surely Centurion Drusus, he's only a lad, and we need every sword and spear hand we can muster. Death is hardly a fitting punishment for this breach of discipline. An argument between boys?" The gravity of the moment was tempered as Balbinus' fingers fumbled around for a garlic clove in the small leather purse hanging from his belt.

"Damn." He looked at the small clove pinched between his forefinger and thumb. It would have to do. He popped it into his mouth, sniffed and looked at his stony-faced centurion. Drusus remained tight lipped, so tight lipped that you couldn't see his mouth in the black stubble darkening his chin.

"Sir?"

Before Drusus could answer Balbinus and return to the matter in hand, the sentencing of Lucius, the door crashed open and a broad, ruddy cheeked face appeared and announced breathlessly, "Centurion Drusus, sir!"

"Calm yourself man." Drusus spoke evenly despite his heart picking up a beat. "What do you have to report, soldier?" Drusus had no recollection of the man's name. His tiny and disparate garrison, gathered from waifs and strays who had come out of hiding since the barbarian invasion had passed by and moved south, had not been together long enough for him to get to know every soldier's name.

"Barbarians, centurion. Men of the White Shields, Attacotti. Swarms of them, everywhere, sir. Approaching from the south."

"Flesh eaters, cannibals. Unholy allies of the Picts." Balbinus observed, completing the picture.

Drusus raised a quizzical eyebrow. "Yes, thank you for that, trooper Balbinus. Just rumours I think you will find about the Attacotti. Anyway, if the rumours are true, Balbinus, you will provide more than enough meat to satisfy these alleged cannibals. Your garlic infused flesh will provide quite a tasty dish for them, I would imagine."

Balbinus sniffed at Drusus' reference to his bulk and looked away.

"As a precaution though, I want everyone to gather in the north gateway tower. And make sure the Lady Calpurnia goes with you. The north gateway tower is defensible still and we can wait there until the barbarians have passed through the Wall on their journey to the north. They shouldn't trouble us. They'll be drunk and laden down with loot from the rich pickings south of the Wall, and they'll be anxious to enjoy their plunder rather than stop for an uncertain skirmish with us. You," Drusus pointed at the soldier who had brought the news, "return to your post. Bring me reports if the barbarians approach the fort. Go now!" The soldier gave a hurried salute and left. "In the meantime, we will need to close this matter of Lucius Verus' punishment. Balbinus, pick two men from the garrison, experienced soldiers, who can conduct the beheading of Verus. They must be men of purpose, of backbone, strong enough to carry out an execution. We need to proceed with the execution quickly and efficiently."

As soon as Balbinus left the room and before anyone could react, Julia was at Lucius' side. She grabbed his arm.

"Centurion Drusus, have you lost your mind? Sentence of death! Whatever Lucius has done, it can't mean he has to die." Julia appealed to Clodius, "You can't want this, surely…" She wanted to add weight to her appeal but couldn't address the youth with the misshapen face by name.

Clodius' reply was a smirk of triumph, difficult to figure out given the state of his face. He knew this dishevelled but beautiful young girl was the daughter of the former commander of Vercovicium, and that added enjoyment to his moment of power. Daughter of an aristocrat begging for the life of his assailant, Lucius.

Before anyone could speak, Macro clamped his iron fist around Julia's arm and pulled her close, with her back against his armoured chest, hand reaching for the dagger at his belt. Julia shrieked, Drusus leapt to his feet, the rickety chair clattering to the floor behind him, the three guards, swords drawn, sprung towards Macro who held Julia in a vice like grip, his pugio, dagger, already at her slender throat.

"Don't! No one move, stay exactly where you are! Lucius, draw my gladius. Do it!" The blade whispered from its scabbard as Lucius reached forward and did Macro's bidding. Drusus made a slight move in Macro's direction. The blade of the pugio pricked Julia's slender white throat and blood trickled under its sharp point. Julia gasped at the sudden pain, her face twisted in disbelief. Behind Macro, Julia and Lucius, the door crashed open and the soldier almost fell into the room. He went to speak but taking in the scene before him, kept his mouth shut. Macro, still holding the pugio point against Julia's neck, turned his head slightly towards the soldier.

"Speak, man. Report." Macro barked.

The soldier opened his mouth to speak, but fish like, no words came out, just a stupid gawp. He looked from Macro to Drusus, uncertain of who to address. He opted for Drusus, whose face was thunderous.

"Hundreds of barbarians, Picts, and others, but mostly Attacotti. Slow moving. Carts laden with plunder. Some barbarians on horseback. A group on foot have broken away from the main party and are making their way up here."

Outside the headquarters, the cries and shouts of his soldiers told Drusus that his men were aware of the approaching tribesmen too. He hoped that Balbinus might appear with the execution party and disarm Macro. His hope wouldn't materialise, as Balbinus was already urging the small garrison to make for the north gateway tower. Saws, hammers, and other tools were cast aside as the men and boys of Vercovicium garrison reached for armour, helmets, and weapons, and hurried towards the north gate.

Macro, eyes fixed on Drusus, stepped backwards towards the door, his pugio still at Julia's throat, her right arm pinioned behind her. Lucius followed, with Macro's gladius clutched firmly in his hand. Julia protested, and her short struggle was met with another warning nick to her throat. Lucius had reacted mechanically to Macro's actions and words. Now his brain had caught up with events, he spoke.

"This can't be right, Macro. I don't want Julia harmed. Why are you doing this? She's done nothing wrong."

"So you would rather stay here and die, Lucius? The girl is our saviour, our escape route. We can get back to where we belong, to where we came from. Our time here is done. Open the door carefully and check outside to see if our way is clear."

Lucius still wasn't sure about what they were doing. Macro would kill Julia if Drusus tried to prevent them leaving. On the other hand, if they stayed…

"You're not going anywhere, Centurion Macro. There's no safety to be found outside Vercovicium. I don't know just what you hope to achieve. If you harm the Tribune's daughter, or you put her in danger out there, then I swear, you'll join Lucius Verus in the afterlife." He took a step towards Macro.

"We'll take our chance, thank you, Centurion Drusus. Lucius, is the way clear?"

"It's clear."

Tightening his already vice like grip on Julia's slender arm, Macro eased their way out through the door. A quick look around showed the absence of anyone outside the headquarters building. The soldiers were now in the relative security of the north gateway east tower, busy preparing to bar the doors and shutter the small windows under the direction of Balbinus.

Macro paused for a moment.

"Lucius, we make for the west gate and take our chances from there. We have to get back to the mansio."

"Mansio?"

"Yes, your great aunt Livia's guesthouse, the Cosy Kettle."

Lucius had no idea what Macro was talking about, but the warm glow from the Great Red Blood Stone of Mithras hanging in the pouch around his neck reassured him to put his trust in his centurion.

The appearance of Drusus, the three soldiers, Clodius Brennus and Alba following them out of the headquarters building persuaded him that doing Macro's bidding would be the best course of action, at least for now, and he hurried after him in the direction of the west gate. Besides, he needed to know exactly what Macro planned for Julia. Would he really murder her once they were clear of the fort?

As for Drusus, he was torn between his desire to follow them or make his way to the safety of the north gateway to join his men. The situation was unclear. If Drusus allowed Macro to escape, and the barbarians went on past the fort, then Drusus would not stand a chance of tracking down and finding Macro, Julia, and Lucius in the emptiness of Caledonia. However, if he pursued them now, he'd be leaving the potential safety of Vercovicium and would take the risk of running straight into the barbarians and certain death. He pursed his lips and frowned his frustration at no one in particular. Perhaps the barbarians would do the job for him if the escapees ran into them outside the fort. A pity if Lady Julia were to die along with Lucius and Macro, a great pity. Drusus had taken a liking to the daughter of the late Tribune. And that liking, along with his plans for Julia, had grown since their escape from the bloodbath at the villa beyond the Wall.

His mind made up, Drusus beckoned to his companions to follow him to the relative safety of the north gateway and its defendable east tower, but not before he sent one of his more trusted soldiers to fetch Lady Calpurnia. The tribesmen's whoops and cheers, along with the bellowing of oxen dragging the plunder laden carts, were louder now as the Attacotti and the Picts made for the Knag Burn gate in the valley to the east of Vercovicium. A gateway added a hundred or so years previously when trading traffic through the Wall had increased substantially and a new customs control point was needed through the border. Besides, the trackway leading north into Caledonia from the north gate had become far too steep to accommodate wheeled traffic. Drusus gave thanks for this gateway down in the valley. It would mean the barbarians circumventing the fort and taking the easier route down through the boggy valley. The stream which ran there, always left the ground marshy and waterlogged. You had to make sure you kept to the firm and trusty metalled road running through the Knag Burn customs post fortified gate, laid over the boggy ground by the ever-efficient Roman military engineers.

Drusus arrived at the ground level entrance to the north gate tower and was met by Balbinus. As soon as Drusus, his three soldiers, Lady Calpurnia and the two boys were inside, Balbinus slammed the heavy wooden door shut and dropped the massive oak bar into the iron brackets set into the gateway wall either side of the entrance.

"All the men are safely inside, sir." Balbinus reported.

Drusus grunted an acknowledgement and hurried off up the internal staircase of the gateway, to appear on the platform on top of the tower with its commanding view in every direction. Stepping to the east parapet overlooking the Knag Burn gateway, Drusus could see that the encroaching tide of barbarians would take time, a couple of hours at least, to process through the narrow customs post. A river of humanity stretched back to the south as far as the eye could see. Hundreds of tribesmen, laden down with what Drusus assumed to be loot, were lost in a jumble of shouting, cursing, yelling warriors, cajoling, urging, and whipping the draught animals toiling heavy legged between the shafts of wooden carts. Oxen bellowed in protest and mules brayed, staggering under mountains of plunder heaped upon their backs or in the carts they were pulling.

As had been reported to him earlier, Drusus turned his attention to the small group of figures which had split from the tide squeezing through the narrow gateway of Knag Burn and were making their way up to the east gate of the fort. Around ten in number, chatting and laughing amongst themselves, clearly unaware of the presence of Roman soldiers in the fort. They were all bent double under large sacks and bags of loot. Spears served as walking staffs, while from their belts hung swords, daggers, and bloodied human heads.

Drusus hissed a command to those around him.

"Keep down everyone. Stay out of sight, no helmets! I don't want tell-tale crests or plumes showing above the parapet giving us away. Absolute silence. Pass the word."

His order rippled away in a hushed whisper repeated to the men to either side of him. Heads ducked low below the parapet, helmets were removed and whispered conversations died away. Discovery meant death. If the barbarians opted to delay their journey home to the north and flush out the tiny garrison of men and boys, resistance would be short lived. More Roman trophy heads would adorn Pictish warriors belts and horse harnesses, whilst

Roman flesh would provide the most macabre kind of feast for the Attacotti.

The small garrison of Vercovicium fort held its collective breath as the group of ten barbarians entered the fort under the barrelled roof of the east gate. Guttural voices, sharp laughs and the clinking bags of plunder slung across backs, echoed eerily across the fort and up to the north gateway.

VIII

Return to The Mansio

As luck would have it, at the very moment the barbarian chatter and laughter paused for a brief second, a soldier in the north gateway tower coughed. Not loud, but enough to catch the attention of a couple of the barbarians now inside the fort. One put his fingers to lips to silence his companions, his eyes darting around the fort interior. The brutish group was a mix of blue tattooed Picts and Attacotti carrying dirty white shields. An unholy alliance of head-hunters, and cannibals. Dark souled creatures, wild haired, clad in leather and fur.

As one, the group lowered their bags and sacks the ground. A rolling clatter, clunk and clink of looted Roman wealth, silver plate, jewellery, gold cups, precious metals and bronze statues was short lived. Relieved of their burdens, the warriors unsheathed swords, hefted spears, and slung shields before them and followed the pointing arm of one their number. All eyes focused on the east tower of the north gateway at the top of the slope on which the fort was built. Steely eyes glittered in anticipation, wild unkempt hair blew in the breeze and grips tightened around spear shafts and sword handles.

Up in the north gate tower, Centurion Drusus chanced a glance down into the fort from behind one of the parapets. The enemy couldn't see him at this angle but he could see them. They were making their up the main road of the fort towards the north gateway, boots crunching along the gravelled surface. From down in the Knag Burn valley came the nonstop noise of hundreds of warriors laden with their booty, talking, laughing, and shouting their way home to the wilds of Caledonia, whose dark mountains lay brooding along the distant horizon.

♦ ♦ ♦

The early autumn countryside stretched away down the slope leading out from the west gate of Vercovicium. A bald, dirt trackway ran alongside the old metalled Roman road, once a busy highway leading west from Vercovicium and running parallel to Hadrian's Wall on its south side, to end at the Irish sea. The track was smooth and they needed to hurry. The pot holed road meant the risk of broken or twisted ankles

Macro led the way, with Julia in tow, her wrist held in his iron grip. Here she was again, a captive being dragged through the wilds of Caledonia, this time by a Roman centurion instead of a Pict war band. Time had ceased to have any meaning for her, playing out her young life in this timeless land stretching out beneath her feet like a prehistoric leviathan, slumbering its way into eternity.

The day was warming up now, one of those late summer, early autumn days. All of Nature's produce hung in the balance between the two seasons. Fruit and berries ripe and fit to burst, at the pinnacle of taste and succulence. In a couple of weeks, the moment of their fulfilment would pass; they would become over ripe and burst, while others would start to wither. The insect world of bees, midges and gnats continue to busy themselves before the first frosts of autumn sparkled and whitened the land, threatening another harsh winter.

The thin whining of gnats around the heads of the three fugitives plagued them as they made their way down the dirt track descending the long slope to the west of Vercovicium. Macro paused their progress with hand held aloft as he caught the sound of voices on the breeze. Very faint but nonetheless familiar to the practised ear of a veteran soldier of Rome. A large party of men on the move back over the sill on which Vercovicium sat. Hundreds of voices. Barbarians..

"We need to move quicker." He released Julia's arm and sheathed his dagger. "If you want to run, girl, feel free, but I wouldn't recommend running from me and straight into the clutches of the barbarians."

Julia shuddered at the thought. Memories of her recent ordeal crowded in on her, like black demons, smiling their barbarity. Faceless spectators crowded onto seats in an amphitheatre, wizened parodies of human bodies in wicker cages, two girls battling on blood-stained arena floor…

"I won't run."

"Sensible girl. Now, we need to make haste. Both of you, keep a good look out, not just ahead but all around."

Lucius did Macro's bidding despite the apprehension creeping up his spine. Macro's nod and outstretched hand suggested that Lucius return the centurion's gladius. He did and Macro sheathed the weapon.

They made quicker progress now that Macro had released Julia from his grasp, and they hurried south along the track with its Roman road running to the right of them. They passed terraced fields growing spelt wheat and barley, crops standing autumn tall, awaiting a harvest which would never come, randomly, other fields of cereal crops had been burnt to blackened stubble by the invading hordes of a few weeks back. Once they left the track, Macro led them through any woodland cover available, and the three of them scanned the surrounding landscape for any sign of tribesmen. They were breaking cover from the scrawny coppice they had passed through when Macro changed direction. Now, they made their way southeast, crossing the great Military Way which runs the seventy-three miles of Hadrian's Wall, from east coast to west coast. Today the B6318 follows the course of the Military Way, a switch back, rising and dipping, as it carries generations of excited Wall tourists and walkers in cars, buses, coaches, and on motorbikes, full of anticipation of their date with Hadrian's Wall. Lucius Mabutt was crossing that same road which wouldn't see cars and tourists for another seventeen hundred years. And as he crossed the road, he looked ahead to where Mr MacRonald pointed to a burnt-out building standing close by. Behind him, Lucius thought he heard the distant hum of traffic from the future, rubber on tarmac; a layer of time covering the tramp of legionary marching boots.

♦ ♦ ♦

The three fugitives approached the mansio, Macro leading the way, gladius drawn and eyes watchful. Lucius followed Julia, checking behind for any signs of pursuit by Drusus and his men, or barbarians, Julia walking between Macro and Lucius, eyes darting in all directions, her head crowded with questions. Macro raised his right arm. Lucius and Julia stopped. Macro made his way ahead to the main door of the mansio. The door, hung from its hinges at a crazy angle, smashed and splintered. It made an odd sight, an open door still clinging to its hinges, hanging open in the centre of a surviving wall, standing in solitary uselessness, the whitewash scorched and blackened by the fire. Macro was far enough away for Julia to risk a whisper to Lucius as he moved to her side, his eyes still scanning their surroundings.

"Lucius, where are we? What is the centurion doing?"

"This is where it started, Julia. Right here at great aunt Livia's guesthouse, the Cosy Kettle."

The whispers continued.

"The, what?" Julia dipped her head towards him.

"The mansio. Guesthouse we'd call it. You must know what that is?"

They looked to where Macro was stepping through the open doorway.

"Of course I know what a mansio is, Lucius," she hissed. "A boarding house, a way stop for travellers, especially imperial couriers on official business. A hot meal, a bed for the night and a change of horses. Wasn't this one called…the Plenum Amphoras, or some such? But why are we here?"

"Because Macro and I came back from the future. I came back to rescue you, and the centurion…well, he came back for his own reasons."

Julia sighed. "Came back? What, from the future? Lucius you went through this nonsense last time, with your exotic black music box, your strange pictures drawn from above us in the sky. No wonder Centurion Drusus thinks you're a magician."

It was Lucius' turn to be exasperated. "Well, at least you don't accuse me of black arts, as he has."

Macro was returning now, his heavy booted steps padding quickly through the ash, suggesting the way was clear.

Julia spoke while watching Macro make his way towards them. "I'll tell you who you are, Lucius. You are a local farm boy, destined to serve in the garrison as a frontier guard at Vercovicium fort. A soldier farmer, following in the footsteps of your father, grandfather, and way back to the time when the Wall was built. Where you disappeared to when I was captured by the Pictish warlord, Talorc, outside the latrine, I have no idea. But it certainly wasn't the future."

Macro arrived, panting from his exertions, and coughing from the still smoking ruins of the mansio. He drew breath and hurried his words.

"Are you ready, Lucius? We need to go right now."

The door to memory opened a little wider and Lucius nodded.

"What about Julia, sir? "

Macro looked at Julia.

"She stays here."

A ridiculous question popped into Lucius' head… "Can't she come with us?" and stayed there, unasked.

Macro read Lucius' mind.

"I say again, the girl stays. And even if she could come with us, how on earth would she react to…cope with the twenty first century?" Lucius opened his mouth to speak but Macro cut him short. "You and I are here through the power of Mithras. You have some understanding, some knowledge of these times, of Roman Britain. You've studied history through the accumulated knowledge of the last two thousand years. What knowledge does she have? She won't have read books about the world two thousand years into her future, will she? She'd likely die if thrown into our world. Now, we need to get on. She has served her purpose and she can make her own way back up to the fort."

Lucius could see the sense in what Macro was saying about the inherent dangers of travel through time, nevertheless, he persisted.

"What about the barbarians?"

Macro looked Julia up and down and laughed. "The barbarians? Don't be ridiculous, Lucius. Look at her. Do you think she looks like a Roman? She would fit in with any group of barbarians. You wouldn't know she was the aristocratic daughter of a Roman Tribune." Macro avoided looking at Julia as he mentioned her father.

Lucius knew Macro was right. Julia made a perfect barbarian. Despite her best efforts, her rudely cropped hair resembled more a bird's nest than a stylishly designed statement befitting her social class. Her oversized Roman army issue woollen cloak would pass for a Pict cloak. A thoroughly uncivilised appearance belying her true identity.

A sudden gust of wind blew a shower of black and grey speckled ash towards them from the burnt out mansio. A bright orange glow amongst a pile of blackened timbers in the heart of the building, told of a fire rekindled briefly. The shower of ashes floated around the three figures standing in the dead ashes of time. with a cloud of past memories floating around their heads.

Macro turned on his heel and walked back the way he had just come. Lucius followed, turning to look back at

Julia, just once. He was deserting her for the second time, and it hurt. Julia stood alone with her thoughts, her feelings of abandonment…her father, her friend Rhiannon and now Lucius. She felt as though her life was an unsealed bottle lying on its side with the contents slowly draining away; or like sand from an amphitheatre floor slipping through her fingers, to leave her empty handed. She would have to find her way back to the fort and her mother. Julia wasn't sure how, but she had no choice. Everyone else may be gone from her life, but her mother needed her. So, lie low for now, but first, she had to satisfy her curiosity. Decision made, Julia plucked up courage to follow Lucius into the burnt-out shell of the mansio, the Plenum Amphora, or that strange unintelligible name by which Lucius called it, to see what he and the centurion were up to.

IX

Trapped

As puzzled as the barbarians were by the wooden door, bolted, barred, and locked from the inside, their drunken stupor, lent a laziness to their puzzlement. The finest Roman wines, like Falernian and Caecuban had proved a heady mix when drunk in vast quantities along with their native barley beer. The best wines looted from the wealthy villa estates and small towns they had overrun, burned, and looted as they made their way south into the richer pickings of Roman Britain. They backed away from the door, for the moment.

On the top floor of the gateway tower, Centurion Drusus had his hand clamped across Lady Calpurnia's mouth. She was a broken woman, a dead husband and now her daughter missing. A totally unpredictable nuisance whose sudden outbursts day and night threatened to reveal Drusus and his comrades to the nearest barbarian warband.

Her fine aristocratic world as the wife of Tribune Caius Metellus, by order of the Emperor, commander of the frontier garrison of Vercovicium, had turned to dust and ashes. In her delusion, she thought the barbarians to be saviours, Roman troops led by her dead husband. Her attempt to call out for help had been pre-empted by Drusus, and her ensuing feeble struggles were like those of an infant in Drusus' muscular embrace.

Voices slurred by alcohol drifted up to the Roman soldiers crouched, heads bowed, breath held behind parapets and shuttered windows. Cruel laughter was accompanied by a return of frenzied banging on the door with sword pommels and spear butts. Lady Calpurnia twitched a feeble protest against Drusus' restraining arms and slumped back again, defeated. Drusus closed his eyes and thought hard about what could happen next. The barbarians might simply give up and rejoin the hordes snaking through the Knag Burn gateway down in the valley. Or they might persist, call for reinforcements, and batter the door until it broke open. As safe as the gateway tower was for the present, it was also a potential death trap if the enemy did break in. Drusus pursed his lips and cursed under his breath. Things weren't supposed to come to this. Yes, it had promised to be a challenging posting, moving from the comfort and civilised world of Nimes in southern Gaul when the call from the Emperor came. But this! Tribune Caius Metellus dead, his daughter captured and abused by barbarians and his noble wife reduced to a nervous wreck. As for himself, Drusus cursed his luck in arriving in this province just at the time when the barbarian world around Roman Britain exploded into chaos.

The pounding at the door had died away. The voices were more subdued and the laughter stopped. Chancing another peep around the parapet, Drusus saw the barbarians drifting away from the gateway. They paused and looked at the assortment of tools scattered around. He ducked his head as a couple of the savages glanced back up at the tower. But they weren't going anywhere. Drusus continued to watch as these unwelcome visitors sought out a suitable spot to lay their weapons and plunder to begin the search for firewood and comfortable places to sit. They were staying here, at least for now. Drusus sighed, ducked down from the parapet, closed his eyes, and laid his head back against grey stone wall.

♦ ♦ ♦

Stepping over and between the debris surrounding the smoke blackened rubble of the mansio, Julia stopped and crouched behind a half-demolished wall to watch Lucius and Macro. Lucius was looking down at Macro who was kneeling in what was once the courtyard garden of the mansio. Dagger in hand, Macro was scraping at the ground. Finally he found what he had been looking for. He stood and pointed down, drawing Lucius' attention to whatever it was he had found. Then, Macro bent to seize hold of a large metal ring, which Julia saw as he pulled open a trapdoor the ring was attached to. He lowered the wooden trap door to the ground without making a sound, straightening up, he took a step towards Lucius and put his hands on Lucius' shoulders. Lucius bowed his head and the centurion lifted the leather pouch from where it hung around Lucius' neck and placed it over his own head to rest around his own neck.

The wind was gusting fitfully now, heavy with the scent of autumn, stirring the ashes of the mansio into spiralling clouds, like dark snowflakes chasing on a winter wind. As Julia crouched behind the low remains of the wall, the ash cloud billowed and grew until a grey gloom descended over the burnt out mansio and the three figures in its ruins. She could just make out the scene as it unfolded before her, despite the ash cloud. The two shadowy figures appeared to descend into the ground and disappear from her view. The last thing Julia saw was the upper body of the centurion as he leant out of the hole in the ground to grasp the edge of the trapdoor and close it over his head.

It was pitch black in the cellarium, the secret underground room, the cellar behind what had been the Cosy Kettle, from where Macro and Lucius had started their journey. Lucius stood, hands outstretched in front of him, reaching into the darkness. No point in moving. He could hear Macro fumbling around in the blackness, looking for a means to bring light into this dark space. His fumbles were accompanied by low grumbling, indistinct, barely audible. And then, a tiny flurry of quick sparks and the sound of Macro striking steel against flint bringing fire to life. Now, the faint orange glow of tinder catching and a soft yellow flame moving through the darkness towards an unseen oil lamp in a wall niche. The flame grew as it found further life stroking the wick in the terracotta oil lamp. Soon the wall niche reflected a glimmer of light into the dark space of the cellarium. Macro's oversized shadow moved across the far wall where the tauroctony flickered its moment in time. The centurion made his way to the next oil lamp and the next. Light grew around the cellarium to reveal Macro's cruciform armour wooden stand which resembled a giant letter T.

"We're back, Lucius."

Lucius looked up at the ceiling. "Back? And up there is what? The Cosy Kettle? The Roman mansio?"

Centurion Macro pointed at the pouch with the Great Red Bloodstone of Mithras hanging from his neck.

"There's no reason to doubt that, Lucius Mabbutt. This," he grasped the pouch, "this holy gem, the Bloodstone of Mithras, brought us back. If you hadn't become a member of our sacred sect, we could never have returned, brother Raven. Your ordeal, your initiation made this possible, as I told you it would when we began our journey."

Lucius cast his mind back to the ordeal of his initiation into the cult of Mithras. Was that only a few days, weeks, even hours ago? Buried alive underground? Lucius was losing track of time and even his own name. Lucius what…Mabutt or Verus? And then there was brother Raven…

"Get changed, Lucius. Your clothes are where you left them, over there on that wooden chest." Macro pointed into the wavering half lit gloom of the cellarium. The tauroctony wall painting of Mithras slaying the Great Bull was clearer now, despite the shadows dancing across it. The god Mithras plunging his cruel dagger into the sinewy neck of the huge creature. The muscles on the bull's neck contracting and expanding under the mortal wound. Blood from the gash flowed and dripped to the earth in fulfilment of the Mithraic creation story. The beginning of all life, the beginning of time itself.

"Hurry up, lad." The acrid smell of burning olive oil filled the cellarium, along with the hiss and splutter of flaring, terracotta lamp wicks.

Lucius removed his woollen cloak, leather belt, linen tunic, and battered Nike trainers, placing them on the wooden chest next to his twenty first century clothes. He shivered once in the chill of the cellarium and dressed hurriedly, dragging on his damp jeans, which smelt of smoke as did his tee shirt and hoodie. With the trainers back on, he was ready to follow Macro's next instruction. Only one item was missing, one item which he dare not mention to the centurion. His mobile phone, now presumably two thousand years away in the distant past, somewhere on Hadrian's Wall, somewhere in Vercovicium. Question was, what would happen to his mobile phone, would it, could it affect the course of history? After all, he'd broken the cardinal rule of returning to the past and doing something which could affect the course of history. Mr MacRonald had warned him. Might there be a terrible price to pay? And, as for the present, what lay on the ground, over his head? Was it the Cosy Kettle or, the Plenum Amphoras? Northumberland guesthouse, or Roman mansio?

"Aren't you getting changed, centurion?"

"Centurion, eh? Well, Lucius, be it centurion, Macro or Mr MacRonald, this is the last time we shall be together."

The flickering orange light from the terracotta lamps brushed over Macro's bronze breastplate. The mythical figures studding the armour, stood in relief against the deeper shadows of the cellar. Lucius stared, as though seeing the bronze breastplate for the first time. He'd never studied it before. Lucius could make out writhing snakes crowning the head of Medusa, surrounded by swirling motifs of laurel leaves, two uprearing winged horses and a pair of threatening scorpions. Here and there, the breastplate sported battle scars, dents and scratches sustained in combat over decades of service under the Eagles, the length and breadth of the Empire.

"Last time we'll be together?" He looked Macro full in the face. "But why? Aren't we going up to…the Cosy Kettle? I don't understand."

Macro was holding the pouch dangling from his neck. He gave the pouch a gentle tug.

"I have to return the Great Red Bloodstone of Mithras to its rightful place, Lucius. Into the dark earth where the temple of our god stands at Brocolitia on the Wall." He gripped the pouch tighter with whitened knuckles. "I have one more journey to make and then it's done, it will be over. We completed our journey, our missions together, Lucius. Our adventure in time, some might say ordeal in time, is done. You became one of the brotherhood of Mithras, a Raven, and that will forever be your link with the past, Lucius, you will continue to live with the past, indeed in the past for the rest of your life. One day you will remember what I am saying to you now, as we part." Macro sighed and looked to the ceiling. "And your Roman girl. She is still up there, alone now. I can take her back to the safety of Vercovicium. I owe her that after the hostage charade. Rest assured, I would not have harmed her. It was different with her father."

Macro's last words made no sense, and Lucius threw Macro a quizzical look. For the rest, Lucius saw sense in that in what Macro, or Mr MacRonald said. His own brush with the past was enough, it was done. His preference now was for the present and the future. Macro read his mind as he moved towards the cellarium steps which led up to the trap door.

"The future is certain, Lucius. I'm sure you are destined for remarkable things, especially in the world of, well, all of this which we call history. The past is always with us, Lucius, it never dies." Macro's words sounded distant as he looked beyond Lucius into some other time and place. A step back towards Lucius, a brief hug, the bronze breastplate hard against Lucius' chest, and one last instruction.

"Do not follow me. Wait for a space of sixty heartbeats, and only then should you open the trapdoor and step out into the world of the Cosy Kettle. Farewell, Raven."

Lucius heard Macro's footsteps as he made his way up to the trapdoor. There was a sudden flood of daylight as the trapdoor opened, a grunt as Macro pulled himself up, followed by a heavy crash as Macro dropped the trapdoor back into place. In the near silence of the sixty heartbeats he counted in his head, Lucius could hear the fetch and pull of his breathing, the spitting lamp flames and the rhythmic whoosh of blood in his ears. The sixty heartbeats counted, Lucius took a deep breath to steady himself. Despite the deep breath, his legs trembled as he made his way over to the steps leading up to the trapdoor. He climbed the steps and rested his palms against the underside of the trapdoor. What glimmer of light was left from the faltering oil lamps didn't reach this far up the cellarium steps and Lucius battled to dismiss the memory of the prehistoric cobwebs which hung all around. You didn't want to brush your hands against those awful dusty webs, or even worse, push your hand through them to disturb any hidden black legged spiders.

There was no sound from the other side of the wooden trapdoor. Lucius drew on all his strength to push the heavy trapdoor up. As the crack to the outside world grew ever wider, Lucius blinked in the sunlight flooding in to the cellarium. The trapdoor reached its zenith after which it fell away and landed with a crash.

"What in the name of God!" Great aunt Livia's voice boomed a welcome of sorts from her back garden in which the secret trapdoor lay above the cellarium. The smell of burning wafted past Lucius as he hauled himself out of the cellarium and stood in the knee deep, scruffy vegetation which passed for great aunt Livia's back garden. Lucius glanced around the tangle of wild rose bushes, the gigantic thistles sporting deep purple flower heads and rampant grass. No burnt out mansio, no clouds of ash. He expected to see Centurion Macro standing amongst the tall weeds and leggy rosebushes, whilst knowing in the same moment that would not be the case. Centurion Macro was now fifteen centuries in the past. Long gone, dust.

"Lucius!" Great aunt Livia was waddling towards him, wiping her hands on the apron tied around her waist. "Thank God you're safe and back here at last. I've had a frightful time. A fire! Arson so the police say. Who would want to do such a thing? Here of all places."

Lucius looked over her shoulder. There had been a fire. Thankfully, the damage was confined to the rear of the Cosy Kettle. The back door leading from the kitchen out into to the overgrown garden, was a charred skeleton of its former self, charcoal black. The kitchen window was equally blackened with cracks running in all directions across it.

"Vandals, arsonists." Great aunt Livia spoke. "It's just a guesthouse, for goodness sake. Anyone would think it was the old days back when barbarians crossed Hadrian's Wall, burning everything in their path."

Lucius took a step towards her, expecting the usual bosomy embrace. At least he was taller than great aunt Livia now and wouldn't find himself suffocated by her ample endowment! She was in no mood for a sympathy vote. Her raised hand kept Lucius back. He shrugged.

"But at least you're safe, great aunt Livia." Even as he spoke the words, his brain, the Lucius Verus one, nagged at him. How could you survive the barbarian invasion and the burning of your mansio? And she made no mention of Mr MacRonald, Centurion Macro?

"Did you see Centurion Macro, er, Mr MacRonald just now?" Lucius cast around, half expecting, half hoping he would see his teacher. Great aunt Livia shrugged.

"Ok. So how long were we gone for, aunt? After we went down into the…cellarium?"

She shrugged again. "About an hour, I'd say. Yes, an hour at the most. The vandals set their fire just after you two descended into the cellarium.."

Gone but an hour from here, and yet days, a week he reckoned, spent in the past?

'So time doesn't match up,' he thought.

With no all-enveloping, suffocating embrace forthcoming, Lucius followed great aunt Livia along the pathway leading around the side of the Cosy Kettle to the front door.

"The kitchen is thankfully, still serviceable despite the damage to the door and window," she said, leading the way indoors. "No doubt you'll be wanting a hearty meal. One of my all-day breakfasts, so favoured by my guests. Then a shower and a good rest."

Lucius never recalled any such creature as a 'guest' frequenting great aunt Livia's bed and breakfast guesthouse, and he had been a regular visitor for ten years during the school holidays. Right now, what he did need was that breakfast, a thorough shower, and a long rest. Lucius needed time, every one of us needs time, the one thing that we never have enough of.

X

Macro and Julia

No sooner had Macro emerged from the trapdoor, than he was walking towards Julia through the fire debris of the burnt out mansio littering the ground. His feet kicked up clouds of ash, and broken pottery crunched under his hobnailed Roman army boots. The short snap of glass fragments underfoot told their own story of the destruction vented on the mansio by the marauding Picts.

Macro was approaching Julia, helmet swinging by its chin strap from his left hand. He spotted Julia and changed direction towards her, halting a couple of paces away. Julia shrank back, shook her head, and lifted a hand to stop him coming any closer.

Macro raised his right hand in acknowledgement. He meant her no harm.

"Where's Lucius?" She looked behind Macro to where the trapdoor lay.

"He's gone, girl. Forever." Macro removed the felt skull cap, wiped the sweat from his balding head, replaced the skull cap before clamping on his centurion's helmet. He was scouring the surrounding landscape as he fiddled with the chinstrap to secure the helmet.

"We can't stay here." He looked at Julia. "Oh, no need to fear me, girl," he chuckled. "I mean you no harm. That…earlier," he gestured a throat cutting action, "that was a charade, mine, and Lucius' way out of trouble. Your Centurion Drusus would have put Lucius to death."

"I know, I heard, I was there." She lowered her hand.

Macro should have felt at least a pang of guilt as he looked at Tribune Caius' daughter. What did it matter? What was done was done. Mithras had willed it. And now Mithras willed the return of the Great Red Bloodstone to the temple grounds at Brocolitia, up on the Wall, then Macro's journey would be complete, his journey at an end. He touched the pouch around his neck, a cautious finger easing the thong away from the wound on his neck.

Julia spoke. "You know Lucius came and went before, I mean, this is the second time I've encountered him. Who is he? Drusus says he's a magician. I have seen strange things. Lucius has shown me things that cannot be explained. A picture from the heavens, as though drawn by an eagle. A black polished stone playing the sound of tiny bells. And he saved my mother from choking to death." Her look demanded an answer.

"You would not believe me if I told you, girl." Macro sidled past Julia, hand resting on the pommel of his word, walking back in the direction of Vercovicium.

"Where are you, we, going?" She called out as headed uphill in the direction of Hadrian's Wall sketched along the distant craggy hills.

There was no answer. Julia hurried after him. He turned to her as she appeared alongside him.

"Hopefully, back to Vercovicium. I can return you to Centurion Drusus, unharmed. You served your purpose. I got Lucius away and safely back to his own time." A horsefly landed on the red raw wound on the back of his neck. He slapped at it and grimaced at the stab of pain.

"All this talk about time and going back. Lucius spoke about it. Back in time? So he comes from the past then?"

Macro sighed and paused in mid-stride.

"Not back, no, but forward." He looked directly at Julia. "What's the point, you wouldn't understand, girl."

Macro continued to walk uphill towards the Military Way, retracing the steps which he and Lucius had made a week ago. He prayed to Mithras that Lucius was now safely back with great aunt Livia in 2005. Lucius, the Raven, and servant of Mithras was destined for remarkable things in his future; he would become a discoverer of, and guardian to the past. Macro touched the pouch hanging at his chest and tightened his grip on his sword handle. He scowled and swatted again at the persistent horsefly plaguing his wounded neck.

Despite his limp prone left leg, Centurion Macro was now into his stride, which in his prime as a Roman soldier could cover twenty-two miles a day on the march with a sixty pound back pack. Those days were gone but he still had a remarkable ability to steadily eat up the miles over the most challenging of terrains. They crossed the road, the Military Way, serving the garrisons and forts along the Wall from east to west and began the steeper ascent towards Vercovicium.

The clamour of hundreds of distant voices grew as the two of them approached Vercovicium. Julia glanced anxiously at Macro's scowling face. The barbarians were still in the vicinity of Vercovicium. Here was a sound heard countless occasions over his lifetime. The raucous din of barbarians gathered in significant numbers. War, plunder, burning, torture, and alcohol provided a heady mix of an ill-disciplined and murderous threat. Through his scowl, Macro looked towards Vercovicium for any signs of life. Nothing. He knelt in the long grass and heather. Julia followed his lead. Macro looked over the burnt-out ruins of the vicus settlement, beyond which lay the Knag Burn gateway way down in the marshy valley to the east of the fort. His house which had once stood in the vicus, was burned to the ground.

Macro pressed his fingers to his lips and signed Julia that she should remain where she was. She nodded. Macro removed his crested helmet and laid it in the grass next to Julia. Bending low, made his way over and through the tumbled, charred remains of the vicus until the valley of the Knag Burn unfolded before him. Where the stone-built gateway, designed to be narrow enough to only allow one cart at a time for customs control, pierced through Wall, hundreds of tribesmen trudged, pushed, and jostled their way through with their plunder. Macro looked to the south where the snake like river of humanity stretched as far as the eye could see. This host would take days to move through the Knag Burn gate. He dare not chance going back into Vercovicium. The girl would have to come with him to the Mithraeum at Brocolitia or find her own way into the fort and back to Drusus. Macro tugged at his bottom lip as he scanned the river of barbarians in the valley. The abandoned fort at Brocolitia with its Mithraic temple hard by, was east of Vercovicium. The barbarians lay across the route to the east and Brocolitia, blocking his path. He tugged harder at his lip and scratched at his grizzled chin, deep in thought. The Scorpion and the Snake itched their irritation and impatience at this delay. Macro turned and ducked low making his way back to Julia. He knelt next to her.

"You will have to make a choice, girl. I go east to my temple. You either come with me or…"

"Or what, centurion?" She waved a hand at the perpetual midges plaguing her head.

"Or you make your way up to the fort. Alone."

The noise from the barbarians crossing the Knag Burn valley rolled up to them. From high above came the trickling tweeting of a lark enjoying the warmth of a sunny autumn afternoon, a strange contrast.

"Your temple, centurion? A temple to your deity, Mithras?"

"Yes. I have unfinished business there." The pouch at his neck was once more cradled in his hand.

Julia pointed a slender finger. "Lucius had that before you arrived at the fort." She shifted on her haunches. "I too possessed it once."

"When?"

Julia marshalled her memories and spoke as the pieces fell into place.

"When you lost it, centurion." Julia pointed up towards the south gateway of the fort. "You dropped it up there by the gateway. I was with my friend." The memory of Rhiannon caught in her throat. "We met you at the milestone. You collapsed there, a ghost, a spectre, a haunted creature. And then we followed you back to the fort. You walked with a limp, that's how I know it was you. You disappeared into the fort but we found your red stone in that pouch which you had dropped outside the gateway. I kept it, in a box under my bed." Julia looked down at the ground.

"Until Lucius tore it from you in the moment of his return." Macro nodded his understanding. "The circle is complete, well nearly." He fumbled with his neckcloth, which prevented the armoured breastplate chafing his throat. It rubbed on the neck wound from the battle at the villa when a savage, taking him for dead, tried to decapitate him. He struggled with the knot. Julia leant forward and with long delicate fingers, eased the knot apart. Macro smiled his thanks and removed the neckcloth and dabbed at his wounded neck. He grimaced as some of the dried blood flaked away, but there was still an open part to the wound. Macro held the neckcloth to it.

"Let me." Julia held out her hand. Macro paused for a few beats before handing the girl the grubby scrap of cloth. Julia flicked the neckcloth open and refolded it, trying to find a cleaner part amongst the grime and sweat stains.

"Better?" Macro winced as Julia dabbed the cloth over the raw wound. He growled his thanks.

Macro, ever watchful, eyes darting, back and forth, pondered their situation. He was still awaiting a reply from the girl. Once he knew what she intended to do, he could set about planning how to get to Brocolitia. His constant scanning of their surroundings took in the south side of Vercovicium and its towering gateway. No sign of life. Had the barbarians slaughtered Drusus and his tiny garrison? Had Drusus and his garrison fled before the barbarians arrived to pour through the Knag Burn gate?

"Ouch!" Macro ducked away from Julia's dabbing hand. "That's enough…thank you." The last said reluctantly. Centurion Macro was not a man to be indebted to a young girl. He took the neck scarf and placed it gingerly on the wound.

"So what is it to be…?"

"I'm coming with you, centurion. It would be safer." Macro grunted in agreement and they settled back into silence. It seemed every fly, gnat, midge, and mosquito seemed in Caledonia had decided to gather around the two of them, crouching low in the undergrowth south of the ruined vicus and the silent fort. Their hands waving to dissuade the whining insects had the usual negligible effect.

"Did you see him die?"

"Who?"

"My father, the Tribune. When the Picts attacked."

Macro played for time, taking the neck scarf from his wound, and examining the cloth closely.

"He died well, girl. As you would expect from a Tribune of Rome."

"That's generous of you. After all, you follow the cult of Mithras, and it was my father's task to eradicate all pagan practices on this section of the Wall. We are Christians, your enemies, surely? My father was your enemy. You saw him die, bravely, you say."

Macro moved uneasily and rubbed at his bent knees. Crouching in the grass and heather was not easy for any length of time these days.

"Picts," Macro hissed as his attention was drawn to a familiar sound coming from the west of Vercovicium, to their left; the sound of hoofbeats and the jingle of horse harness, the promise of another threat? A steady rhythm coming nearer with each heartbeat. Julia heard it too. She was far from unfamiliar with military sounds. The encroaching rumble told of a sizeable number of horsemen. A sizeable number had to mean Roman cavalry, and as Macro and Julia stood, the first sign to confirm their conclusion, was a figure bent over the neck of a horse plunging its way up the grassy hillside towards them. A figure wearing a Roman helmet and a reddish-brown cloak trailing out behind him. Grasped in his left hand was a silvered eagle-topped standard. The horse was slowing as the hill steepened and more horsemen were coming into sight behind him, likewise helmeted and cloaked. The Scorpion itched, the Snake answered and the Bloodstone glowed warmly in its pouch. Mithras made his unseen presence felt. There were around thirty cavalrymen now, the number growing with every heartbeat. A sight to raise the spirits. No need for Macro to rest his hand on the pommel of his sword.

"Well, well. Mithras be praised." Macro bent to pick up his helmet. Felt skull cap in place, he jammed the helmet onto his head and without bothering to tie the chin strap, he waved at the horsemen, so close now you could see the breath pluming from the horses' flared nostrils and make out the features of individual troopers. Macro noted the numbers as they grew to around sixty horsemen, fully armed and disciplined. The leading cavalry group slowed their mounts to a walking pace and now the animals picked their way carefully through the undergrowth, their riders' gazes fixed on the south gate of Vercovicium. The first rider they had seen tugged his horse's head round in the direction of Macro and Julia. He walked his horse cautiously towards them, drawing his spatha, long cavalry sword, as he did so. You trusted no one in these turbulent times, even though the man standing before him wore the transverse red crested helmet of a centurion. Resting his sword across his knees, the cavalryman edged his horse a little nearer to Macro and Julia. Behind him, the jingle of harness and whinnying of horses, now slowing to a walk, moved up the trackway towards Vercovicium. A figure broke away from the main party and joined the soldier approaching Macro and Julia. The newcomer was clearly a senior officer, despite his mud-spattered uniform. A red cloak, a gold-coloured helmet topped with an even deeper red plume of exotic ostrich feathers. The soldier holding the eagle-topped standard saluted the newcomer, then spoke from beneath the rim of his helmet, a hook-nosed tanned face with narrowed eyes.

"I'm Signifer Flavinus of the Ala Petriana," he announced. His horse snuffled loudly down the length of its nose, nostrils quivered and flecks of white spume flew when it shook its head. "And this is Legate Decimus Metius Manillus, former commander of the Legion Twentieth Valeria Victrix at Deva, now commanding the Ala Petriana."

Legate Decimus Metius Manillus was a tall man, seeming to dwarf his horse, itself a larger than normal beast, standing at some fifteen hands. The Legate's feet, sporting bright red leather boots, looked like they were close to brushing the ground, such was his height. Jet black curls spilled from under his golden helmet and lay thick across his red cloaked shoulders. Red and gold, the colours of Rome, red the colour of Mars, god of war.

Macro marvelled at the introductions, a formality and grandeur which sat nonsensically alongside the circumstances around them. Signifer Flavinus' horse pawed at the ground, impatient to join the stream of cavalry passing behind, making its way up to the south gateway of Vercovicium. The wooden shaft of the standard he grasped firmly in his left hand, was topped by a crossbar from which hung a red flag, fringed at the bottom by gold-coloured tassels. Above that, a silvered shallow disc with a scalloped edge, held an image of the Emperor's face. A bright silver imperial eagle topped the standard.

"And you would be…?" Signifer Flavinus nodded at Macro, Macro looked past the Signifer and addressed the Legate directly.

"Macro Cornelius Varus, former chief centurion of the Legion Sixth Victrix, sir."

Legate Decimus nodded and pointed at Julia. "And the girl? Your slave, judging by her appearance." He took in the grubby oversized cloak and the messy short, cropped hair. Julia opened her mouth to protest, Macro pre-empted her.

"Daughter of Tribune Caius Metellus, former commander here at Vercovicium." The Legate nodded again.

"I know of the man. Appointed to this part of the frontier Wall. Former you say?"

A shouted order from the head of the cavalry troop brought the horses to a halt. Macro placed a discouraging hand on Julia's arm as she went to speak again.

"Yes, Legate. The Tribune was killed in action to the north of the frontier. We had all been seeking safety in Caledonia after the barbarian invasion."

"And you made your way back here to Vercovicium along with the girl, sorry, the Tribune's daughter?" He smiled at Julia, aristocrat to aristocrat.

Macro nodded. The Legate turned and looked up to where Vercovicium squatted on the craggy horizon with Hadrian's Wall stretching to the west, and to the east, dropping away sharply into the Knag Burn valley.

"Vercovicium appears to be deserted, sir, apart from the presence of a handful of barbarians. There's some smoke, probably from a cooking fire. But to the east, there is a barbarian host crossing through the Knag Burn gateway," Macro volunteered. It was Legate Decimus' turn to nod an acknowledgement.

"My duty is clear. I will take the Ala Petriana into Vercovicium to secure it first. Then we'll deal with your barbarians, Centurion Macro."

Ever more Roman cavalry were arriving from the west until, by Macro's estimate, there were around two hundred of them. Eventually, the jostling for space settled down as the cavalry troop formed up in a line two abreast, stretching back down the hill leading up to Vercovicium. Macro could not remember the last time he had seen so many seasoned soldiers of Rome gathered into one place. These were professional troops, not frontier guards collecting taxes and patrolling the customs points along the Wall. Legate Decimus answered Macro's unspoken question.

"We were patrolling far to the west of Deva legionary fortress in the mountains of the Deceangli tribe when the barbarians attacked. I knew nothing of what happened until I returned to Deva to find the fortress deserted. A few surviving locals told me what had happened." He screwed his eyes up and looked up at Vercovicium. "I need to secure the Wall frontier until relief arrives from Rome. Vercovicium will serve as my temporary headquarters for now." A sharp tug on the reins turned his horse's head round in the direction of Vercovicium and he nudged the animal's flanks with his knees to get it moving. Legate Decimus called over his shoulder as he moved off.

"Bring the Tribune's daughter with you, Centurion Macro. I'll be needing your services. Every blade counts if we are to hold Vercovicium and await the relief column from Rome." And with that, the Legate cantered away to rejoin his cavalry. Ahead of him, Vercovicium erupted into noise as Centurion Drusus and his meagre garrison, burst out of the north gateway tower and made short and bloody work of the gaggle of barbarians who had settled down there. Drusus and his men had spotted the horse soldiers of the Ala Petriana from atop the north gate and realised it was safe enough to come out of hiding.

Centurion Drusus was wiping blood from the blade of his sword on a corner of his cloak when Legate Decimus and his men clattered through the south gateway. Drusus sheathed his blade and noted the evident seniority of the Legate as Decimus brought his mount to a halt.

"Centurion?"

"Drusus, sir." He snapped to attention.

"Centurion Drusus. I take it you are in command here?" Legate Decimus took in the ragged and assorted bunch of Drusus' soldiers gathering behind their centurion. Men and boys, Decimus noted. Frontier soldiers, more farmers than soldiers.

"Sir. There are forty-two of us. We laid low. Hundreds of tribesmen, Picts and their allies are returning north through the Knag Burn gate. Some of them, as you see, made their way up here." Drusus pointed at the crumpled bodies nearby.

Decimus removed his magnificent red plumed helmet while his cavalry fanned out through the fort.

"Yes, Centurion Macro informed me of their presence, just now." Legate Decimus placed his helmet on his lap and stroked the red feathers of the plume with care. The ostrich feathers lay delicately curled across his thighs and his highly polished scale armour rippled as he moved, like the shiny scales of a fish.

"Macro?" Drusus' brow furrowed.

"You know the man? He's on his way up here. With the former Tribune's daughter."

"Sir is there a young lad with them. Name of Lucius?"

Holding his helmet securely by the chinstrap, Legate Decimus slid with practised ease from his saddle and patted his horse's neck. His eyes were busy taking in the scene around him and he shook his head in answer to Drusus' question. There were more pressing matters to attend to than questions about some boy in the company of the Centurion Macro and the girl.

"Centurion Drusus, I'll need you to get your men…and boys into order. You will all be under my command until the relief column arrives from Gaul. Emperor Valentinian won't be in the frame of mind to abandon his province of Britannia any time soon. News of this conspiracy, this treachery by the garrison of the Wall, will reach Rome. The Emperor is busy on the Rhine frontier holding the Germanic barbarians at bay, nevertheless…"

Drusus wasn't taking in the Legate's words. His attention was pinned on the south gate through which he expected Macro and Julia to appear at any moment. But where was Lucius? He could wait. Macro and Julia would suffice for the present, each for distinct reasons.

"Yes, Legate," came his mechanical response. "Balbinus!" Drusus relayed Legate Decimus' orders about the men to his garlic chewing second in command, excused himself to the Legate and made for the south gate, checking that his sword moved freely in its scabbard.

Legate Decimus raised an eyebrow at the man's sudden departure and looked doubtfully at the plump soldier who, with head tilted back, spat a glob of something up into the air and smiled in satisfaction as he watched it arc gracefully through the air before landing with a splat. The Legate shrugged his disgust and led his horse up the main street in the direction of Vercovicium's headquarters building at the heart of the fort.

◆ ◆ ◆

His quick, hob nail booted footsteps echoing back from the barrelled roof of the south gateway, Drusus strode through the half-light and appeared outside the fort, sword in hand. The burnt-out shells of the settlement buildings, houses, shops, taverns, and workshops obscured his view to the south until he reached the end of the main street running through the vicus. The scorched fields of blackened stubble down the hillside merged with the grasses and undergrowth of the natural terrain. The blackened fields contrasted sharply with the bright colours of the autumn landscape. Much of the undergrowth to each side of the dirt road leading up to the vicus and the fort, was trampled flat where the Ala Petriana had made their way into Vercovicium earlier, not chancing the treacherously pot-holed official road running parallel. Drusus shaded his eyes against the low light of the autumn afternoon sun which made it difficult to pick out detail in the land to the west. To the east, down in the Knag Burn valley and out of sight, the north bound barbarians kept up their incessant din, oblivious to events unfolding at the fort overlooking them from the Whin Sill Crag. Drusus cursed. No Macro, but he caught his breath as an indistinct figure moved against the hazy countryside. The figure took shape, willowy and topped by short, cropped hair.

"Julia." Drusus' heart thumped a heavier beat for a few breaths. Of Macro and Lucius there was no sign. He sheathed his sword and hurried down the slope to meet Julia. When he reached her, she threw herself into his arms.

"Thank God." She looked up into his face. He fought the temptation to run his hand through her cropped hair. Other matters were to the forefront of his mind. He looked down the slope behind Julia.

"Centurion Macro, is he not…?"

"No. He left me. Told me to make my way up to the fort when the cavalry arrived."

Drusus looked around, eyes narrowed. Shadows were lengthening in the pale light of a soft autumn afternoon. A gentle touch from a kindly season which would last a few short weeks until the freezing Caledonian winter woke from his slumbers and placed his icy grip across the land and all its living creatures.

Drusus turned his face down to Julia who was trying gently to release herself from his 'too long' embrace.

"And which direction? Where did he say where he might be going?" Julia squirmed out of Drusus' arms but smiled at him as if to soften the blow. She liked Drusus, but…

"Brocolitia, if that's how you pronounce it. Yes, that was it, Brocolitia. Something about a temple."

Drusus knew of the temple, the Mithraeum lying in the shadow of the abandoned fort. It had been one of the many pagan sites close to Vercovicium which Tribune Caius had been charged with closing down those long months back. Macro, the centurion turned merchant, retired, and living in the vicus outside Vercovicium, the man of mystery, rather like the boy Lucius. Both seemed of another world. His memories were cut short by Julia's question.

"My mother, she is still alive and safe?"

"Yes, she is." Drusus took one last look around, despite knowing that Macro would be long gone by now and on his way to Brocolitia. Anyway, travelling alone, he would probably fall prey to the Picts or their companions in crime. Drusus shrugged and beckoned Julia to follow him up to Vercovicium. Under a kind autumn sky and brushed by a warm breeze, neither of them had any idea of the deadly, silent storm arriving on the south coast of Roman Britain which would engulf them in the coming weeks. This was a period in our history which would continue to snap and snarl at all it touched as these islands continued their descent towards what would become known as 'the Dark Ages.'

XI

A Final Journey

Away to the east, beyond the riotous, celebrating hordes of barbarian tribesmen returning to their Caledonian wilderness north of the Wall, the land lay empty and lifeless, apart from the lone figure of Macro easing his aching body in the direction of the Mithraeum at Brocolitia. The day was nearly done. His legs pained him but it had been a good day, a day to celebrate; he had avoided the roaming bands of raiders, Pict, Attacotti, army deserters and an assortment of brigands who now peopled the burnt out and looted lands of the former Roman frontier. And Lucius was safe now.

Macro's tattooed forearms itched the unspoken questions of the Scorpion and Snake, his left calf ached unbearably and his breath came in shallow gasps as he ascended and descended the switchback hills and crags surmounted by the looming presence of Emperor Hadrian's Wall. A fitful wind brushed and bent the tops of the knee-high grasses and vegetation lining his route. He paused at the summit of the next hill, to his left, the Wall stood stony tall, blocking from sight the wasteland of unconquerable Caledonia to its north. He remembered what he had said once to Lucius,

'Here we are near the edge of the world, the world of the Ocean…near the edge of time.' Macro smiled. 'Near the edge of my time, too.' The Mithraeum at Brocolitia was not far now, he should make it before dusk.

Moving down the hill, Macro looked ahead to the milecastle lying on the slope of the next ascent. It was one of the eighty milecastles on the seventy-three miles length of Hadrian's Wall. From where Macro was, he could see the wooden shingled roofs of the two barrack blocks which had once housed the tiny garrison of anything between eight and twenty frontier guards. The barbarians had not wreaked their senseless savagery on this small fort, else the barrack roofs would have been destroyed. The steep slope up to the milecastle meant Macro needed to take a short break. He perched uncomfortably on a rocky outcrop. Rested after a few breaths, he made his way up the slope and through the open gateway of the milecastle. The wind moaned as Macro entered the nearest barrack block through the open door. The dim half-light revealed a scene which told of sudden abandonment by the frontier guards. The area just inside the barrack doorway had stabled the soldiers' horses. Piles of fresh horse manure bore testimony to the soldiers' hasty departure. Beyond the stable space stood wooden bunk beds, their straw mattresses littered with a scatter of coarse army issue blankets. Two more blankets lay cast aside on the stone floor. The beds looked as though their night time occupants had thrown the covers aside in haste. Bunk beds telling of an eight-man garrison, now vanished. The wooden table in the middle of the cramped, untidy room was strewn with crude pottery drinking vessels and wooden platters, set ready for a breakfast which never happened. A small, grey mouse skittered away from the bread crumbs covering the table top, hurried down the table leg and disappeared into a dark corner. Macro smiled at its frantic escape, picked up a terracotta flagon and sniffed the contents cautiously. He wrinkled his nose as the tang of rancid wine bit the back of his throat. He put the flagon back on the table and sat on the wooden bench alongside it. Macro sighed, removed his helmet, and laid it on the table. The felt skull cap remained in place, giving him a monkish appearance. Outside, the wind sighed too as if nodding its sympathy at the loneliness Macro felt. One more task to carry out in a lifetime of service to Rome and his god. Outside, an open door to a storeroom banged insistently as it picked up the rhythm of the growing wind. Everything and everyone has a final journey which it cannot escape, Macro thought as he leaned an elbow against the table top. Yes, it was gloomy in this barrack. It smelled of urine, horse dung, sweat, smoke, leather, and oil. Damp lay everywhere, the walls, the floor and even the bedding. There was an underlying smell of olive oil from the burnishing of weapons, sword, and spear blades, the cleaning and rust proofing of steel armour, a workshop smell. And overriding those smells was the farmyard stench of horse manure. On Hadrian's Wall it wasn't unusual for cavalry units to keep their mounts under the same roof, alongside them in the barracks. Horses were a source of warmth in winter and stood ready to saddle up at a moment's notice, stabled right inside the barrack door. Macro caught sight of a couple of bags of horse fodder stacked against the far wall. Would this milecastle be garrisoned ever again? Or would Rome abandon finally her northernmost province? Questions to which Macro knew the answers, as every history teacher worth their salt should know.

410 AD. The 'Rescript of Emperor Honorius' telling the Romano Britons to look to their own defences. For the present, a mere fifty years, just one lifetime before that final break, the history of Roman Britain was stuttering to a close, like a series of dying spasms rather than one cataclysmic death throe. Macro laid his forearms flat on the rough table, palms down. Even in this dim light, he could see the tattoos on his forearms fading. It was difficult to make out the outline and detail of the Scorpion and the Snake. The wound under his armpit was damp and sticky. The stitches weren't holding, he was bleeding again and infection was beginning its journey through his body. He needed to go now. The Mithraeum at Brocolitia was close.

Macro would need to dig. He cast around the musty gloom of the barrack, his eyes alighting on a battle-damaged sword propped up against the wall next to one of the bunk beds. With the lower half of the blade missing, the sword, a gladius, gave the impression of being half buried in the floor. An image leapt out of Macro's near two-thousand-year-old memory. A popular story from history. King Arthur and the sword in the stone. He chuckled at the comparison, rose from the bench, and retrieved the broken gladius, the sword in the floor.

A howling gust of wind brought with it a sharp staccato squall of rain across the barrack roof, accompanied by the furious banging of open doors and loose wooden window shutters in the abandoned milecastle buildings. An unwelcome interruption to the peaceful gloom of the barrack room. The rain turned to icy hailstones rattling fiercely on the roof, the changing gusts of wind driving them into a crazy dance, this way and that. Macro moved to the door and looked out. The autumn world of lush grasses, weeds and vegetation lay under a frozen thin white blanket of hailstones. A herald of the harsh Caledonian winter to come. The hailstorm stopped as abruptly as it had begun. Macro picked up his helmet, placed it on his head and fastened the leather chin straps under his grey grizzled chin, for what would be the last time. As he stepped out into the white blanketed icy world, the returning sun had begun to melt the carpet of hailstones lying as far as the eye could see. For now, the landscape sparkled wetly like a bejewelled giant's cloak. As the hailstones melted, the ground became slushy, and despite his heavy hobnailed boots, Macro had to watch his footing until he reached the summit of the hill beyond the milecastle. Below him, Hadrian's Wall marched away over the sweeping hills and crags, disappearing into the distance to the east. There lay the long-abandoned fort of Brocolitia, and just below its brooding earthen ramparts and rotting wooden palisade, the tiny Mithraeum which marked the end of this journey, and all his journeys.

♦ ♦ ♦

Mud squelched underfoot as Centurion Macro made his way across the boggy ground surrounding the Mithraeum. The ice white magic of the hailstone carpet had gone. The low temple stood surrounded by bright sunlit puddles. The heavy oak door was missing from the entrance and the grey stone walls were smudged with soot left from the fire set by Tribune Caius and his men. The tiled roof had given way, crashing into the interior of the Mithraeum, its shattered remnants lying ankle deep across the temple floor. Daylight flooded in where once the darkness of the cave like temple interior had been relieved only by the faint light of torches and candles. The destruction was plain to see and hear as Macro crunched his way across the tile strewn temple floor towards the far end where the three altars to Mithras had stood. No longer upright, they lay toppled onto their sides. The temple had been desecrated rather than destroyed. The tauroctony frieze on the wall behind the three toppled altars, showed signs of damage where sword points had slashed and chipped at the scene of Mithras slaying the Great Bull. The Emperor Valentinian had wished to discourage pagan worship across the Empire, rather than try to wipe it out. He knew that would have been an impossible task. The old gods still had a timeless hold across the Empire, especially in the ranks of the Roman army and the loyalty of the army was crucial to any Emperor's survival. The new religion of Christianity was growing organically decade on decade and one day would prevail. There was no need to attempt the impossible at this time and go to war with deep rooted pagan beliefs. This was of no comfort to Macro. Done with surveying the wreckage around him, he turned and made his way back outside.

The oak sapling was still there, in time to become the landmark two-thousand-year-old venerable oak tree, much marvelled at over the centuries, much photographed in later years. Its fame grew after the wanton destruction of the iconic tree at Sycamore gap. The oak tree at Brocolitia marked close to the spot where Father Macro and his band of brothers had hidden the Great Red Bloodstone of Mithras the previous winter. And now the Great Red Bloodstone of Mithras would be returned and Macro's soul could finally rest in peace. Centurion Macro stood next to the sapling, head bowed, his eyes closed and remembered.

"Here." Macro pointed with his centurion's vine staff to a precise spot on the ground close to the oak sapling.

One of the Brothers pulled a folded Roman army entrenching tool from under his cloak. The small spade unfolded, he dropped to his knees and began to dig. Despite the hard soil under the newly laid snow, he dug quickly with steady practised strokes. He had dug the ditches and piled earth for ramparts of forts and marching camps across the length and breadth of the Empire for thirty years in his time as a legionary serving under the Eagles. Soon, there was a deep hole in the ground. He stopped, wiped the back of his hand across his sweating brow and looked up at the stocky figure of Father Macro who nodded his satisfaction. The piled chunks of damp earth at his side lay stark black against the snowy ground.

Macro produced a small, iron bound mahogany box from under his cloak, opened the lid and placed the Red Blood Stone inside, snapping the lid shut and fastening the clasp. The soldier stood up and Father Macro knelt. With devotion and regret, he lowered the small box into the hole, an arm's length deep, the side of his head coming to rest on the cold ground. He stood up, braced himself against the wind, and pulled his cloak around close.

"Cover it." He nodded at the freshly dug hole.

"Yes Father." There was love, respect and obedience in the reply.

The soldier set about his task as Father Macro turned to the others.

"We will return in better times, safer times, Brothers. For now, the sacred stone is hidden from the Christ followers, those desecrators, destroyers, well poisoners and thieves."

With the hole backfilled, the Brother patted the earth flat with his spade and stood.

"The Red Blood Stone came from beyond the eastern frontier of the Empire, beyond the eastern borders of Persia, the home of Mithras.

It was brought from the land of India and now it rests safely in the cold ground of the furthest northern border of the Empire. May the spirits here watch over it, may Coventina, goddess of the sacred well hard by, guard it closely."

Macro watched the soldier scrape the thick, cloying peat from the entrenching tool, fold it and bundle it back under his cloak. When they would meet again, safe from the watchful eyes of the Christ worshippers, no one knew. Macro raised his arms to bless the group.

Alone this time, Macro knelt on the wet ground and dug into the dark earth with the broken bladed gladius. He made short work of digging a hole, light peaty soil is easy enough to dig into, especially when it has been previously disturbed when he had returned to the Mithraeum to rescue the stone from the clutches of the Christian Tribune Caius who had desecrated the temple. Macro laid the broken gladius down and used his hands. He paused mid scoop, a handful of wet peat cupped in his hand. His memory was vague. Had he not rescued the Great Red Bloodstone of Mithras only to lose it outside the south gateway of Vercovicium fort? At least that's what Julia told him. The scooping hands remained poised. And then Julia had lost the stone to Lucius, who in turn had returned the stone to Mr MacRonald, and now Centurion Macro could rebury it in its rightful place. The circle of life, death and time was complete. The poised hands, full of dark peat could resume their holy task.

Dig, scoop, repeat until the bottom of the hole became waterlogged, puddling and threatening to back fill. The leather pouch would rot. No mahogany box this time, no band of brothers, no witnesses to the sacred act of concealment, consignment into the care of Mithras. Macro gave a sharp tug on the leather pouch. The cord around his neck broke and he cradled the pouch reverently in his left hand. Looking to the autumn sky, he caught a movement, a bird in flight and descending with slow beats of its wings. The oncoming shape, set against the now high resting clouds after the icy fury of the hailstorm, was unmistakable. Those wide and imperious outstretched wings, effortlessly bringing Hispana in the direction of the Mithraeum. Macro rose from the damp ground, stood erect and drew his gladius. His outstretched right arm thrust the sword up in salute as Hispana turned her head side to side looking for a suitable place to land. The point of Macro's gladius described a sweeping arc as his outstretched arm tracked Hispana's path across the sky until she alighted on the weed covered rampart of the old fort overshadowing the Mithraeum. Only when she alighted did Macro sheath his weapon, cry "hail to the Ninth Legion," and turn back to the task in hand. Sinking to his knees in a squelch of mud, Macro lowered the pouch holding the Great Red Bloodstone of Mithras into the dark, wet hole. There was a slight plop as the heavy pouch dropped into the puddle at the bottom. Macro closed his eyes and offered a prayer to his god Mithras for the safe keeping of the holy gemstone. Hispana took a moment from her customary preening to watch as Macro used the broken weapon to shovel the pile of dark earth back into the hole. Hispana's hooded eyes blinked slowly once before she returned her curved beak to her ruffled feathers. No longer carrying the nine thunderbolts gifted her by Jupiter himself after the death of the Legion Ninth Hispana, she would still live on into eternity in the skies above Caledonia and later, Scotland. Tourists driving, walking, rambling, or resting and catching that rare glimpse of a Scottish golden eagle, would point, marvel, and talk excitedly about their magical moment. Little could they guess just how 'magical' that moment really was. A two-thousand-year-old moment of magic, unknown to anyone.

Macro, centurion, merchant, and Father of the Brotherhood was done. He rose to his feet unsteadily. The tattoos on his forearms might be fading, their itching certainly wasn't. He resisted the temptation to scratch them. The blood seeping from the wound under his armpit was warm and his left calf ached abominably from its wound. He knew it was a part of the journey. The tattoos would disappear, pain would grow, poison spread, his spectral self would move through shadow and half-light towards the River Styx where Charon, the ferryman, awaited him on the far bank.

Macro looked to the sky. The day, like his life, was drawing to a quiet end. The sun was making one last appearance, clear of clouds and dropping down to the tops of the shadowy hills to the west. Like a molten gold coin, the sun blazed without warmth, its lower edge seeming to rest on the lip of the world. Macro nodded his satisfaction. Sol Invictus told him of Mithras' pleasure at the return of the Great Bloodstone to the holy earth by the Mithraeum. Now Macro was free, now he could rest in the land of the dead, finally at peace with himself and his god.

In the muddy space between the brooding ramparts of the fort and the tumbled scorched remains of the Mithraeum, Macro found the perfect resting place. Grimacing, he drew his gladius and lay down. It was always challenging to lie down wearing a heavy bronze breastplate, you ended up like a beetle on its back, waving its legs fruitlessly in an effort to get up. For this bronze clad beetle there would be no rising again, ever. The grimace remained fixed on Macro's pained face. He laid his gladius lengthwise down his chest and crossed his arms over the blade, like the effigy atop a medieval knight's tomb. He had removed his helmet and lain it by the side of his head. Not long now though, thought Macro. A rumble of thunder complained somewhere to the north. Hispana, still watching the scene, shifted her weight from one taloned foot to the other as Macro lay prone, staring at the heavens. A couple of wing beats and Hispana hopped from where she perched imperiously, down to the centurion, landing on his chest. She scrabbled with hooked talons, trying to get a foothold on the smooth surface of Macro's bronze breastplate. He smiled at her efforts under a flurry of frantic wingbeats and a couple of discarded feathers as the thunder in the north moved closer. Finally settled on Macro's chest, if a little precariously, Hispana fixed Macro with her predatory stare. A chill was closing around Macro's heart, tightening its grip for the final farewell. It was difficult to breathe and the pains from his wounds stabbed into the numbness creeping through his limbs. Movement was impossible, apart from glimpses of the sky through his fluttering eyelids. Above him, a dark grey solitary cloud hung high in the heavens, like a messenger from the gods. Supernatural lights flickered back and forth through the cloud, a gathering energy, swirling into a vortex; an embryonic thunderbolt threatening a terrifying birth. Thunder grumbled across the heavens, a portent of what was to come.

Hispana blinked her understanding and tapped her curved beak against Macro's bronze breastplate. It was her final goodbye to the veteran centurion of the Sixth Valeria Victrix Legion, one time merchant and Father to the Brothers of Mithras. There was no way that moisture in her left eye could be called a tear; after all, eagles don't cry. As Hispana took flight, a sharp crack accompanied the bolt of lightning lancing downwards from the lone cloud above to strike the centre of Macro's bronze breastplate. With no pain, no trauma but more with a sense of wonderment, Centurion Macro passed from this life to the next where Charon the Ferryman waited, hooded and skeletal on the far bank of the River Styx. But with no coin to pay the ferryman for his service, Macro's spirit might be condemned to wander unseen in the land of the living by day, and to fast in the fires of Hades by night.

XII

Place of The Yew Trees

A strange peace descended over war ravaged Caledonia, autumn worked her artistry from the dark hills of the distant north where the forests stood still and silent, down to the lowlands where the summer plants and flowers took their rest and handed over their red, yellows, blues, and purples of summer to the autumn golds of autumn. In the marshes, green ferns hung heavy with their luxuriant leaves drooping down to the damp ground. Coppices of larch and elm stood sleepily, grateful for a temporary rest from the early autumn blustery winds. Autumn, the season which yawns wide before the deep sleep of winter. Bees seemed to buzz more slowly while insect and animal life prepared for their winter survival. Birds busied themselves with preparations for a journey to warmer climes, or readiness to face the harsh rigours of winter. Rain squalls and hailstone flurries chilled both bodies and souls. The promise of winter.

Lucius had disappeared with his friend, Centurion Macro, two weeks ago. The countryside around

Vercovicium was peaceful and it seemed the flood tide of barbarian war bands had ebbed away back north, taking with them their looted plunder, raucous war chants and drunken vandalism out through the Knag Burn gateway. It was safe enough now for Julia to venture a little distance from the walls of Vercovicium. Today she was outside the south gateway, making her way through the wreckage of the vicus, where buildings stood in various states of destruction. Stone buildings were burnt out blackened shells, wooden ones were piles of ash and charred beams. And even now, the odd wisp of smoke curled from where the burning had been the fiercest. The detritus of possessions discarded by the barbarians as worthless, lay scattered everywhere. Broken amphorae, smashed pottery, shattered furniture, cheap jewellery, and personal possessions lay half buried in the black ash carpeting the ground in and around the vicus. The smell of burning was everywhere. Julia walked down the slope leading away from the fort and sat down. She turned her face towards the setting sun and closed her eyes. The world seemed at peace, but then it had seemed at peace before. This was a good place to sit, away from the fort. Julia was growing wary of Drusus' over familiar attentions. His standing too close, the occasional hand laid on her forearm, the over long comforting embrace whenever Julia grew sad about her father's death, her mother's decline, or the loss of her friend, Rhiannon. Despite the horrors of the last few months, Julia loved this place. The familiar noise of soldiers going about their business in the fort behind her, were a comforting reminder of the time before the upheaval and horrors of the barbarian invasion. A peace tinged with sadness and grief folded its arms around her with a promise of better times to come.

The warmth of the sun on her face made her drowsy, she closed her eyes and the day dream returned. Julia heard the voice yet again. She kept her eyes closed because when this happened on previous days, opening her eyes meant the voice faded. Each time she heard the voice, it sounded nearer. Today, it was so close you hear the swish of footfalls through the long grass and the voice came close enough to be like a whisper in her ear. The voice resembled that of Lucius, but deeper, an older Lucius, a greeting and then a question, asking if she needed help. A lazy autumn bee buzzed by her ear. Without thinking, she waved a discouraging hand at it and opened her eyes. The voice, like the bee, disappeared on the gentlest of breezes moving up the slope and past Julia, brushing the long grasses where she sat. The westerly breeze was a welcome relief where Julia was accustomed to sit outside the south gateway these last days. However, when the breeze blew from the east, it brought the stench of waste from the sewer outlet of the fort latrine. That, mingled with the farmyard smell of horse manure which pervaded the whole fort since the arrival of the two hundred strong Ala Petriana cavalry unit, hung in her nostrils day and night. Julia breathed in deeply and closed her eyes once more, her thoughts returning to recent events.

Lucius and the other boys had been detailed to clear the sewer outlet as a punishment. That was cut short when Lucius attacked another boy with a shovel smashing the boy's face to a ruin. Lucius was condemned to death by Centurion Drusus for that offence. To save Lucius, Julia was taken hostage by Macro. He had dragged her, accompanied by Lucius down to the ruins of the burnt out mansio, just south of Vercovicium, where Lucius had disappeared.

"Lucius, the boy, more a young man now with that shadow of a beard, Lucius, who came and went, appearing and disappearing like a wandering spirit, the owner of strange objects," Julia thought. Perhaps he was indeed some sort of magician, as Drusus claimed? As if the thought of Drusus had summoned his presence, Julia heard him calling from the south gateway. Her reverie broken, Julia stood and waved an acknowledgement to Drusus. Smoothing her grubby tunic, she made her way up to the south gate where Centurion Drusus waited. Perhaps the voices would return. She glanced over her shoulder to where the voice had come from and stopped for a moment, her forehead wrinkling as she tried to recall the phantom building standing in the mid-distance, on the south slope dropping away from Vercovicium. Not a building she could remember seeing before outside Vercovicium, it stood close to where the disembodied voice had come from. She shook her head and turned back to where Centurion Drusus stood, arms folded, outside the looming south gateway.

♦ ♦ ♦

"We will leave in two days' time, once the horses are fully rested and provisions for the journey packed. It was a hard ride back from the land of the Deceangli by the western Hibernian sea when I learned of the invasion, the catastrophe. Moving south will be safer than staying here at Vercovicium, I have decided."

Drusus shifted uncomfortably as Legate Decimus, arms folded across his chest, made the announcement to those gathered in the headquarters building. Drusus was not convinced, and his conviction was stiffened less as Legate Decimus continued.

"I am confident that the Emperor will have already launched a recovery operation. Rome has faced uprisings in these islands before, ever since the time of the rebel queen and traitor, Boudicca. The barbarians, true to form, will have sated themselves on slaughter, plunder and wine and will be returning home to the north and the west."

"As you witnessed when you first arrived here, Legate," Drusus volunteered.

"Indeed, centurion. Through the er…"

"Knag Burn gateway, sir. Down in the valley to the east."

The Legate nodded and continued.

"We will travel quickly in order to get as far down south in the province as possible. I want to meet up with any relieving force crossing the Channel from Gaul and offer them the services of the Ala Petriana in restoring the law and order here in Britannia. And even if we don't meet the expected relief army from Gaul, the walled cities, and fortresses like Eboracum and others further south, will afford better protection than forts like this on the Wall."

Drusus raised a questioning finger.

"Speak, centurion."

"Are you planning for us all to move south, sir? After all, the Ala Petriana are mounted troops, while I only have a handful of horses between forty-two men of the Vercovicium garrison."

"Eight, to be exact." Balbinus added. Drusus frowned at Balbinus who completed his sentence with due formality, "sir."

Drusus continued. "We also have civilians here to consider, Legate. Lady Calpurnia and Lady Julia."

"Mmm…well, given their social position, they will come with us, Centurion Drusus. Make sure they're mounted as a matter of priority. Your foot soldiers will have to keep up as best they can."

Drusus opened his mouth to voice a protest which hadn't found the right words at this moment. Moving south to greater safety seemed a clever idea but so did staying put at Vercovicium. The Ala Petriana along with his soldiers made a considerable garrison, numbering some two hundred and fifty soldiers.

"Question, Centurion Drusus?"

"No, Legate, nothing of import."

"Good. See to the necessary arrangements. We leave at dawn tomorrow."

Drusus noted with amusement how the rickety chair Legate Decimus had taken over, threatened to send the Legate tumbling to the floor when he finished handing out his orders for the next day.

Drusus glanced at Balbinus, who was about to evacuate a spent garlic clove onto the floor. Balbinus noted Drusus' glance and opted to swallow the mushed clove instead.

◆ ◆ ◆

It was a cautious cavalcade, a mix of mounted troopers and foot soldiers trailing in their rear, which left Vercovicium by the south gateway as the sun blushed the low clouds to the east with a rosy hint of dawn. Led by the standard bearer of the Ala Petriana, the silver eagle topped standard held high, they passed down the main street of the vicus with its charred timbers poking up from a sea of grey and black ash like accusing fingers pointing heavenward. With no pack animals, the garrison had to carry what provisions they had either on broad shoulders or slung across the backs of the horses behind the riders. Cloaks were pulled around shoulders against the slight chill of an early Caledonian morning. Breath plumed from the nostrils of horses, champing at the bit, anxious to get going and stretch their night legs. Morning coughs clearing dry throats and sleepy lungs, hacked back and forth along the column, and the odd sneeze told of winter chills to come. Some kept their cloaks wrapped tightly about themselves as though the comforting warmth of a night's sleep could be continued into daylight hours. A few men managed to reunite themselves with their night's sleep, dozing inside the folds of their great army cloaks. Roman cavalrymen were practised in the art of sleeping in the saddle while on the move. From overhead came the trickling twitter of an early morning lark, the eternal bird song oblivious to the trials of humans, oblivious to the march of time carrying its ever-present threat of death.

"It should be safe enough to follow the main road down to Eboracum," Legate Decimus announced to no one in particular. Perhaps he needed to reassure himself with the sound of his own voice. Truth was that no one could predict where safety lay in the province. It could only be a matter of guesswork, and still no word from the central government in Rome. As the cavalcade clopped and clattered its way along the paved road leading south from Vercovicium, Drusus recalled his journey on this same road only two years ago with Tribune Caius, his family and bodyguard troop, heading in the opposite direction as they travelled towards the Tribune's new posting at Vercovicium. So much had happened since then. Once again, Drusus' thoughts meandered until settling on Julia riding ahead in the column, her mother alongside. Julia had certainly changed in the last two years, from young girl to young woman, from spoilt aristocrat to gladiatrix, from carefree, privileged childhood to hunted fugitive. Gentle pressure from his knees guided his horse up alongside Lady Julia who was trying to engage her mother in conversation, to no avail. Lady Calpurnia was a ghost rider, staring ahead into nothingness. At night, she shrieked, and by day she mumbled nonsense. Drusus felt that familiar tingle of pleasure, of anticipation as Julia turned to greet him with a smile. He remembered how it had felt when he cupped her in his arms, riding two up when they escaped from the villa beyond Hadrian's Wall.

Julia offered him a hint of a smile. "Centurion Drusus. It seems we may be returning to the protection of Rome, under Legate Decimus' guidance. He cuts a dashing figure, wouldn't you say?" Julia was reminded of her own father in a mix of sorrow and pride.

"It would seem so, Lady Julia." The twinge of jealousy would pass. "Let us hope that Eboracum proves safer than Vercovicium."

They both stared at the road ahead, swaying in time to the back-and-forth motion of their horses' slow pace.

"We should have recovered my father's body. It was wrong to have left him to the barbarians and the wild beasts and scavengers." Julia shuddered at the thought of her father's mortal remains being torn apart and his bones being scattered across the bestial landscape of Caledonia. "A good Christian burial, that's all. May God rest his soul."

Drusus nodded, aware of the fact that Julia had laid the blame at his feet for not going back to the villa and retrieving the bodies of her father and his bodyguard when they first returned to Vercovicium. The girl knew nothing of military matters. Such an enterprise would have been doomed to fail. He changed the subject.

"Your mother?"

"It feels like she will never recover from this ordeal. She is broken. I can't even tell if she understands that her husband is dead." Julia threw her mother a sideways glance, sitting slumped in her saddle, bowed hooded head nodding along with the plodding rhythm of her horse's progress.

"And Lucius? Where did he and Centurion Macro really go? You told me that they headed east along the Wall. I think there's more to the story than that. Do you know, Lady Julia? What really happened at the mansio?" It was a repeat of the question he had already asked her back at the fort when she returned alone from the mansio. Julia swallowed hard at the memory of what she had seen there. She wasn't about to tell Drusus that Lucius had disappeared into the ground along with Macro who then reappeared, returning to the fort with her. Silence was the best path until she could frame an answer. Drusus however, persisted. He reached forward to grab the reins of Julia's horse and tugged the animal to a halt in the middle of the roadway. The other riders in the column flowed around them on either side. Drusus rested his folded hands on the pommel of his saddle and leaned forward to peer round at Julia's expressionless face.

"Well?"

"They took me as far as that mansio, the Plenum Amphoras, south of the fort. Then they released me."

"And?"

"And what?" Julia was still playing for time. Her answer had to be good, not like the flurry of disjointed excuses colliding with each other through her brain at present.

"After they released you, Lady Julia, what then? Where did they go?" Drusus was insistent.

"They disappeared.."

"Disappeared, what, into the air? You told me they both made their way east. Which story is it? I suspect, no, I am certain that Lucius is a magician of some kind. And you, Lady Julia, a good Christian soul…mmm."

"No, no, sorry, I forgot. At the mansio, they told me to stand still and not to follow them. Then Centurion Macro told me to return to you, at the fort."

"Stand still, where? What does that mean? Where exactly did they go?" Drusus sighed and leant further forward in his saddle and flicked his horse's reins as if wearied by the conversation.

"They walked, I don't know, eastwards I guess. Yes, east." Julia affected a smile, hoping that this would satisfy Drusus. Drusus returned an equally insincere smile and sat back in his saddle. He clicked his tongue and urged his mount forward with a gentle pressure from his knees. Julia did likewise.

"Thank you, Lady Julia. At last. Just one more detail you seem to have forgotten, though."

Drusus looked hard at Julia.

"What?"

"If Centurion Macro left you at the mansio and made his way east with Lucius, away from Vercovicium, how is it that Legate Decimus saw you with Centurion Macro and spoke with him outside the south gate of the fort?"

They rode on in silence.

◆ ◆ ◆

The tramp of weary feet, the steady clop of hooves, the rattle and jingle of armour and harness was a familiar accompaniment to cavalrymen on the move for a few days. Sometimes the road they travelled was metalled, paved and firm, easy for a mile or two, then it would sigh and fall into disrepair, a challenging mix of mud, rock, gravel, and potholes. It was as if the road traced the history of the province on its journey through time. From the organised military stamp of early occupation by the legions of Rome, to the decay and disrepair of the last century. The road, once mocking marsh and forest, now lay humbled and crumbling under the heavy hand of time. The column splashed through streams and small rivers, clattered, and tramped over stone bridges single file following the line of the road traversing timeless prehistoric fords.

Around them, the land lay gloomy and sullen. Broken and smouldering farms and homesteads were scattered alongside the road for mile after mile. The fields stood high with wheat and other cereal crops, high and unharvested. The crops would rot where they stood with no one to harvest them, and next Spring would bring months of famine to the land. Wandering groups of livestock, sheep and cattle either moved away at the column's approach, or stood dumbly chewing the cud, eyes fixed on the column as it passed by, looking in vain for their farmer or shepherd. Stray dogs, in packs and alone, barked defiance and fear from a safe distance. There was no sign of human life anywhere. Where they crested hilltops, the land around was laid out like a map, but in dark valleys they felt smothered by the brooding threat of Caledonia as they were hemmed in by dark, silent forests. This was the land of the unconquered and unconquerable Picts.

And so the days passed and when night fell, they camped amongst the ruins of empty farms, their camp fires spilling flickering orange light across the ground where they slept under cloaks, huddled together for warmth beneath the cold light of stars in an autumn sky. The moments before dawn brought a chill warning of the winter to come.

Centurion Drusus made it his job to sleep as close to Lady Julia and her mother as possible, but always at a distance which acknowledged the warning look in Julia's eyes. The tethered horses snuffled and snorted now and then through the night. Their human companions coughed, snored, and called out in dreams from under their heavy woollen cloaks. Lady Calpurnia battled her nightmares with cries of anguish for a lost husband, and a life lost since her arrival in this barbarous land. Some of the men would rise to relieve the call of nature, the splashing streams punctuated by yawns and coughs loud enough to wake those nearest, who mumbled and turned the other way under their cloaks. Julia chose to resist the call of nature, fearful of what the darkness beyond the camp perimeter with its guttering fires might hide. By morning, her bladder ached and she would seek shelter behind the nearest tree, or bush to relieve herself.

Each dawn brought them nearer to Eboracum, the mighty fortress dominating the north of Roman Britain. Tall granite milestones counted down the distance to what they hoped would be safety. On this morning, after a short ride from their night camp, a milestone gave them the good news that Eboracum was only five miles distant. Spirits raised, men chatted loudly now, rather than in the subdued tones of the last few days. Laughter returned and the horses, picking up the new atmosphere, strained at their harnesses, eager to make quicker progress.

"I have no idea, centurion." Legate Decimus and Centurion Drusus were riding knee to knee at the head of the column. The Legate was replying to Drusus' question about what they might expect to find when they reached Eboracum.

"It certainly won't be anything like it was as a full legionary fortress of nearly six thousand men. That was three hundred years ago when it was constructed by the Ninth Hispana. Some say the name Eboracum owes it origins to the Celtic description, 'place of the yew trees.' The Emperor Hadrian stopped at Eboracum on his way to Caledonia to initiate the building of his great Wall."

'Hispana,' there was a name Drusus had heard recently, a cry from the lips of Centurion Macro as he pointed heavenward at the eagle swooping to wreak fiery destruction on the Pict warband swarming towards the villa north of the Wall while Drusus, Balbinus and their precious charges, Lady Julia, and Lady Calpurnia, made their escape.

Five cavalry troopers clattered past, led by the Ala Petriana standard bearer, Flavinus; outriders scouting ahead, Flavinus minus the standard which he had handed to another trooper remaining with the column. The two officers watched as the five horsemen disappeared into the distance and out of sight over the brow of a dip in the road, cloaks billowing behind them.

"The Divine Hadrian, not the only Emperor to be associated with Eboracum." Legate Decimus said as he turned in his saddle to face Drusus, throwing him a quizzical look. Drusus rose to the occasion.

"The Emperor Septimius Severus passed away…"

"At Eboracum, correct, centurion." The Legate was one of those who appeared to dislike anyone finishing a sentence, preferring to do so himself.

The countryside here, south of the Wall, was kinder, it rolled rather than threatened with the ruggedness of Caledonia. The 'Emperor' conversation closed when Drusus added a last point, hoping to prove worthy of his part in the conversation about the importance of Eboracum in Roman Britain's history.

"And the blessed Emperor Constantine, hailed as Emperor a half century ago, bringer of Christianity to the Empire." No interruption from the Legate this time, just a curt nod.

Trudging along at the rear of the mixed column of horse and foot, Clodius Brennus, his minion, Albus and the two-score garrison from Vercovicium hung back from the dust kicked up by the horses of the Ala Petriana. Clodius' battered face was on the mend and would soon revert to its former brutish normality. His battered pride however would take longer to heal, if ever. Bullies don't take kindly to their comeuppance.

"He'll meet his end somewhere, hopefully at the hands of a head-hunting Pict." Clodius' voice was restored, only a slight trace of a lisp from a slightly swollen mouth. "I don't understand just where he disappeared to." As if to reinforce his remark, Clodius looked around pointlessly.

Albus opted for the safety of a bland reply. "Yes, just gone." He waved a hand aimlessly. Best not to resurrect further Clodius' humiliation at Lucius' hands.

Four days they travelled and four nights slept under the stars in whatever shelter they could find. The road they followed south towards Eboracum cut through dark forests and open countryside. Sometimes the treeline crowded in close to the road sides, saplings, tall grasses, and weeds creeping over ground in previous years kept clear by local garrisons. The vegetation tumbled into silted drainage ditches running either side of the agger, the raised earth bank on which the road, like all Roman roads, lay. Tall nettles thrived, a deep lush green, spears tipped with purple flowers. Ditches had been kept clear in the past, trees and vegetation cut back to the shadowy world of forest, at least a hundred metres from the raised bank carrying the road. There were no sudden ambushes from the depths of forest and wood with drainage ditches kept clear back then. A vastly different world now.

The long column emerged from the shadows of a gloomy, crowding forest just a few miles to the north of Eboracum. Signifer Flavinus and the four outriders appeared in the distance, heading back towards the column. Legate Decimus raised a hand and the column halted. The walking stragglers to the rear had a chance to close up with those on horseback. Dust settled. Flavinus reined his horse in and trotted forward, raising an arm in salute. His four companions stopped behind him. Plumed helmets nodded as the troopers leant forward to pat their horses' sweaty necks.

Flavinus turned in his saddle and pointed back in the direction from which he and his companions had just come.

"Eboracum, Legate. Barely two miles now." A broad grin creased his face. "We could see the fortress walls clearly. No sign of activity between here and Eboracum, sir." He paused and thought for a beat.

"One more thing, Legate. Fresh trails of black, smoke are rising above the walls of the fortress. Recent fires, and not from buildings or wood. Denser."

"We'll find out what is happening soon enough, Signifer Flavinus. Continue to scout ahead but keep the column in sight."

"Legate." Flavinus clapped his right fist to his chest and wheeled away back in the direction of Eboracum.

♦ ♦ ♦

Their approach to the massive fortress of Eboracum was marked by the mausolea, tombs lining the roadside. The occasional small mausoleum, or simple grave marker in the case of poorer citizens of the city lay here, at the furthest distance from Eboracum's walls. Roman law forbade human burial within towns and cities. The wealthy and powerful spent their afterlife in expensive monumental tombs which could be as high as four men standing on each other's shoulders. Designed to stand for all eternity, statements to the spirits of the dead; 'Dis Manibus.' Men and women lauded and successful in their lifetimes, remembered for all time, their names and lives recorded in bronze letters on marble and granite.

Making their way across the gentler countryside of cultivated fields and farmland, before them Eboracum squatted on a rise, dominating the river and the surrounding countryside as far as the eye could see. Massive walls crowned the natural ridge with a series of enormous ditches surrounding the whole fortress city. An unmistakable statement of Roman power, Eboracum, the capital city of the north. Those in the party, such as Clodius and Albus, eyes wide with wonder, walked past the increasingly bigger, more ornate, and more imposing stone and marble mausolea. Their short lifetimes on the Wall had not prepared them for such grandeur. There was nothing like this at Vercovicium, or at any fort on the Wall. Yes, simple wooden or stone grave markers, perhaps the odd tombstone of former soldiers, beautifully carved and brightly painted, but nothing on the scale they saw now. The road was in a better state of repair the nearer they got to the city fortress. No potholes here, no evidence of robbed paving stones. The authorities in Eboracum had clearly maintained some sense of civic pride, keeping the roads leading out of the city in good working order. Even on the best kept Roman road, the surface was covered in the remains of waste from various beasts of burden, from thorough bred cavalry steeds to humble draught oxen and mules. Fresh dung lay over the dark stains of centuries worth of animal droppings, while dried out hay and straw from the animal waste filled the cracks between paving slabs or was strewn across the road from ditch to ditch.

Centurion Drusus riding alongside Legate Decimus, sniffed the air and wrinkled his nose. The sudden burst of chatter from those around him suggested they too had picked up the cloying smell of burning meat. Despite the increasing popularity of inhumation, favoured by the Christians, everyone had attended a 'bustum,' a cremation at some point in their life. Burning human bodies gave off a rich smell, similar to roast pork. You always tried to position yourself upwind at a cremation.

The burst of chatter in the ranks brought a sharp rebuke from Legate Decimus in the form of a raised hand demanding silence. The walls of Eboracum loomed higher and higher as they neared the north gate. To their right, the great expanse of the River Ouse, flat and grey, wound its way timelessly past the fortress. Signifer Flavinus cantered back and reined in before his Legate who moved forward to meet him.

A sharp parade ground salute was followed by an equally sharp report.

"Sir, the gates to the north entrance are open. I can see no sentries, either on the walls or on the gateway tower. It's too quiet."

Legate Decimus turned in his saddle, right hand resting on the animal's rump, its black tail swishing at the endless cloud of flies, a cavalry trooper's constant companions.

"Centurion Drusus."

Drusus walked his mount up next to the Legate.

"Sir?"

"Go with Signifer Flavinus and twenty men. Find out what is happening or has happened to Eboracum. Don't venture too far inside the north gateway though. Just far enough to make a brief reconnaissance."

Drusus in turn twisted in his saddle to look back down the line of cavalry for Julia. She sat, like her mother, shoulders slumped, head down and hooded. Drusus felt for the young girl. Daughter of an aristocrat, brought to the far reaches of the northern Empire and plunged into bitter strife, invasion, and war; a gladiatrix who had lost her father.

"Centurion?" Legate Decimus' voice pulled Drusus back to the present.

"Sir." Drusus raised a hand in acknowledgement. "Balbinus! Twenty men, on me, now."

Duly instructed, Balbinus turned away to carry out his orders. When he returned with the twenty mounted men, he, Drusus and Flavinus cantered away in the direction of Eboracum's brooding north gateway. The ride up to the towering gate left them dwarfed and craning their necks up to the battlements crowning the great walls of the fortress. The towers spaced along the walls were huge and imposing, multangular towers the height of seven men, and on the top of the towers, defensive platforms for Roman artillery pieces. No sign of life, no sentries on duty, no movement of any kind, just drifting trails of smoke. There was that smell, more pungent now, burning human flesh coming from the fires and as they rode into Eboracum under the cavernous, vaulted roof of the north gate. Another smell mingled with that of burning meat, that of sickness and decay. Some of the troopers covered their mouths with hastily untied neck scarves, while others cupped their hands over mouth and nose. The interior of Eboracum fortress opened out before Drusus and his men as they entered through the gateway. The source of the fires was evident now. Piles of bodies lay heaped in the main street, the via decumana. A sudden gust of wind brought black smoke rolling towards them. Horses shied and tried to turn away, men coughed as the smoke blew into their faces. The gust died away and the black smoke pillared upwards once more, as if settling back after the sudden appearance of Drusus and his men.

They halted and Drusus dismounted, Flavinus and Balbinus followed suit. Drusus signalled the rest of the party to remain on horseback and walked forward. Behind him the drawn-out metallic hiss of swords sliding from scabbards added to the feeling of unease. Drusus kept a dignified hand on the pommel of his sword. The main street, lying like an arrow piercing through the gateway behind them headed straight for the heart of the fortress. The place was deserted apart from a few ghostly figures flitting in and out of the alleyways between the buildings lining the street. The high stone walls of Eboracum strode away from either side of the north gateway to continue their circuit of the city. Eboracum, like Vercovicium had the playing card plan shared by forts, fortresses, towns, and cities across the Empire. Drusus glanced up. There were no sentries pacing the walkway atop the walls.

Black smoke from the funeral pyres roiled between alleys and buildings, sometimes suffocating Drusus, and his men, sometimes clearing briefly. Ahead lay the basilica at the centre of Eboracum, the main and grandest building in the city, the nerve and power centre of any Roman town, or city the length and breadth of the empire. It towered over the temples, houses, shops, and lesser buildings clustered around it. The garishly bright colours of the statues adorning the triangular pediment topping the huge building seemed to mock the drab buildings lining the streets around it. Any signs of life in the city could be described as 'half-life,' living ghosts hiding in the shadows of the dying city fortress. Ghosts, gibbering to themselves as their shadows flickered against the walls of deserted buildings. Living corpses dragged the plague dead by their ankles towards the piles of victims awaiting the flames of the funeral fires. Early autumn fallen leaves skittered along the gutters of the streets, stopping to gather in small drifts against the bodies of the dead lying there.

XIII

Silent Enemy, Deadly Killer

A group of grey ghosts shuffled towards Drusus from the direction of the basilica, accompanied by a discordant chorus of moans and cries carried on that same breeze which ushered the fallen leaves into the gutters where corpses lay like discarded bundles of rags.

"What in the name of Mithras…?" Flavinus' question was cut short by Drusus' raised hand. The ghostly figures greeting them were hooded, eyes flitting around furtively above rags masking faces. Drusus was uneasy but walked forward sticking to the middle of the road, the reassuring scrape of military boots behind him telling him his companions were close.

"What in the name of Mithras, indeed," thought Drusus as he drew his sword against the approaching spectres. Coughs, some papery, some rasping, some a chesty rumble, and all behind muffled faces, half covered by scarves or rags above which fearful red rimmed eyes stared at the soldiers advancing towards them, swords drawn and at the ready. One of the spectres stopped, raised both hands, and stepped forward. A rasp, a parody of a voice floated over to the Romans.

"Stop! No further, brothers." The chorus of coughs from his companions lent a macabre echo to his words.

Drusus narrowed his eyes at the tattered ghouls gathered behind their leader. Flavinus whispered from behind Drusus.

"We should go, I fear the worst, centurion."

Drusus ignored Flavinus, sheathed his sword, and spoke.

"Who are you, what are you?" He raised his chin as he addressed the ragbag of humanity. The leader took a step closer, close enough for the smell of his breath to cause Flavinus to step back and cover his mouth with the corner of his cloak.

"The stench..!" Flavinus turned his head away. Drusus stood his ground despite the fetid smells coming from the group. Let Flavinus cover his mouth like a child. Centurial dignity dictated that Drusus should not follow suit. The stench reminded Drusus of the latrine at Vercovicium. Something rotting. Death and decay hung in the air. Behind the ragged group, figures continued to flit back and forth between buildings wreathed in black swirls of smoke.

"Funeral pyres, centurion." The leader of the ghost group recognised Drusus' transverse crested helmet as that of a centurion. "We are burning our dead, Eboracum is dying…we are dying. You must not come any closer. Turn around and leave the city, centurion. All you will find here is death. Eboracum has fallen to the plague." That would account for the smell of diarrhoea mingled with smoke and death. They were already dead, shrouded in rags, grave ready.

Drusus succumbed to the stink assaulting his nose, and mimicked Flavinus, grasping the corner of his cloak, he held it up to cover his mouth. Behind him, sudden scuff and scrape of hobnailed boots and jingling harness told Drusus that Flavinus and his fellows from the Ala Petriana were mounting up and preparing to leave. Drusus turned round as a shouted command from Flavinus was followed by a clatter of hooves on the paved road as the cavalry galloped back in the direction of the north gate. Balbinus, loyal as ever to his centurion moved alongside Drusus. If Balbinus had a chewed garlic clove to spit out, he would have done so. As it was, good, cultivated garlic cloves had been hard to come by in recent weeks, and the wild cloves he had managed to pull up from the roadside, or from under the shelter of Hadrian's Wall, were thin and weedy, barely worth the effort.

"Your story?" Drusus thrust his thumbs into his belt, took a deep breath and addressed the scarecrow hunched in its rags.

♦ ♦ ♦

Signifer Flavinus yanked hard on the reins of his mount, nearly colliding with his commander's horse which shied back a couple of paces. Legate Decimus' annoyance with Flavinus abrupt arrival was short lived as Flavinus spoke between gasps of breath.

"Plague, the city has fallen victim to plague, sir."

The soldiers behind Legate Decimus close enough to have heard Flavinus, moved uncomfortably in their saddles as their horses pawed restlessly at the ground and shuffled uneasily as though they sensed the gravity of the message.

Tense faces peered out from under the rims of helmets, anxious looks exchanged with comrades.

"Plague." More statement of disbelief than question, Legate Decimus was marshalling his thoughts, planning his next move. He pinched the bridge of his nose between forefinger and thumb and screwed up his eyes. When he opened them again, he was ready, decision made.

"Signifer Flavinus. Your men will rejoin the column. Pass the word back. The Ala Petriana is to return north, in the direction of the Wall." To add emphasis to the command, he flung his arm back and pointed north. Julia, holding the reins of her mother's horse, moved to the Legate's side. Her mother's face a vacant contrast with Julia's look of concern.

"What is happening, Legate?" The rear of the cavalry column was already turning amidst calls and shouts from the riders and making its way back up the road towards Hadrian's Wall. Flavinus nodded at Julia and galloped after the retreating column. Cries and shouts of dismay from the Vercovicium garrison who were on foot mingled with the thunder of hooves of the departing horsemen. Legate Decimus watched Flavinus go and spoke without looking at Julia.

"A retreat, Lady Julia, a prompt retreat. It seems that plague has laid its dark hand on Eboracum." Romans knew about plague. The great plagues over the centuries had ravaged and decimated the Empire since the late second century, proving as disastrous to civilisation itself as any barbarian invasion, civil war between rival generals claiming the throne or economic catastrophe.

Legate Decimus leant forward to gather the reins of Julia's horse, but she yanked the animal's head away out of his reach.

"And where's Centurion Drusus then?" She looked past Decimus in the direction of Eboracum. She knew the answer but insisted, nevertheless. "We can't just abandon him."

"Your centurion is not my concern, Lady Julia. Come to that, neither are you and your mother." Legate Decimus threw a glance in the direction of his cavalry troop who were fast disappearing back along the road leading north. He pulled at the reins and his horse stepped back a couple of paces from Julia and her mother.

"Make your choice." With that, Legate Decimus tugged the reins, pulling his horse's head round in the direction of the retreating Ala Petriana and cantered after them.

"You can't just ride off and leave him!" Julia called out. The trail of dust from the Legate's horse's hooves was her only answer.

At her daughter's words, Lady Calpurnia seemed to awake from a deep slumber and spoke for the first time in days.

"Him? Who, my husband, Caius, where is he? Is he here? Is my husband alive? He is here, isn't he?" Head up and red rimmed eyes scanning left and right, her outcry took Julia by surprise. Before she could reply, Lady Calpurnia dug her heels into the flanks of her horse and galloped away in the direction of Eboracum, a rag doll, mute for the last couple of weeks, suddenly springing to life. Too shocked to speak or move for a few beats, Julia stared in disbelief as her mother spurred her horse on towards Eboracum, her arms and legs flailing, looking as though she would be thrown from the animal at any moment.

A sudden rain squall whipping in across the countryside with its unharvested fields and silent mausolea had the retreating Ala Petriana clutching at their cloaks for protection whilst the needle-sharp driving rain rattled against shield and helmet. Oblivious to the sudden downpour, Julia pushed her knees into her horse's flanks, flicked the reins and the beast sprang into action. Her mother was fast approaching the north gateway of Eboracum.

♦ ♦ ♦

The hunched spectre before Drusus spoke. The bad breathe of disease pricked at the centurion's nose. The rain squall to the north hung in dark tatters from beneath the scudding grey clouds.

"The garrison deserted Eboracum just before the barbarian invasion, centurion. They left the fortress gates wide open. The Picts and their allies stormed in just after dawn." He paused whilst a wave of coughing had him hawking and spitting to clear his throat. Hooking his rag mask down from his mouth, he wiped some spittle from his thin lips with the back of his hand. "We were powerless to resist, even though some like me are retired veterans from the Sixth Valeria Victrix. We hid." The man looked down, ashamed of his admission. "My time under the Eagles has long gone. I too was a centurion, like you." The man pointed at Drusus' helmet crest.

"Continue, brother." Drusus smiled at the man in recognition of their comradely bond.

"The Picts wreaked their havoc, slaughtering and looting in equal measure. They drank themselves into a ferocious stupor. Then, as suddenly as they had appeared, they were gone, laden with the treasures of Eboracum on their backs and Roman heads from their belts. Savages!" He tried to spit but his throat was as dry as an empty husk. Again he lowered the rag covering from his face and this time, Drusus noted with alarm the running sores disfiguring his face, erupting around his thin mouth. Plague sores.

"Then came the outriders."

Drusus raised an eyebrow.

"Outriders from the relief army. A welcome sight, at first." Drusus' raised eyebrow found a little more eyebrow to raise further in question.

"The Emperor has sent General Severus with an army from Gaul. The outriders told us that the general had already landed at Rutupiae on the south coast and was marching north to the Wall, bringing relief, but also bringing with them the plague. The reinforcements for General Severus' army were brought from the eastern front of the Empire, probably Syria, where all our plagues have come from since the great plague during the reign of the Emperor, Antoninus Pius." He paused to gather his breath. "We are walking dead, centurion, walking dead…" A wracking cough followed by another trail of bloody spit from his lips, finished the sentence for him.

Balbinus spoke from behind the corner of the cloak covering his mouth.

"Samhain, the time when the living and the dead meet, the shadow world. We are there, Centurion Drusus." The ancient Celtic beliefs, seasons, deities, and mysteries had not died under the booted feet of the Legions bringing the splendours of civilisation to Britannia. Rome ruled, but alongside that iron fist, Celtic life flourished, was immortal.

"True, Balbinus. And if we don't go soon, we will be joining these…spectres." As he and Balbinus turned back to where their horses stood, heads lowered, reins dangling, they were stopped in their tracks by an apparition galloping through the north gateway. A wild creature, on horseback, hair whipping forward to cover her face, cloak billowing, horse's mane streaming out before its nodding head, a fantastical figure, like a Fury from mythology. And like some demonic rider out of Hell, the wild apparition headed straight for Drusus and Balbinus. Leaping out of the path of careering horse and rider, they turned to see Lady Calpurnia continue her journey towards the centre of Eboracum, in the direction of the basilica.

"By the gods!" Despite his nominal label of Christian, Drusus still swore by the old gods, the timeless divinities who had set the Romans apart from all other races and brought them to empire. Cover all possibilities and eventualities. He turned to where his and Balbinus' mount still waited patiently by the north gate.

"Do we follow?" Balbinus asked, knowing that he had no intention of going deeper into the dying city. The huddled group of ragged plague victims shuffled around, unsure of what was happening.

"No," was the curt reply from Drusus to Balbinus' pointless question. As they turned towards their horses, a second mounted figure hurtled through the gateway in pursuit of Lady Calpurnia. Drusus stared in disbelief as Julia galloped past, knowing that to follow the women meant almost certain death. Plague is no respecter of social standing, class, military rank, youth, or age. They were already in mortal danger having ventured this far into the stricken city. Plague infected the air they were breathing. To go further and stay longer invited an almost certain agonising and drawn-out death, the body wracked with weeping sores, bloody froth coughed up from infected lungs. The Romans knew all about the plague. Very few caught and survived the plague. Drusus pushed Balbinus in the direction of the horses and turned to the ragged group with its ex-centurion.

"May your god, or gods, go with you and bless you, brothers." The years of life under the Eagles of Rome, of military steel which had stiffened his backbone and hardened his heart, left Drusus short of any more words to address the dying men before him. Drusus was as familiar with death as he was with life. It happened, you were born, you lived, you fought, ate, slept, and then you died.

He turned on his heel to follow Balbinus who had already hurried to their horses. With a last look behind him at the unfortunate, doomed souls in their huddled group, Drusus sketched a salute in their direction, for the benefit of the one-time retired centurion, mounted his horse and cantered after Balbinus who was already leading the way out of the doomed city of Eboracum, 'the place of the yew trees.'

♦ ♦ ♦

The Eboracum Drusus and Balbinus left, lay dying under a darkening autumn sky. Shops, taverns, houses, former barracks, and bathhouses stared from sightless windows at the empty streets criss crossing the fortress in traditional Roman planning. Inside the buildings lay the dead, singly, in pairs or in family groups. A grid iron pattern of main roads, side streets and even some alleyways conforming to the unbending rule of right-angled urban planning favoured by the Romans across their vast empire. Syria or

Spain, Britain or Morocco, towns and cities were laid out in a familiar fashion so that wherever the traveller found himself, familiarity with his new surroundings was the watchword. Now, the vast urban plan, designed for a teeming, thriving city had turned to a vast nothingness. In that nothingness, the dying stalked the streets where ragged, emaciated dead bodies lay unburied or in burning funeral pyres. Rats from the sewers moved quickly around this city of the dead, the new citizens feasting on the former citizens, and ownerless dogs roamed the streets in search of food. Countless corpses offered a ready meal.

Only a few temples in Eboracum remained open; but even the combined holy powers of Jupiter, Minerva, Serapis, Isis and even the new Christos god weren't enough to lift the dead hand of plague from the city. Supplications, sacrifices, and burning of incense from the scattered handful of priests added smoke to that of the funeral pyres. Near the temples dotted throughout Eboracum, a heady mix of frankincense, myrrh, rosemary, and cinnamon wafted a strange sweetness into the smells of death and burning.

Outside one of these temples Julia reined in and dismounted. There, at the bottom of the temple steps stood her mother's horse. Its flanks heaving with the exertion of the mad gallop which had brought it here. It stood head down, its nose snuffling at the few weeds growing between the flagstones fronting the temple. Julia's mother was nowhere to be seen. Julia sensed rather than saw the ghostly figures moving in the alleyways leading away from the small square in which the temple stood. The heady scent of burning rosemary floated down the steps of this temple and caught in Julia's throat making her cough, a smell both acrid and sweet in the same moment. And along with the smell of rosemary, voices carried down the steps to where Julia stood. Chanting voices, interspersed with loud cries. Pulling her cloak close about her, Julia looked up to the portico of the temple and mounted the steps. At the top of the sweeping marble steps, Julia paused to turn around and look down the road leading back to the north gateway. So, where was Centurion Drusus? She had passed by him and the plump soldier, Balbinus, as she galloped through the gateway in pursuit of her mother. She coughed as the acrid aroma of the burning rosemary pricked at her nostrils. Where was Drusus? She needn't have bothered asking herself that question. Centurion Drusus and trooper Balbinus were back on the mausoleum lined road out of Eboracum, heading in the direction of Vercovicium to escape the contagion engulfing the city fortress. Drusus prayed silently to no divinity in particular that they hadn't lingered long enough in the city to have been touched by the dead hand of plague.

The scraping of a heavy wooden door on marble floor made Julia turn her head. The bony fingers of two hands were clutched around the edge of a massive time worn oak door, twice the height of a man. The bony, yet powerful fingers flexed twice as the owner sought a better grip on the edge of the door. The scraping from the bottom edge of the door drowned out the sounds from within the building. The door was now nearly fully open, the scraping turning to a last protesting screech at the final tug of the bony fingers. A figure emerged from the shadows of the temple interior. Julia cast one last anxious look over her shoulder, praying that Centurion Drusus and Balbinus would appear, and as she turned to look back, a voice spoke and the figure moved towards her.

"What is it you seek, daughter?" A straight question, a clear and deep voice, full of authority, and carrying no trace of the cough wracked hoarseness of a dying plague victim. The man was tall, bony, and angular but nevertheless giving the impression of great strength. He pulled back the cowl from his bald head and folded his arms across his chest. A priest of sorts, Julia thought. He wore a long gown from neck to the ground, his feet hidden under the voluminous folds of the burgundy red garment hanging tent like from his square shoulders.

"My mother, I seek my mother. Is she here? She must be." Julia waved a hand towards where her mother's horse stood patiently. The man nodded, unfolded his arms, and beckoned Julia with a bony forefinger. He smiled a welcome at Julia.

"Come. She's within." He turned and melted into the gloom behind the temple doorway, the bottom of his gown swishing across the marble floor. Julia looked behind once more and followed the man inside the building.

The semi darkness filling the vast expanse of the temple interior faded as Julia's eyes adjusted away from the daylight of the outside world and this new half seen world. At the far end of the room was a seated statue of a huge, bearded god, his throne a dull gold, faded and in places, peeling. Around the walls of the temple stood tall wrought iron candle holders with a dozen or so candles dripping wax down the stands and onto the floor. Shadows from the lamp stands stretched out impossibly long across the floor of deeply worn mosaic patched with stone flags where the mosaic had worn away. Niches lined the half-seen walls stretching either side of where Julia stood, waiting for a sign, a signal from the figure in the long gown. You couldn't make out colours in this gloomy space which echoed with hushed voices from the far end of the temple and from the dark shadowed walls. Closer by, two armed figures stepped forward, and at a quiet word from the man Julia now believed to be a priest, they walked over to the wooden door and pulled it shut. The thud from the closing door echoed around the cavernous space of the temple.

"Welcome, sister, to the holy precinct of the god, Serapis." The priest bowed. Julia's eyes continued to dart around the shadowy world she had stepped into. Movement in the deeper shadows at the far end of the temple caught her attention. Indistinct figures were grouped together in a tight huddle around something. The something shrieked and appeared to struggle, causing the tight huddle to fall apart for a moment and then close in on the centre of their attention. The soldiers behind Julia, seized her arms and marched her towards the far end of the temple where the shriek had come from.

"He's here! I know he is! You lie, pagan scum!"

The two soldiers were pinioning Julia's arms so brutally that she cried out in pain.

"Mother!" She pulled forward in the grip of her captors. Ahead, Julia watched as an uneven struggle began between her mother and the figures surrounding her.

"My husband, the Tribune is in here. I know he is! Let me go, you savages!"

Mother and daughter were locked in their own struggles with their captors. The two soldiers holding Julia stopped short of the group battling to control Lady Calpurnia. She seemed to have drawn on a maniacal fury hidden deep within as she kicked, tore, and screamed at the group trying to restrain her. Something had wakened her from the near-death trance of the last few weeks. She knew her husband was here. He hadn't died at the villa when she and Julia had escaped. He was here, isn't that what the officer with the red plumed helmet, the Legate, had said? Lady Calpurnia's battle with those around her, was short lived. Her outburst was brief and now, her frailty left her as limp as a bundle of rags in the hands of her captors. Despite Julia's repeated cries, Lady Calpurnia paid her no heed. She hung, rather than stood, in the grip of the two men. The priest stepped forward between Julia and her mother and spoke.

"Look at me, woman." The others of the group moved backwards, bowing in the direction of the priest. He stepped forward and grabbed his prisoner's chin, forcing her head up, her face pallid and expressionless, her eyes closed against the world. The slap when it came, whipped Lady Calpurnia's head sideways, her grey hair flying wildly. She opened her eyes, as if waking from a deep sleep, and blinked at the priest.

"Know this, woman. You are in the holy precincts of the god, Serapis." He gestured at the huge figure enthroned in the apse at this end of the temple, designed to tower over, awe, and intimidate worshippers. A colossal figure, its full beard curling down to his chest. Hair, equally tightly curled in the classical Greek style falling to his shoulders. On his head, a crown like object, a basket symbolising the collection of grain at harvest time. Serapis the provider, Serapis the blend of Greek and Egyptian gods. The right arm of the god lay on the armrest of his throne, below its veined and muscular forearm, the hand hung down, fingers relaxed. In the god's left hand was a scroll which he held aloft, imperious, all powerful, all seeing. The priest pulled the cowl from his head. His was a face with strong cheek bones and a hooked nose with close set eyes.

"Who is this husband you spoke of? A Tribune, you said."

Lady Calpurnia tried and failed to straighten her back to summon up aristocratic pride to her voice. Her words were whispered from behind a curtain of straggly, unkempt grey hair, as she stared down at the floor, her shoulders slumped in resignation, her short burst of energy spent.

"Tribune Caius Mettelus, Commander of Vercovicium fort. Appointed by the Emperor himself."

"Ah, I see, to help defend our northern frontier." The priest continued. "A hero of Rome. And yet," the priest moved the curtain of grey straggly hair to reveal Lady Calpurnia's haggard face, "and yet unable to save us from the barbarians and rebel scum." He cupped her chin in his hand and lifted her face up to look into her eyes. "Perhaps a coward. Did he betray us, did he betray Rome? I heard most of the Wall garrison soldiers went over to the enemy, opening fort and milecastle gates to the barbarians, and joining in the looting, burning, destroying, and killing. Treacherous cowards, not heroes of Rome protecting her frontier."

Lady Calpurnia gathered what little spit she could muster from her parched mouth and aimed it at the priest's face. She missed and the spittle landed on his chest.

"My husband is no coward, a brave and honourable man, a good Christian, dutiful to God and Emperor."

The priest brushed the spit from his chest and smiled.

"A Christian? And would you be a Christian too woman, like your good husband?"

"Do you have him, is he here?" Lady Calpurnia's shriek echoed back from the dark recesses of the temple and was lost in the lofty heights of the vaulted roof so high you could not see it from the floor. Two pigeons, lost in that darkness above, flapped their wings for a few beats and settled again. The murmurings and chants from dark corners of the temple ceased at the shriek and then picked up again. Prayers and supplications for the dead and the dying in plague stricken Eboracum, pleas for the god Serapis to save Eboracum.

"The defiler of our ancient gods and the bringer of plague. Christians, followers of the Christ. Since men turned from the old gods, those who built and protected Rome, the Empire has fallen to war, invasion, and plague."

A brooding sense of doom hung in the air, carried on the sickly-sweet smell of burning rosemary and the murmured prayers from unseen worshippers cloaked in the shadows.

"Your god, your Christ, hasn't saved us from plague and barbarian invasion, woman."

"No more has your pagan stone statue behind us," came the mumbled response.

"We shall see. Serapis requires more than prayers and incense. Even within the confines of this temple, we are not safe from the plague. It will destroy us eventually. For all we know, you two may have brought it within these temple walls even now. I may have it, those around us might be carrying it. No one knows who might be harbouring this deadly, unseen enemy. This is a brief respite, a temporary refuge from the mass grave which is Eboracum." The priest paused, ran his fingers through his beard in thought and continued.

"Sacrifice, that's the answer. Yes, a Christian sacrificing to Serapis would be a powerful thing. Come." He beckoned to the guards holding the two women to follow him with their prisoners. As they approached closer to the seated figure of Serapis, Julia stared up at the monumental, enthroned marble figure. Its cold carved stony face stared impassively down the length of the building towards the wooden doors at the entrance. At the bottom of the steps leading up to the god Serapis, stood two iron incense burners on waist high tripods. The priest turned to look at Julia and her mother. The heavy cloying incense thickening the air made Julia's eyes water.

The priest continued. "In the old days, before the Emperor Constantine cast away the old gods for the Christos, the great Flavian amphitheatre in Rome saw a fitting end to your early Christian martyrs. On the sand of the arena, criminals, prisoners of war and Christians were executed or thrown to the wild beasts to be torn to pieces. The Christians were often granted the chance to repent and swear allegiance to the Emperor and to Rome. A simple act of sprinkling incense on a burner," the priest reached into a bowl, pinched some dark powder between forefinger and thumb, "would be enough to save your life. No words of loyalty to the Emperor, just a sprinkle of incense." He dropped the pinch of incense into the smouldering embers in the burner. A brief whoosh of bright flame, a puff of white smoke, and the smell of exotic frankincense filled the air. Julia struggled against the grip of her guards, fearful as to what might happen next.

"If you both scatter incense," the priest pointed at the still smouldering contents of the incense burner, "your offering will sit well with Serapis. He will deliver us from the plague. He will both protect and heal those within his temple and in the city. Will you do this?" He looked from mother to daughter and back to the mother. Somewhere up in the darkness of the high vaulted roof, the pigeons flapped briefly once again and cooed in some other worldly paradise. Pigeons don't die of plague, pigeons pay no heed to the passage of time bedevilling the brief candle of human life.

Lady Calpurnia was spent, exhausted and broken. She shook her head. Julia said nothing. Her mind raced. What was the priest planning? His next question was not long coming. He addressed Julia directly.

"Are you a virgin, untouched by man?" Julia's head shot up before the priest had finished his sentence. Before she could take in his question and frame an answer, he turned back to her mother.

"You are clearly not untouched by man." He pointed at Julia while addressing her mother. "Your daughter here is more than enough to show me that you are clearly not a virgin. You broke your vows, I'll warrant."

Julia spoke for her mother who continued to hang lifeless between her guards, like a ragged sheet hanging from a line to dry. "Vows. What vows? The only vow my mother has ever.."

"Silence! Your mother will make offering to Serapis. She must scatter incense and renounce her belief in Christ. We have tried every way possible to enlist the god Serapis' help in fighting and ending this plague. We have to try everything." The priest reached into the bowl for another pinch of frankincense, nodded at the guards holding Julia and stretched out his hand out towards her. The guards released their grip on Julia.

"You first, girl."

Julia stared at the outstretched hand proffering the frankincense. She would not recant, would not deny her faith. The priest lowered his arm slowly and dropped the pinch of frankincense back into the bowl. He dusted the few remaining particles of incense sticking to his finger and thumb back into the bowl with his free hand. Not one mite of this expensive incense could afford to be wasted.

"Very well. There is another way, another path we can follow."

Julia felt her arms pinioned behind her back once more. Her heart thudded against her ribs as she looked from the priest to her mother, still hanging lifeless between her guards, a rag doll with the stuffing torn out.

"As you will not recant your belief, and your mother is clearly incapable of doing anything, it would seem, we will honour Rome in the old way. I have a woman who is not a virgin, so.."

Julia's guards increased their grip on her as they felt her tense herself at the priest's ominous words. He folded his arms and continued in the fashion of a teacher simply imparting facts to students.

"The Temple of Vesta in Rome, I'm sure you have heard of it and its place in history." Julia nodded, not because she knew or understood what he was saying, but because she needed to know what was coming next. She glanced around the vast gloom of the temple, whipping her mind into forming an escape plan. Fruitless and pointless, as she knew deep inside her. The priest continued his lesson.

"The Temple of Vesta, holding the eternal flame of Rome on a hearth guarded day and night by the priestesses, the Vestal Virgins. The eternal flame of Rome, burning since the time of the Kings of Rome. War, pestilence, famine, and plague are kept at bay by the eternal flame. If the flame dies, disaster follows for Rome."

"What has that to do with us?" Julia ventured, blinking away the tears pricking her eyes.

"Girl, I'm helping you to understand the reason why your mother will die. The Christian cult in Rome, under the Emperor's orders, has closed the Temple of the Goddess Vesta. The eternal flame has been extinguished." The priest brought his face close to that of Julia. A bony fingertip traced the trail of tear down her cheek. When he spoke again, she noticed his yellowed, broken teeth between thin, cruel lips, barely visible fringed by his beard as they were.

"Why do you suppose war, invasion and plague have been visited upon us? Eboracum is dying, Britannia is dying, the Empire is dying." His voice rose. "Your Christ god has brought disaster to the entire world. The old gods must be appeased. Sacrifice is needed."

Julia fought for breath enough to protest but the words would not come. She swallowed over and over again trying to gain control. She hadn't felt fear like this since being thrown into the arena with Rhiannon. The fear heightened as silence descended, silence apart from the shuffling of many feet as the ghosts hiding in the shadows against the temple walls moved towards the priest and his two captives. He turned his head left and right to address the ghostly figures encircling him.

"Firstly, the wife of a Tribune of Rome, doubtless an aristocrat. Secondly, not a virgin. Like the noble born priestesses of Vesta who broke their vows of chastity, the woman will be buried alive, a living grave. Her sacrifice will lift the plague and drive away the barbarian infestation."

Before Julia could summon the energy to scream, a hand clamped across her mouth, stifling any sound. The priest turned from her and called out in a language Julia didn't recognise as she struggled and fought to free herself from the rough hand covering her mouth. There was a flurry of movement accompanied by excited voices as the small group of watchers made their way to the rear of the seated statue of Serapis. Julia threw her head from side to side with as much violence as she could muster and taking the guard on her left by surprise he lost his grip on her just enough for Julia to bite deep into the fleshy part between thumb and forefinger of his hand. The guard yelled out, released his grip to grab his wounded hand and Julia seized her moment to break free. Her freedom was short lived. Three strides into it, her escape was brought to an abrupt halt when she was sent crashing to the floor by the outstretched foot of a shadowy figure in the group around the priest. Julia's forehead thumped onto the marble floor and she blacked out.

When Julia came round, she put a tenuous hand up to her forehead, fingertips searching out the painful lump where her head had cracked against the unforgiving temple floor. A hard shape akin to an egg stood out from her forehead, above her right eyebrow.

The marble floor was cold. Julia raised herself into a sitting position and looked around. She was alone. There were distant mumbled voices coming from further towards the rear of the temple. A low rumble, like a heavy object being moved steadily across the floor. Marble on marble, a marble slab hauled over the marble floor to expose a dark space below, a basement.

Holding her breath, and battling to keep as quiet as possible, Julia crouched on all fours, stifling the urge to cry out in pain as her knees pressed onto the unforgiving marble floor. She bit her lip and shuffled forward to get a better view of what was going on. The priest was speaking, a voice full of kindness, a voice coaxing, offering hope.

"He's there, below you, below us. Your husband has been hiding under the temple since the plague started. You can rejoin him. Please, please." In the smoky gloom Julia couldn't make out the top rungs of a wooden ladder which protruded from the entrance to the basement, but she could just make out the priest with outstretched hand. The shadowy figure of Lady Calpurnia moved forward to the top of the ladder and grasped it with her clawlike hands. The ghostly tableau of shadowy figures were murmuring their approval at what was taking place, prayers, supplications. A sacrifice to Serapis and to all the old gods, Mithras, Isis, Jupiter, Mars Ultor, all of them being appeased by the death of the aristocratic Christian descending into the bowels of the temple. An end to invasion and plague, an end devoutly to be wished for.

Julia was about to stand and rush to her mother's aid when the sound of slight scuff behind her was followed by a hand clamped over her mouth. Her feet scrabbled on the marble floor as she was dragged backwards the length of the temple towards the main door.

A voice hissed in the gloom behind her, carried on a whiff of garlic.

"This way, Lady Julia." It was Balbinus.

♦ ♦ ♦

Dusk was brushing its timeless, tireless hand across the vastness of Northumberland. The sun had completed its daily journey and rested just below the edge of the world. Shadows stretched out from the rooted feet of trees and crept across the wild scrubland and abandoned fields, the mausolea by the roadside brooded in the half shadows, wild flowers began to droop and drowse and insects buzzed and whirred their way into the autumn dusk.

Eboracum lay behind the two groups fleeing for the relative safety of the northern frontier. One group, the Ala Petriana, reunited and led by their commander, Legate Decimus, had eased their initial headlong flight from Eboracum, reining in their labouring mounts and bringing them back to a canter, then a trot and finally, a walk. A raised hand from the Legate found them resting now. The horses shook their heads and snorted their relief as riders slid from their saddles while their mounts tails swished back and forth in a vain effort to scatter the inevitable flies, while hooves pawed at the new ground searching for fodder. The rest for soldiers and horses alike was brief and soon the cavalry troop was on the move again, desperate to put distance between themselves and the plague behind them.

A warning cry from Signifer Flavinus, riding alongside his commander, broke through the hubbub of snorting and neighing mounts and soldiers' chatter. Men followed the direction of Flavinus' pointing arm down from the ridge they were on and into the valley below. The valley was teeming with men, both mounted and on foot; barbarians carrying dirty white shields. The Attacotti swarming through the valley slowed their progress to a stop as some of their number gesticulated wildly, waving swords and stabbing spear points towards the Roman cavalry on the ridge above them. Unsure of the number of Romans fringing the ridge in the gathering dusk, the Attacotti continued shouting and gesticulating with raised weapons at the Ala Petriana. They could make out enough detail of the ridge top enemy to realise that these were no ordinary frontier garrison troops, limitanae, but an elite, professional cavalry regiment. Legate Decimus could tell by the

Attacotti unwillingness to advance up the slope of the hill that the barbarians were wary.

"How many, Flavinus?" Decimus turned to his Signifer.

Flavinus squinted into the gloom of the valley. "Around three, perhaps four hundred, sir."

Legate Decimus scratched at his chin and eased the tight helmet strap biting into his chin. "I don't want to suffer unnecessary casualties by engaging with this rabble of looters."

"And flesh eaters, sir." Flavinus was curious and unnerved in the same moment.

"Yes, thank you, Signifer. Tell the men behind us, those hidden from the enemy, tell them to leave now and head east for two miles and then…"

"And then, sir?" Flavinus kept his gaze fixed on the milling Attacotti.

Legate Decimus was a recent arrival in Britannia and hadn't quite got his bearings of the geography of the land. He screwed up his eyes and thought hard. Heading back south, towards Eboracum and beyond was out of the question. Plague was the silent enemy, taking friend and foe alike, killing individuals, hundreds, thousands and even tens of thousands of people. And as for meeting up with General Severus and the relief army, they were the very people who had brought the plague to the shores of Britannia. He looked down at the barbarians swarming uncertainly below him, some still waving their weapons at him and his troops. Clearly there were barbarian war bands still on the loose; there were those who still drunk and disorganised, hadn't returned home to their tribal homelands since the invasion.

"Yes, and then head north east back to, er.. Segedunum at the far end of the Wall. It's close to Pons Aelius on the coast where we may find sea transport to take us to Gaul."

"Gaul, sir?" Flavinus braved the question. "But isn't that where the plague..?"

"Yes, yes, Signifer. I know, but at the moment, it's the best option we have. Maybe the only one." Legate Decimus made no attempt to hide his irritation with Flavinus' interruption. In such times of crisis, no one had grasp of the bigger picture. After all, it could take the best part of a month for the picture to become clear. News travelled slowly fifteen centuries ago.

"What we do know is that we can't remain here. Quite clearly the barbarians haven't all returned to their tribal lands, and General Severus' relief army has brought with it an enemy just as deadly as the barbarians, as we witnessed in Eboracum. Get the men who are still out of sight on the move, Flavinus. We will cover their departure and catch up with them later."

"Sir." Flavinus tugged on his mount's reins and wheeled away to carry out the Legate's orders.

Legate Decimus' ploy worked. The main body of the Ala Petriana headed off under Signifer Flavinus and Decimus followed with the remaining troopers when he was certain the Attacotti had no intention of following. From horizon to horizon the shadow world of Caledonia was darkening towards nightfall.

♦ ♦ ♦

XIV

The Attacotti

Clodius Brennus and his ghostly sidekick, Albus, weren't as lucky in their encounter with the men of the dirty white shields, the human flesh eaters known as the Attacotti. The foot soldiers of the Vercovicium garrison who had made their way down to Eboracum under the command of Legate Decimus, proved easy prey for the Attacotti war band leaving the valley from which they had observed the Roman cavalry up on the hill. Despite their shouts of defiance and much brandishing of weapons, the Attacotti weren't up for a fight with well-armed and disciplined cavalry of the elite Ala Petriana. Like their allies, the Picts, Scots, and Saxons, they were out for plunder and not death under the hooves of Roman cavalry and so they made their way back to the road after the Roman cavalry disappeared from the hilltop. On that road, dust still hung in the evening air marking the passage of men with the scatter of discarded shields and weapons telling of fear, of panic. The Attacotti had the scent of easy pickings and those on horseback picked up the pace following the trail of tell-tale dust. Behind them trotted the rest of the men of the dirty white shields in anticipation of the taste of human flesh.

When they fled from Eboracum, most of the former garrison of Vercovicium elected to throw away the encumbrances of their weapons. Such was their haste to outdistance a plague which they thought might be following them, born on the wings of some demon from hell. Shields, swords, and spears lay discarded by the roadside and in weed choked ditches leading back north to the Wall. With no officers such as Legate Decimus or Centurion Drusus to keep discipline, the farmer soldiers wanted to put as much distance between themselves and the plague washing up from the south of the province as they could. The very word plague struck terror into everyone, it might be snapping at their heels however fast they fled.

And so the straggle of soldier farmers seeking sanctuary back at Hadrian's Wall and their home of Vercovicium, was strung out along the road, some men looking back over their shoulders as though expecting to see death personified, the plague itself sweeping along after them like an incoming tide moving ever closer with every swell of the ocean.

It was Albus who first spotted their pursuers as he turned his head at the sound of the distant clatter of hooves on the road. Eyes wide in terror at what he saw, fear strangled his throat and stopped him from calling out a warning. No need, the others had turned too at the growing thunder of hooves. Some cried out, the younger soldier farmers among them shrieked in fear. Many in the forty strong group, abandoned the road, their instinct to take to the open countryside. A few stumbled into the ditches lining the road while others who managed to jump across, tried to put as much distance as they could between themselves and the Attacotti. Clodius Brennus and Albus opted to stay on the road. For their part, the Attacotti whooped and hollered their delight at the sight of such easy prey. Those on horseback drew swords, or readied spears for the kill. The Attacotti on foot were already leaping across the roadside ditches and fanning out across the shadow land following the fleeing Romans.

Clodius Brennus and Albus found themselves labouring to keep up with the men. Albus was weak and skinny, his companion was weak and fat. As Albus turned to look back, his foot caught on a broken paving block on the road and he fell. Whatever he was shrieking was lost to Clodius Brennus as he fought to keep his plump legs going. His breath was laboured. He wheezed now, his wheezes mixed with sobs of terror gripping his throat. He wanted to cry out but needed every ounce of breath and fight to keep his legs moving. Clodius wasn't going to risk a glance back to see the fate of Albus, even if he had the strength to do so, strength and spirit were fast ebbing away. From either side of the road back to Vercovicium came the cries and shrieks of Romans being butchered, intermingled with the victorious whoops and shouts of the triumphant Attacotti. Some Romans died meekly, hands held up in supplication, others died with a weapon less show of resistance, naked forearms raised in futile defence against sword edge, spear point and war axe blade. The youngest lad, with the strawberry-coloured birthmark on his left cheek, lay whimpering in a weedy ditch until a spear thrust ended his terror and sent him into the spirit world. Those slaughtered immediately were the lucky ones. Clodius Brennus had the misfortune not to die. A kick to the middle of his back from a mounted barbarian, sent him stumbling, hands outstretched onto the unforgiving surface of the road. Turning his tear stained face up to the grinning warrior looking down at him, Clodius Brennus blubbered incoherently from the face broken and battered by Lucius Verus. A blow to the side of his head from a spear butt put him out of his terror and misery, for the moment. The Attacotti warrior dismounted, laid down his dirty white shield and tied the unconscious Clodius' hands behind his back.

As evening dusk melted into night, the Attacotti lit their fires alongside the road from Vercovicium to Eboracum, fires lit for comfort, warmth, and food preparation. There would be no funeral rites, no solemn burial for Clodius Brennus, no grand mausoleum, not even a simple wooden grave marker remembering the life of this one-time auxiliary of Rome. Instead he, and the captive remnants of the garrison of Vercovicium, would become that which he had been tasked with shovelling and clearing from the outlet sewer in the fort of Vercovicium on Hadrian's Wall courtesy of those feasting on their flesh and gnawing at their bones. These same bones would be left scattered around the feasting area of the Attacotti with not even enough flesh left for the carrion to strip; discarded bones, bleaching under the sun, weathered by the wind, and washed away by the rain.

♦ ♦ ♦

The hand clamped across Julia's mouth, smelled of sweat and leather, the smells of a soldier. She knew who it was once she heard Balbinus' voice and allowed herself to relax a little in the iron grip of Centurion Drusus. Balbinus spoke again.

"Clear."

They were near the temple door and light from outside washed palely across the marble floor. Julia stiffened again as she realised Drusus' intention. She was being rescued, but what about her mother? The far end of the huge temple was now lost in Stygian darkness and no sounds came to Julia. She wasn't going to allow Drusus to rescue her and leave her mother. The centurion's hand clamped a little tighter as he felt his captive stiffen. Keeping his voice low, he whispered into her ear. She felt his hot breath on her cheek as she bucked against his words.

"I know she's in there, your mother, I know. We can't save her but we can save you, and now ourselves. We have to leave Eboracum, now!"

Julia's muffled protest blew hot into the palm of Drusus' hand covering her mouth.

The sharp rasp of Balbinus' gladius drawn from its scabbard had Drusus turning his head in the direction of his companion. No need for muted voices now. Balbinus' words followed fast on the heels of the rasp of his sword.

"We have company, centurion."

"Hear me, Julia. I have to let you go. I can't fight and hold onto you at the same time. Your fate will be in your hands. If you turn back into the temple to go to your mother, you will surely die. If you stay with us, perhaps we will live. Your choice."

"Five heavily armed men, centurion. I can't see any others. They look like temple guards, Syrian type of armour, I'd say. They've seen the horses and now they're looking up the steps towards the temple door."

Drusus dropped his hand from Julia's mouth. "Choices yet again for you, Lady Julia." He unsheathed his sword followed by his dagger which he handed to Julia.

"You can either go and rescue your mother," he pointed his sword in the direction of the giant statue of Serapis barely visible in the smoky gloom of the temple, "or join us and get to the horses."

Balbinus took another peek around the bulky door. "Centurion. They are coming up the steps."

The five armoured men, temple guards as Balbinus had guessed, were treading cautiously up the flight of steps, heads turning this way and that, searching for the riders of the four horses.

"We have the slight advantage of our momentum down the steps." Drusus whispered. "And surprise. Run for the horses, don't stop to fight, just storm into them. With luck they will fall backwards down the steps, perhaps. It's in the lap of the gods." He didn't look at Julia, didn't wait for an answer. She had her choice. He made his move. Drusus joined Balbinus behind the wooden door and they both stepped outside. With one last agonised look to the far end of the temple where her mother was trapped, Julia hefted the dagger and sprang after her rescuers. As she emerged at the top of the steps, in front of her Drusus and Balbinus had barrelled into two of the temple guards catching them off balance. The men tumbled backwards down the steps in a clatter of armour and dropped weapons. The remaining three guards recovered their wits and stood ready, braced on the steps and weapons raised. For a count of thirty beats, the five men faced each other across the temple steps, dark smoke rolled up the street to drift past the temple. With it came snow-like powder, a grey ash which settled on cloaks and on helmets, speckling everything it touched wherever it fell. Balbinus spat away the ash which had stuck to his lower lip; ash from the funeral pyres still burning across the city. One of the waiting temple guards wiped his eyes with the back of his hand against the smarting caused by the cloud of ash. Drusus seized the moment and lunged at the man with his sword. Too late the temple guard dropped his hand from his eyes and tried to ward off the attack through blurred vision. Drusus' aim was true and his swift sword thrust dispatched the guard neatly in a clean kill. The guard tumbled backwards clutching his reddening throat. In the same instant, Balbinus engaged another guard in a flurry of sword blows. Balbinus' overweight frame had often brought a triumphant smile to an enemy assuming an easy victory. That was the case now, as Balbinus' bulk belied his swift reflexes and deadly sword play. His enemy's smile was soon replaced by a look of horror and disbelief as Balbinus parted the man's sword hand from his arm. Balbinus didn't stop to finish the man off, no need, instead he kicked out at a guard getting to his feet. As the melee moved down the temple steps towards where the horses stood tossing their heads restlessly at the commotion above them on the temple steps, Julia skirted the action and ran down the steps towards them before they bolted. She gathered up the reins of the horses and turned to see if Drusus and Balbinus were coming. As she turned, her head exploded into a flashing world of lights, stars, and chaotic colours. A temple guard who'd recovered his wits delivered a backhanded swipe whipping her head round and she collapsed at his feet. His contempt for a mere girl was his undoing, for as he turned to engage with Drusus and Balbinus, Julia stabbed up at his exposed thigh with all the strength she could muster. The dagger blade went in deep and the guard fell clutching his wounded leg. Rhiannon would be proud of her. Julia twisted away and sprang to her feet. Drusus and Balbinus, chests heaving from the close and brief combat, nodded their appreciation at Julia. The man writhing at their feet was bleeding out fast, his femoral artery ruptured by Julia's handiwork with the dagger. The grey ash from the funeral pyres was lying ever more deeply now, like the first fall of fresh snow, dirty grey, not pure white, but still soft, and puffy underfoot. Balbinus was already mounted and throwing glances all around to check for further obstacles to their escape. The ghost city offered no further hindrance to their departure, indeed it was so quiet that you could almost hear the ash fall as it settled like a grey blanket across Eboracum. The still silence which accompanies the fall of snow, a silence seeming to herald something else to come apart from winter.

"Cover your mouth as best you can. Keep out the ash and hopefully, the plague. Let's ride. Stay close, Julia." Drusus had barely finished his sentence as he kicked his heels into the flanks of his horse which broke instantly into a gallop, neighing wildly, head up, mane streaming.

Julia needed no encouragement, even though she glanced back to where her mother's horse stood patiently waiting for its rider who would never appear. She urged her horse into action and followed her rescuers as they clattered along the dying streets of Eboracum, the horses' hooves kicking up clouds of grey ash, towards the north gate and the road back to Vercovicium.

♦ ♦ ♦

The three grey ghost riders slowed their mounts to a walk as the last, and smallest of the mausolea and roadside grave markers petered out. Eboracum, The Place of the Yew Trees, city of the dead and dying was behind them, along with its stench of death and smoking funeral pyres. As the three riders walked their mounts back north towards Vercovicium, they set to brushing the ash from themselves. Drusus was trying to wipe the dust from his bronze breastplate, without much success. Riding hands free, he reached up to his helmet, undid the chinstrap and eased the helmet off. With a look of disgust, he swept his hand across the transverse red crest in a vain attempt to remove the grey dust. Balbinus was rummaging in his ash covered saddle bag for any vestige of a garlic clove, unconcerned about the niceties of his appearance. The grey dust would blow away, disperse in time, there was always enough wind and rain in this wilderness. His sausage fingers emerged from the saddle bag empty. He sighed. He was out of wild garlic bulbs. The only concession he made to the clinging dust was to lick, hawk and spit the filth from his lips. As for Julia, she cried silently for her mother, the tears washing the grey dust from her cheeks. For Lady Calpurnia, held within the mighty walls of the temple of Serapis in Eboracum, the end would come slowly. Her last glimpse of the world gradually becoming smaller, narrower as the huge marble trap door on the temple floor closed over her head gradually. The thin strip of dim candle light finally snuffed out as the huge marble slab was dropped into place, the sudden darkness and silence swallowing her. A sacrifice to the god Serapis, a hope that the ravages of the plague overwhelming Eboracum would abate and show surviving citizens some mercy. In the pitch black of the underground tomb, Lady Calpurnia reached out her hands seeking her husband.

"Caius, are you there? Is that you?" she whispered. "They told me you were here. Answer me, Caius. I pray to God Almighty that I can find you. Caius...are you here?" Her Christian God laid the blessing of madness on her to ease her final hours.

PART 2

XV

Face Masks and Old Bones

The A68 road runs like an umbilical cord joining England to Scotland, a route old beyond living memory. It is a scenic journey for long, straight stretches, largely following the course of the Roman road known these days as Dere Street. What the Romans called it, we will never know. The landscape it runs through is timeless, prehistoric in some parts but what we would call the modern world in others. The driver of the Land Rover knew this route like the back of his hand yet nevertheless had the snaking blue trace of the A68 tracking upwards on his sat nav, a toy, a habit, a backup. As the smooth tarmac under his tyres ran away in the rear-view mirror, he cast his mind back to the first time he made this now familiar journey. As the newly appointed curator of the recently revamped and renovated Housesteads fort museum on Hadrian's Wall, he learned soon enough that a regular visit to the National Museum of Scotland in Edinburgh would be part of his remit following his appointment as curator at the relatively early age of thirty-four. There were lectures and seminars about recent finds, discussions around the future of archaeological practice along with the occasional offer from the National Museum of Scotland providing artefacts for temporary display in the Housesteads museum. The item being loaned this time by the National Museum of Scotland was a recently uncovered and surprisingly well-preserved weapon which had been found in a hitherto undiscovered human skeleton dating to the late fourth century AD. A particularly strange burial which showed no trace of a grave having been dug, no evidence of a coffin, or any kind of preparation by human hand. There was no stone lining, no rust stains in the soil from iron nails to indicate the presence of a wooden coffin. Nothing. Not even the ubiquitous carved stone grave marker giving details of the deceased along with the customary blessing, Dis Manibus, 'to the spirits of the dead.' What the archaeologists were able to determine was that this was the grave of a soldier, a centurion. Along with the well-preserved skeleton, an ornately decorated bronze breastplate was accompanied by the rusted remains of an iron helmet with a bronze mounting for a centurial transverse crest. The prize artefact, a gladius, lay across the man's chest, his arms folded over it. The centurion gave every appearance of having simply lain on the ground and died, his body enveloped and swallowed by the ground.

The driver glanced at the sat nav, more from habit than necessity, as the approaching road sign told him the next left turn would take him to Risingham where the mighty earthwork of ditches, grassy banks, and stubbornly enduring remains of the Roman fort, Habitancum, still dominated the surrounding landscape. Habitancum, one of countless Roman forts in Britain, forts so old they had forgotten who built them. As on previous trips north to

Edinburgh, the sign drifted past on the left and disappeared into the distance in the rear-view mirror. Lucius Mabutt gripped the steering wheel a little firmer, pursed his lips and promised himself yet again, "next time, definitely." Habitancum had played a significant part in his life, as had this area of north England calling him back for a third time, now as an adult, archaeologist, and museum curator.

Music from the radio, Classic FM, eased its way back into his thoughts. Lucius had always been a huge rock and punk fan when he was younger but preferred the more challenging tones of a classical music station these days of mellowing mid-thirties. Anyway, classical music suited the countryside he was driving through. Something vast, something unmeasurable about both. Timeless. Like the looming darkness of the Kielder Forest now crowding in darkly towards the nearside of the A68. As Beethoven's symphony No. 6, The Pastoral, announced its brash arrival, it brought to mind that primordial fear which engulfs humans when they are faced by the unfathomable depths of the darkest forests. We share that with our ancestors, fear of the dark, especially that of the deep forests.

The sat nav informed Lucius there was still an hour and fifty-seven minutes left of his journey. His fingers tapped in appreciation of Beethoven's stunning musical interpretation of a day in the countryside with all its moods and changes. Life was good, it didn't get much better than this. Great music, great drive on a largely traffic free road and the prospect of a fascinating meeting at the National Museum of Scotland in Edinburgh only... he glanced at the sat nav, yup, one hour and fifty minutes away.

♦ ♦ ♦

The long trestle table lay between rows of shelving towering above the three people gathered around the human skeleton laid out with stark precision before them. The fluorescent strip lighting between the high shelves might be good enough for everyday purposes, but for today they were far from sufficient. Four successive sharp clicks brought to life four powerful angle poise lamps, one at each corner of the long table. The trestle table and its three masked watchers stood in the dazzling circle of high intensity powerful lights. So powerful, so intense was the lighting around the table, that the fluorescent lights stretching along the ceiling paled into nothing more than the glimmer of a glow worm at twilight. Beyond the brightly lit table shadows lay deep amongst the shelving housing countless cardboard boxes of archaeological finds. The final resting place for fragments of human life; jewellery, pottery shards, glass, farm implements, weaponry, armour, scraps of leather and the detritus of humanity's past. In many boxes lay the dusty, fragile pieces of bone from long dead souls. Lucius felt the puff and suck of warm air around his mouth and chin as he breathed behind his face mask. A harsh memory of the Covid pandemic of 2020 which swept across the world from its origins in the east. As an historian, Lucius recalled those plagues too which had swept across the Roman Empire, brought from the east by returning soldiers, or merchants venturing as far as India and China in their timeless search for luxuries to sate the appetites of the rich and powerful Roman elites. Trade in the ancient world was a two-edged sword.

He glanced at his colleagues, noting the slight puff and suck of their masked mouths as they breathed. The pandemic had taken his mother. Her lifelong respiratory problems had proved too much when exacerbated by an attack of Covid 19.

The yellowed bones of a skeleton laid out neatly on the table were those of a man; not tall, reduced now to a clinical jigsaw puzzle arranged with thorough precision, his detached lower jaw bone giving him a comically macabre appearance. The dislocated jaw lay gaping in an impossible ghoulish and timeless laugh. And there, alongside the skeleton, laid out in an almost military fashion, were the man's last possessions. A distorted rusted iron helmet, flattened to an almost unrecognisable parody of itself, a surprisingly well-preserved bronze breastplate, a military dagger, rust fused inside its metal sheath and the remnants of a soldier's belt. Six phalerae, disc shaped military medals, lay each side of the breastplate, their leather harness long since decayed. At the skeleton's feet, lay a handful of rusted hobnails from his long-rotted leather caligae. The star of the show though was an eighteen inch long, Roman gladius. Fresh from a painstaking conservation and renovation, the blade topped by a worn ivory handle.

"Shall we begin?" Without waiting for an answer from her two companions, the tall, willowy woman wearing a knee length white laboratory coat, face mask and blue latex gloves, picked up a stylus like instrument and bent over the lower part of the skeleton's left leg. She twiddled the stylus between her fingers and spoke from behind her mask.

"Look closely here." The twiddling ceased as the sharp point of the stylus indicated an area of yellowed bone on the fibula. Lucius strained to see the sharp stylus point as it hovered above the thinner of the two bones running the length of the calf. He bent forward to get a clearer picture. There was a noticeable 'v' shaped nick in the slender bone, and evidence of calcification around it where the bone had healed itself. Professor Sarah Taylor pulled her glasses down from where they rested in the bird's nest tower of hair crowning her head. With her glasses resting on the tip of her nose, she leant closer, almost obscuring Lucius' view of the fibula in question.

"See here," her words seemed to be spoken to herself, "evidence of trauma at some time in this man's life, inflicted by the sharp point of a sword, or more probably, an arrow head. Hardly surprising, given that he was a soldier. And there's more." She removed her glasses, stood upright, eased her back and bent to the task once more, replacing her glasses. This time her attention moved up to the right-hand side of the ribcage. She tapped the stylus gently against ribs three and four, just under the armpit area. Lucius shifted his gaze to where the stylus rested between the two upper ribs. Again there was evidence of trauma in the shape of gouges on the surface of the ribs where something sharp, spear or sword point had forced its way between the ribs and into the side of the upper ribcage. Professor Taylor warmed to her task.

"The individual would have died as a result of this trauma to the chest. The heart would have been damaged, given the direction of the blade as indicated by the damage to the ribs. A mortal wound. A punctured lung would equally have spelt death, long and lingering. If by a miracle the man had survived, these areas of damage to the rib bones would have healed in time. These clearly never had the chance to heal over. A fatal wound."

Was that a whiff of burning pine cones? Lucius opened his mouth to give the question life but shut it in the same instant. Then the distant rumble of hooves telling of a cavalry charge. Memories recalled from a classroom in his past. Even without that prompt, Lucius knew this man, knew he could give flesh to these bones. Professor Taylor looked up from the meticulously arranged skeleton and sniffed. It wasn't unusual down here in the bowels of the museum finds storage rooms to be mystified by an occasional unearthly smell. After all, some of the finds had rested in their cardboard boxes on the tiered shelves for decades. Fragments of cloth, remains of leather shoes from the Middle Ages, it was musty down in this world of the dead, Hades' catacomb, where the living moved through their temporary lives, trying to put the pieces of an incomplete jigsaw back together. The jigsaw of our ancestor's lives and deaths.

The Professor's continuing observations broke into Lucius' musings. Her words were accompanied by the metallic tapping of the pointer stylus, rhythmic and insistent. Tap, tap, tap…

"And then there is this unusual dent in the centre of this fellow's breastplate." Tap, tap, tap..

Lucius followed the insistent pointing of the stylus and peered at the dent on the once burnished bronze breastplate with its Medusa head, surrounded by swirling motifs of laurel leaves, two winged horses and a pair of threatening scorpions. There, in the centre of Medusa's forehead, was a dent the diameter of a ten pence piece.

"Closer examination of this dent shows it to have been caused by something like a lightning strike, an electrical charge of extremely high voltage rather than a sharp point from a spear or sword. There's been almost a fusion here, rather like a soldered joint in metalwork, a repair. Signs of a partial, instantaneous fusion which appears to have failed. A mystery."

Professor Taylor's words were becoming a background noise, almost a distraction accompanying

Lucius' thoughts. Not only thoughts but memories too. A few days after his return to great aunt Livia's guest house those years ago, in a footnote to the national headline news, there had been a report of the death of a teacher, stabbed outside a London school. Despite surgery in an attempt to save his life, Mr MacRonald, a long serving teacher at the secondary school on the Caledonian Road, had taken a turn for the worse, succumbing to the knife wound he received whilst on after school gate duty. A sad story, the teacher's death set against the background of an unusually violent thunderstorm. The storm brought spectacular lightning, thunder, and localised flooding to the area around the hospital, one bolt striking the hospital radio mast at the same moment Mr MacRonald passed away. That was nearly two decades ago. Since then, Lucius Mabutt had pursued his love of history, following the path of university, degree, archaeologist and finally his appointment as curator of Housesteads Roman fort on Hadrian's Wall. A full circle. It's what Mr MacRonald would have wanted, and what Centurion Macro foretold…

"The future is certain, Lucius. I'm sure you are destined for remarkable things, especially in the world of, well, all of this which we call history. The past is always with us, Lucius, it never dies."

"A prize discovery." Professor Taylor took a step back from the long examination table, pulled herself up to her full height and took in the skeleton, her eyes scanning it from skull to the tiny metatarsal bones of the feet. "The mystery is how did this find escape detection for all the years that the Carrawburgh Roman Mithraeum and its nearby fort of Brocolitia have been painstakingly raked over by successive generations of archaeologists? Not to mention the nighthawks with their illegal metal detecting activities." She used the pointed end of the stylus to delicately scratch an itch on her head through the mass of piled curls.

"Then there's the other mystery surrounding the trace element lining the dent on the breastplate. Research has so far been unable to classify, to categorise the substance. We could say that it's an element hitherto unknown to scientists." In the silence which followed, one of the powerful angle poise spotlights fizzed. It wasn't the only electrical charge present in the room.

Here was a quandary for Lucius, not unlike those he had experienced in the past when talking to the living about the dead of two thousand years ago. Before him lay the bones of Centurion Macro, of that there could be no doubt. Should he announce in some bizarre way that he knew this man? Would such an announcement qualify him for immediate psychiatric attention? A manifested mental health problem in an archaeologist and museum curator? The work has evidently got to him, others would say. Dealing everyday with dusty deaths from the past. Concern for peoples' mental health was very much an issue these days. Then there was the question of Mr MacRonald; were the centurion and the teacher not the same person? Lucius had heard that Mr MacRonald had been cremated, and yet here rested the bones of Centurion Macro? Lucius shook his head to clear his mind.

"Mr Mabbutt…Lucius?"

"Apologies, Professor Taylor. I.. er, I was miles away." He smiled a pointless apology behind his mask.

"Clearly. Is everything…"

"Ok? Yes, I'm fine. Just looking for answers… to your, er, questions about this man." He nodded at the skeleton.

Professor Taylor hooked a slender forefinger into the top of her mask and pulled it down to rest below her chin.

With blue latexed gloved hands she picked up the gladius lying alongside the skeleton and moved it to the end of the table at the foot of the skeleton. Here was more room and the sharp intensity of the light from one the angle poise lamps threw into sharp relief the corroded surface of the weapon. The three figures bent over the gladius and studied its ruined blade. After a couple of beats, Professor Taylor turned the sword over.

"On this side of the weapon, the results of intensive x-rays show marks which we deduce as some form of engraving, etching onto the surface of the steel blade."

"A gladius typical of the first and second century AD Roman army use." Lucius felt impelled to add his knowledge of the obvious to his professional colleagues who were equally well versed in weaponry of the Roman era. The point of the stylus resumed its journey, this time over the pitted and lumpy surface of the gladius. Professor Taylor resumed her commentary.

"So, this side of the gladius we know had something engraved on it. Most likely the name of the owner and probably his military unit. Possibly an invocation to a religious deity? A few letters were just discernible as a result of the x-ray. From the hilt down the length of the blade we retrieved the following letters." Professor Taylor reached into her lab coat pocket and pulled out a piece of paper.

"Let's see now…" She peered at the piece of paper.

"Erm…the letters are, c, o, letters ne and l grouped together, p, r, s, and s again. Then we draw a blank until the end of the sequence, and noticeably clear on the x-ray, the Roman numerals VI. That number will undoubtably refer to a military unit."

"Legio VI Valeria Victrix." Lucius spoke without thinking. Professor Taylor frowned over the rim of her glasses.

"Pardon?"

"Er…I'm guessing, Professor Taylor. Just an assumption really but given that we know the Legion VI Valeria Victrix was stationed in the province.." His voice trailed away.

"The discernible letters at the end of the engraving would support your observation." She didn't elaborate further. Lucius declined the opportunity to tell his companions that the gladius owner's full name was Macro Cornelius Varus, Primus Pilus of the Legion VI Valeria Victrix. He declined even further to inform them that his old History teacher, Mr MacRonald had also owned that gladius, in what we call 'time.' Arrogance and presumed knowledge about such matters as 'time' make poor bedfellows.

"It will prove to be the star attraction at Housesteads museum, I'm sure." The voice from behind the third mask was that of Paula Mason, curator of The National Museum of Scotland. The masked face, reminiscent of pandemic and plague. Lucius dragged his thoughts away from the approaching question of how many plagues had afflicted the late Roman Empire.

Back to the present. "When can I expect the gladius to be delivered to the museum?"

"Within the next fortnight, given that the research is now complete. Professor?" The curator's masked face turned to Professor Taylor.

"We can work on the gladius engraving without it being here at Edinburgh. We have the X-rays. I'm sure we can make sense of those letters we have deciphered." The

Professor fixed a steely eyed contact with Lucius. "Tightest of security for this show piece." She pointed at the sword. "We don't want a repeat of the 1933 disaster when the priceless ruby was stolen. The skeleton of the centurion will accompany the gladius, for the sake of context. That includes the pieces of armour and the helmet."

Centurion Macro was going home, home to Vercovicium.

Lucius nodded his pleasure at the news and wrestled with the memory that before him on this table and lying next to Centurion Macro, was the sword with which he, Lucius, had ripped open the throat of the barbarian Pict when he first descended into the chaos and carnage of late fourth century Vercovicium, AD 367 to be precise. If truth is stranger than fiction, and if his two companions relished a 'stranger than fiction' adventure in time travel, he could reveal to them what was engraved on the blade of the gladius. Their reaction? They would be shocked to hear of his mental health issues and would smile pityingly at him. They'd say his fanatical addiction to archaeology and history had crossed the line from fact into fiction. Lucius had learned over the years to keep his thoughts and memories to himself.

"Any questions then?" Professor Taylor was moving the rusted hobnails from Macro's boots with her fingertip, as though trying to neaten them further. Lucius shook his head. Professor Taylor peeled her blue latex gloves from her hands and unhooked her mask so that it hung from one ear, like a ridiculous earring. Lucius and Paula Mason followed suit and the three of them moved away from the table displaying Centurion Macro's skeleton, bones, armour, and sword.

Professor Taylor smiled. "Next Thursday then, Lucius. Be ready to receive this gentleman for display at Housesteads. He will be delivered along with an armoured glass display case for his gladius. It should prove a delight for your visitors. Might even encourage the buying of more replica plastic Roman swords from your shop! In fact, if the display proves popular, we may well invest in a full-size replica. We'll see."

♦ ♦ ♦

The busy roads of a city hurrying about its business, vehicles, and pedestrians criss crossing paths and streets, soon disappeared into the rear-view mirror as junctions, roundabouts and traffic lights thinned out to allow for less of a stop start journey back towards Housesteads back down the A68. Grim grey buildings, garish advertising posters and stubborn city planted trees were replaced by the inviting sweep of a dual carriageway promising an uninterrupted journey back to Hadrian's Wall and the museum at Housesteads. The miles of the return journey were swallowed up to the accompaniment of Classic FM, in turn soothing or invigorating the mood of the driver. The triumphant, strident blasts of 'Purcell's Trumpet Voluntary' added to Lucius' feeling of personal pleasure in securing the loan of Centurion Macro for Vercovicium. Records of the museum told him of earlier loan triumphs, a single sapphire earring, mysteriously lost, and what he knew to be the Great Red Bloodstone of Mithras. Given the scandal surrounding the disappearance of the latter, Housesteads museum was lucky to be given a further opportunity with the loan of the gladius after ninety odd years. It was a strange world in which the curator of a museum had already handled objects before they became artefacts and spoken with the skeleton of a Roman centurion lying in the bowels of the National Museum of Scotland. Time…

Time was passing, along with the miles as Lucius approached the turn off for Risingham, or to give it its Google maps grand name, Habitancum Roman fort. "And why not," Lucius thought, "just a quick diversion to break up the monotony of the journey." Decision made, and with a quick glance in the rear-view mirror, Lucius pulled off the A68 onto the side road leading to Habitancum. The smooth ride of the A68 was replaced with a bumpier, slower progress, hemmed in by hedgerows and shallow grassy banks lining uneven, uncultivated fields. To the left the dark woods of Cragg Estate, ahead, a gentle curve to the right. Habitancum loomed low at its south east corner. Steep sided ditches and rising mounds lay below the more obvious remains of the ramparts with clumps of trees gathered on the hill overlooking the fort to the north. Lucius pulled over, turned off the ignition and stepped out of the car. The only music here in the world outside his car was the timeless sigh of the wind and distant cries of high-flying birds. He closed the car door, locked it, and made his way up towards the weed choked ditches, beetling high banks and ramparts sloping up from the road. Lucius paused. One bird cry seemed more insistent, more powerful, and more personal than the others. He looked up as an eagle glided earthwards, wings outstretched, predator's eyes fixing the lone figure paused between his car and Habitancum Roman fort.

"Hispana." Lucius whispered to himself. The bird landed so close to Lucius that he could have reached forward and touched it.

"How long? Two thousand years?" Hispana blinked at him, a blink of recognition. Lucius still had the frame of a gangly youth but his hairline was starting to recede. The smooth white skin showed where his hair had retreated in the face of advancing time. The slight balding and the stubbly beard enhanced his museum curator character. A head, always busy on the inside, far less concerned with what the outside appearance showed to the world.

Hispana turned her back on Lucius and faced north. She took a moment to preen under her wings and took flight. Not skywards, but a low trajectory, gliding on outstretched wings, skimming the ditches and ramparts of Habitancum to land about a hundred metres away. Was she injured? Lucius clambered up and down the earthwork ramparts and ditches and made his way to Hispana. After two or three similar false starts by Hispana, Lucius decided to return to his car and follow the eagle via the trackway skirting Habitancum to the west and then leading north east. And so the strange journey continued. Lucius searching out farm trackways between fields and open countryside, peering over the bonnet of his Land Rover, keeping one eye fixed on Hispana, now flying onwards, then returning but always heading north east, guiding him.

The afternoon wore on, Lucius' zig zag journey, bumping over rutted farm tracks concerned him. He should have been back at Housesteads museum around now, a glance at the dashboard clock told him it was four-thirty, when drizzle started to bead on the windscreen. One swish of the wipers cleared his view only to lose sight of Hispana. He was driving up a gentle slope towards a solitary tree on the horizon, a large tree, unusual for this part of the world. An olive tree.

Lucius stopped his Land Rover, reached onto the back seat to retrieve his rainproof jacket, and stepped out of the vehicle. Tugging on the jacket he walked up the slope towards the olive tree. Closer inspection of the tree showed a gnarled and twisted trunk around three-foot in diameter. An old tree, an ancient tree, a good two thousand years old. How on earth had an olive tree of such a venerable age had ended up here in the northern wilds of Northumberland? Lucius had no idea, although in another life or time...there were horses, people fleeing something.

Ahead, Hispana sat imperiously atop what appeared to be a short section of tumbled wall. Something wasn't right here and in the same moment, too right. Lucius' memory went into free fall behind the professional, objective gaze of the archaeologist's trained eye. Distant memory locked horns with present cold observation. His eyes scanned back and forth, taking in the bumps and hollows surrounding Hispana. Human activity at some time had served to shape and control this landscape. The question was, at what time? The archaeologist's eyes sought to interpret with a field walkers' close inspection, looking for tell-tale signs.

Lucius hurried up to where Hispana was still perched on the low remnant of wall. Picking up the line of the wall as it traced away either side of him, Lucius decided it marked an enclosure of some sort. A gap in the line of the low wall was filled by a crowd of dark green nettles where perhaps a gate once stood. A horseshoe shaped enclosure with…Lucius homed in on some straight lines showing in the grass further up the slope. Straight lines, so a building of some sort? An old, abandoned farm house, perhaps? A farmer's cattle byre? Sheep pen? Lucius strode across the area delineated by the trace of the wall and stopped in front of the ghostly straight lines. The drizzle was light, only beading his coat and hair. Lucius looked at his watch. Ten to five. In ten minutes, he should have been back at the museum. It was time to go. He could check archaeological records of this area north east of Habitancum later. Any structures of note, trial trenches, fieldwalking finds would appear in the records. For now, he'd have a cursory look before heading back to his Land Rover. A walk through the wet grass showed a probable long rectangular structure divided into around eight to ten sections, his trained archaeologist's eye told him. Most probably animal pens then for a hillside farmer. He kicked at a pile of fresh earth, the result of mole or rabbit activity and loose soil showered up. Lucius did a double take. Lying amidst the scattered soil were some bits of familiar dirty red brick colour. His brow furrowed, Lucius bent to pick up a piece. He knew in an instant. This was a fragment of Roman roof tile. Lucius' pulse picked up in a beat and was racing ahead of his thoughts. With the tile fragment held between forefinger and thumb, Lucius took a fresh look at his surroundings. As he had known the skeleton of Macro, so he knew this place too. The ancient olive tree. Memories crowded in, clamouring for attention. Right beneath his feet lay the remains of a Roman villa where a drama had played out two thousand years ago; a drama of which he had been part.

♦ ♦ ♦

The news, when it broke, shook the world of archaeology, a Roman villa, north of Hadrian's Wall. Currently accepted historical knowledge was that no Roman villas had been built in the north of Britain, certainly not as far north as Hadrian's Wall, or beyond. The land, like the Caledonians, was untamed and untameable despite the efforts of various Emperors sending, or leading huge armies against the Picts of Caledonia. Anyway, poor soil and a harsh climate meant that the Roman idea of a productive farmland could never be realised. Villas abounded in the south and south east of Roman Britain, the more civilised part of the province, with its rich farmland, and kind climate. This villa discovery lay even further north, beyond Hadrian's Wall, beyond even Habitancum, (Risingham) fort. Lucius Mabbutt explained to professional colleagues that his discovery of the villa had been based on a hunch, a bit of casual field walking leading to the discovery of Roman roof tile fragments. Initial disbelief was soon replaced by a flurry of activity as an archaeological team from York University gathered together trowels, spades, brushes, buckets, and wellington boots in preparation for what promised to be a unique 'dig' beyond Hadrian's Wall, the Roman villa where there shouldn't be a Roman villa.

XVI

Spades, Shovels, Trowels, and Brushes

"Do you believe in time travel, Lucius?"
Lucius and the site director, David Cole, were standing way up the slope to the rear of the site of the villa. The olive tree stood impassively behind them, oblivious to their temporary passing presence in its two-thousand-year-old existence. A miraculous tree, sprung from a centurion's vine staff, not just any centurion, or any vine staff. The vine staff, that mark of rank, power, and punishment, had been the property of the centurion present at the crucifixion of Jesus Christ. Reassigned from his legion, the Tenth Fretensis in the province of Judea, to the province of Britainnia, the centurion had thrust his vine staff into the ground here sometime in the mid first century AD as the legions of Rome had pushed into Caledonia for the first time. For what reason, we will never know, one of history's untold stories lost in the mists of time. The vine staff, having taken root mysteriously, had grown into a

venerable olive tree. It stood as mute witness to the scrabbling, frantic and brief lives of humans over two thousand years, from the first carefully constructed Roman villa, with its spades, shovels, trowels, and wheelbarrows, to its careful excavation with its…spades, shovels, trowels, and wheelbarrows.

"Well, do you?"

Lucius was miles away, or perhaps millennia away. Straining to pick up sounds from the distant past; the roar and clash of battle, the cries of the wounded and dying, fire raging and men shouting. The here and now sound of his companion's voice nudged him into a reply.

"Sorry, I was.. in a different place, time. You were saying?"

"I was asking if you believe in time travel, Lucius?"

"An intriguing question, especially for us archaeologists. Even more intriguing if you're a time traveller, of course, like me."

The site director laughed at Lucius' joke. "Well, I always say that apart from all the theories about time travel, such as passing through time zones when we're flying, those of us who make a living scraping at the earth with a trowel, are we not time travellers?"

Lucius picked up on the idea. "Yes, we peel back layers of time, literally." He warmed to his subject. "High speed time travel is removing top soil with a bulldozer, medium speed time travel is the trowel, slow time travel is the brush…"

"And infinitesimally slowly with a toothpick at some fragile, delicate find." The site director looked pleased with his contribution.

"Won't be needed on this site, even if we could get a mini dozer up here," Lucius pointed out.

"Nope, the topsoil is shallow enough to get down to the archaeology soon enough," Cole agreed.

They watched as the already muddied team of 'diggers' moved back and forth between the two trucks parked below the villa site, carrying an assortment of buckets, spades, shovels, brooms, and brushes up the rutted pathway to the villa site. Amongst the 'diggers' Lucius swore he could make out two ghostly figures, side by side coming up the path. A centurion, transverse crest atop his helmet, and young lad dressed in a tunic. The figures faded. There were no sounds of battle, no cries of anguish or roars of rage and anger, only the chatter of the diggers busy with their preparation of the site.

"Certainly was a huge stroke of luck for you to come across this site. A chance kick at the ground and, hey presto, pieces of Roman roof tile." As if to prove his point, David Cole stubbed the toe of his boot into the ground, bringing up a clod of soil. He moved the clod this way and that with his toe, breaking it down into smaller bits in an exaggerated display of trying to find something, an archaeological clue. He sighed, ceased his toe poking, and turned to Lucius.

"Nope, nothing. Looks like you were extremely fortunate indeed, Lucius." Cole smiled at his fellow archaeologist. Lucius responded with an equally expressionless smile.

In what had been the courtyard of the villa, a finds tent was being erected and collapsible wooden tables unfolded and put up. The ground work was going ahead at a fast rate. The dig would begin tomorrow morning. Lucius offered his apologies, saying that he needed to get back to the Housesteads museum. The Roman gladius and its owner was due to be delivered and he had to make the necessary preparations for its arrival. Leaving the villa site, he made his way out through the weed grown space where once the villa gateway had stood gateless with only a rickety farm cart to defy the Picts swarming outside. Lucius looked down at the ground where he thought he and Macro had stood those centuries ago. Behind him, David Cole was barking orders at the crew who would begin excavating the villa site next day. Walking back down the rutted pathway leading up to the villa, Lucius decided that here, truly little had changed. If he turned around and faced back up the rutted slope in the direction of the villa, he could sense Centurion Macro at his side, Hispana gliding ahead of them towards the low wall where two Roman soldiers stood guard at the gateless entry to the villa courtyard. Time was…well, a funny old thing, past, present, or future…it is, was and will be… a funny old thing.

♦ ♦ ♦

You only knew the former bed and breakfast had been called the Cosy Kettle if you had visited it in the previous decade before 2024. The sign hanging outside was long gone, the shell of the building stood in a suffocating tangle of undergrowth. A haven for weeds, knee high grasses, waist high nettles with glorious purple flowers crowning their tips and shoulder high brambles, thorny and guarding the property like Nature's own barbed wire. Great aunt Livia's wild rose bush was now lost in a greater wilderness. Above head height, ivy snaked its fingers up to the gutters of the former guesthouse, probing cracks, and crevices in the walls. Grasses pushed up through the gravelled surface of what used to be the car park. In the corner, great aunt Livia's Ford Anglia stood rusting on long flat tyres, the sides of them looking like black crepe paper where the wheel rims lay heavy on the perished rubber. Paint peeled from the body work and the chrome bumpers were rust pitted and flaking.

Lucius stepped out of his Land Rover after spending some moments studying this other world from his youth. Despite the grass and weeds, gravel crunched underfoot as it had always done. He walked over to the Ford Anglia and, shading his eyes, peered through the driver's side window. There was the spindly steering wheel which had threatened to cradle great aunt Livia's ample bosom. Wispy spider webs festooned the interior, the plastic seats were cracked and covered in dust. Lucius decided against disturbing the spiders and ghosts. No tug at the obstinate, rusty hinged door today. Perhaps next time…

He made his way past the front door and the windows, now boarded up, looking like giant wooden sticking plasters, and pushed through the weeds following the path to the rear garden, overlooked by the fire blackened rear wall and kitchen door. And here was the mystery, occasionally visited, never resolved. Amongst the wilderness flourishing across the back garden, was an area of ground sporting a huge question mark. Lucius bent and picked up a weighty circular iron handle, the type used to pull up trap doors. The iron ring was rust coated but still solid. Lucius wiped the rust-coloured dirt from his hand down his jeans. An iron trap door handle with no trap door, just solid ground beneath his feet. As he scoured the ground where he knew a trap door had once led below ground to a cellar, a 'cellarium' as Mr MacRonald had called it, a memory insisted on being heard.

"Cellarium? What's that? A cellar perhaps? Lucius thought.

Mr MacRonald wrestled with the huge, circular iron ring handle set into the trap door. Great aunt Livia stood with customary hands-on hips as the teacher cursed and pulled at the stubborn handle.

"You're losing your strength, your fitness, my fine Centurio," she mocked.

"Quiet, damn you woman. See to your duties." The admonishment died on his lips as he glanced up at Lucius.

"Well, boy?" …..

No need to clear weeds from where the trap door had once been. The weeds lay broken and crushed from Lucius' earlier searches for the portal to the past, here in the back garden of the Cosy Kettle. The ground was firm beneath Lucius' feet, unyielding, belying any suggestion of a cellar, or anything other than Nature's hard packed earth. And yet…he turned the trap door handle around in his hands, looking for an answer. The heavy iron ring was dumb, and dumbly it thumped onto the disappointing earth as Lucius dropped it back onto the solid ground. Lucius turned and stepped his way back through the tangle of undergrowth and memories which had once been the Cosy Kettle. He made his way back to the Land Rover.

Behind the wooden boards nailed across the reception room window, a figure moved close enough to press its face up against a crack of daylight, its eye blinking, following the Land Rover as it sped away back to Vercovicium.

A whisper, "he'll come back, Lucius always comes back." Great aunt Livia brushed a ghostly tear from a ghostly eye and made her way to the dusty, cobwebbed shell that had once been the Cosy Kettle kitchen to prepare non-existent dinners for non-existent guests.

♦ ♦ ♦

Museum duties at Housesteads kept Lucius away from the dig at the newly discovered villa north of the Wall for three days. There was the arrival of the Roman gladius and its owner's skeleton to deal with. The gladius in its glass display case, hung vertically by a thin wire attached to the sword pommel, its blade tip hovering above the base of the display case. In its brightly lit world of LED lights, you could just make out a few letters engraved on the rusted blade. A photo of an artist's reconstruction of the sword, and a notice giving brief details about the artefact completed the exhibit. To the left of the gladius display cabinet stood, or rather lay, the glass case containing the skeleton of Centurion Macro.

"Once of this parish" thought Lucius as he looked down at Macro's oversized glass coffin standing at knee height on the museum floor. The skeleton lay on a thin bed of pale orange gravel, the helmet, breastplate by its side, hobnails from his caligae arranged like well-ordered rusty dots at his feet.

The museum had been closed for the afternoon to allow for the delivery of its latest exhibits. What sunlight there was, filtered in through the small windows set high up in the walls, dappling the interior of the building in pools of light. One of these pools of light lay across the top of Macro's 'coffin.' It bathed the centurion's skull in a warm glow, highlighting its yellow hue.

"Sol Invictus," Lucius spoke into the empty museum. "Mithras greets you, Centurion Macro. You are blessed. You are home." Lucius smiled at the memory of his friend and teacher. If it wasn't for the detached lower jaw bone beneath its skull, a parody of a raucous laugh from a dead man, it was a peaceful moment witnessing a spirit at eternal rest. Tomorrow, the museum would open again and the world would come to view the marvel of Centurion Macro and his gladius. For now, Lucius Mabutt turned out the lights in the museum and left, locking the door behind him.

♦ ♦ ♦

No sooner had Lucius stepped out of his Land Rover, back at the villa dig, than he caught sight of David Cole waving at him, not a casual greeting but a furious demand to hurry up to where the site director stood at the top of the slight rise on which the archaeological site lay. His voice carried down the slope, adding urgency to the wild waving of his arms. Lucius decided that today the wellington boots could stay in the Land Rover and he'd chance slipping and sliding up the muddy trackway leading to the equally muddy excavations. And now Cole was hurrying across the exploratory trenches already dug into the ground as the first phase of making sense of what archaeology might be present below the surface of this field.

"Lucius!" Coles' voice was something more than insistent. The arms were no longer waving but used for precarious balance as he slalomed between trenches to arrive breathless before Lucius. He paused to regain his balance and dignity.

Cole gulped before hurtling into a monologue. "This is Howard Carter all over again! That moment in the world of archaeology which people will marvel at and talk about for generations to come. The moment which is every archaeologist's dream." He swallowed his excitement again. "You won't believe it, Lucius. You simply won't believe what you have uncovered, well, what we've actually uncovered. Come, come." Cole grabbed Lucius' arm and pulled him up the slope, along the former trackway leading to the villa. Like a couple of ice skaters locked together in an ice dance, they slipped and slid their way up to the excavation.

Cole had calmed down, more through the necessity to draw breath to tackle the slope than by choice.

"Yes, Howard Carter and the tomb of Tutankhamun. There he was, Carter, with three companions in the rubble filled corridor leading to the tomb. He made that tiny breach in the top left-hand corner of the door to the inner tomb and, by the light of a solitary candle, he peered in at the dimly lit contents of the tomb. As you know, Lucius, Carter was unaware of the fact that he had discovered King Tut's final resting place." Cole paused and breathed deeply before continuing.

"I think we might just have our Howard Carter moment right here. Follow me, Lucius."

A glance to his left and right, informed Lucius' professional eye that the trenches in which hunched and muddied figures scaped with trowels, brushed with brushes and hoisted buckets of spoil up onto the ground from the bottom of trenches, that the excavation was well advanced. There was no stratigraphy here, no settlement pattern overlying previous human activity. This was a single wing Roman villa lying under a few inches of top soil and the diggers were making quick progress unearthing the foundations of the building.

"Mr Cole." A digger wearing muddied dungarees and wellington boots, stood up in the trench in which she had been kneeling. A raised, muddy hand held a small round object between thumb and forefinger.

"Just uncovered this," she said tapping the small round object with the tip of her trowel.

Cole leaned forward to take the find, which the digger placed in the palm of his outstretched hand. "Let's see," he said using the ball of his thumb to carefully prise away some of the mud encrusted small object. Lucius moved closer and watched as Cole's thumb eased away the dirt.

"Mmm…feels for all the world like a small bronze head." The thumb worked away to reveal a fine-featured face, topped by a hat, a floppy, conical one. David Cole continued his running commentary while his thumb worked away at the remaining mud encrusted artefact. Around them the sounds of chattering diggers and scraping trowels provided the perfect background for what came next.

"This'll be Mithras, don't you think, Lucius? Judging by the distinctive shape of this.." He paused and felt the conical top of the hat. The bronze head, now largely cleared of dirt, had the luxurious green patina which adds beauty to what would have been brightly polished and gleaming like gold.

"Been hacked or wrenched from the body of the figurine. Look at this jagged line around the neck." He showed Lucius the damaged neck. "Someone clearly wasn't happy with this god. So, deliberate damage then. Hardly accidental, not given the twisted nature of the break" He peered intently at the neck, his thumb tracing the ragged edge of the neck. "Hardly unusual given the religious turbulence of this period of the Roman Empire. A late fourth century date for this villa, according to the few coin finds."

Lucius felt it might add a certain indefinable quality to the conversation if he informed David Cole of his position as a Raven, a brother initiate into the mysteries of Mithraic worship. Perhaps another time…Lucius smiled to himself.

David Cole misread the smile and drew breath before his next announcement.

"And in the words of the song, 'You Ain't Seen Nothing Yet,' Lucius."

"Sadie, take this to the finds tent for cleaning and cataloguing, please. I presume you've logged and recorded its position here in the trench?"

"Yup, all sorted, Mr site director, sir." Sadie mocked a salute, smiled at her boss as she stepped out of the trench and took the bronze head from Cole's open palm.

Dropping into the trench, Cole invited Lucius to follow suit. Lucius watched as Cole picked up Sadie's trowel and knelt down on an exposed portion of mosaic floor. Leaning forward on one hand, Cole scraped away at the dirt covering what appeared to be part of a design at the centre of the mosaic floor. A layout common to most Roman mosaic floors. Where soil had already been cleared by trowel and brush, Lucius could make out the edge of a geometric design, the lower quadrant of a circle. The trowel scraped faster across the uneven mosaic floor.

"I know what this is, Lucius, and it'll shake the world of archaeology. You won't believe it."

The insistent metal against stone scrape, scrape of trowel edge on mosaic floor working its way towards the centre of the floor, set a beat which matched the racing of Lucius' heart.

"See, here," a pause followed by more scraping, "folds of a long gown." The point of the trowel, flicking earth aside from the mosaic, worked its way up to reveal more of the gowned figure and eventually the left side of the figure's face emerged. A narrow line of black mosaic tesserae, travelled downwards from where the left ear lay hidden under intricately detailed shoulder length hair. The trowel, that wooden handled humble wonder of time travel, continued its journey to uncover another line emerging from the man's head, to be topped off by a letter P above the gowned man's head. Cole stood, breathing heavily from his exertions. Sadie's trowel hung from his right hand. Neither Lucius nor he needed to find words to describe what lay before them. They knew enough to complete the picture at the centre of the mosaic floor. The figure of Christ with the Chi Rho monogram behind his head. Cole pointed at the Chi Rho motif at the centre of the half-excavated mosaic floor.

"That's our Howard Carter moment, Lucius. Not only have we, you really, uncovered a Roman villa north of Hadrian's Wall, but we have unmistakable evidence of Christian worship, at that. Ground breaking archaeology, Lucius, ground breaking. A Tutankhamun moment."

Lucius heard Cole's words but his attention was taken by the hill behind the villa. The distant sounds of ancient battle played all around, topped by the voice of Macro urging him to flee, to climb that hill and follow those on horseback who had already escaped the imminent slaughter of all those left at the villa.

"What's burning? Something is on fire. Where…?" Lucius cast around for the source of the smell of burning wood.. not wood but straw.

"Sorry?" Cole looked puzzled. "What burning, Lucius? Nothing on fire here. You must be imagining it."

"No, I can.." Lucius sniffed at the air as he continued to turn his head seeking the source of what smelled like a growing conflagration.

"I remember now! The pile of hay at the back of the villa. It was on fire. I think the Picts had caused it, fire arrows or whatever." His tense, puzzled look was met by an equally puzzled look from David Cole.

"Picts, Lucius?" He looked across the mosaic floor which bore scorch marks looking very much like the result of collapsed burning roof beams. "Well, fair enough, there's definite evidence to suggest that the building collapsed as the result of a fire. Not an uncommon end for villas in the final years of the Roman period." The point of the trowel did the work again of guide as Cole aimed it at the charred marks criss crossing the Chi Rho mosaic floor.

"Well, I suppose your theory, suggestion about the Picts burning the villa down, probably sometime in the late fourth century, is a valid guess. I'm hoping we can add some more artefacts to the little bronze head of Mithras. Would be nice to get a clearer picture of what went on here."

Lucius nodded in agreement. The smell of burning straw and the sounds of battle were fading. His life, his lives, lay all around him; a journey from this villa back to Hadrian's Wall, the Cosy Kettle and Vercovicium fort where he was now museum curator.

David Cole greeted Sadie as she returned from the finds tent and took her trowel from him. She dropped into the trench and the rhythmic scrape of her trowel on mosaic floor resumed as Lucius and David Cole walked back across the former courtyard to where the villa gateway had stood fifteen centuries ago. Here, they shook hands and parted company. The site director made his way over to the finds tent where he would examine the bronze Mithras head further and try to give it context. The curator made his way down the trackway to his Land Rover. He needed to get back to Housesteads museum and the newly arrived display of the human remains of Centurion Macro

Cornelius Varus and his uncannily well-preserved Roman gladius. As Lucius got into his Land Rover he told himself that his need to sleep on a camp bed in the museum, 'for security purposes,' wasn't the real reason he hadn't been home to sleep in own bed since the new display arrived from the Museum of Scotland. It wasn't about security, it was about the powerful pull of the past, the ghosts of Hadrian's Wall were calling.

XVII

The Jigsaw Pieces of Time

"This really is a very stupid and unnecessary idea," Lucius thought as he turned over on the flimsy camp bed for the thousandth time that night. He couldn't sleep, indeed hadn't slept for the last, what, nearly two weeks since the arrival of the new display from The National Museum of Scotland. He lay on his back, hands folded across his chest and stared up at the ceiling. The middle of the camp bed sagged under the weight of his hips and he feared that one of the supporting springs might snap at any moment. Then the other springs would snap in rapid succession and he would end up stranded between the metal frame, backside nearly touching the floor, as helpless as a beetle on its back. And no one to help him untangle himself from the wreck of the collapsed camp bed.

He didn't need to be here. Modern museums were veritable fortresses of alarms, sensors and other such security paraphernalia making any museum the equivalent of Fort Knox. Lucius was about to turn on to his side to relieve the boredom of his restless night when a protesting spring warned him think better of it. Back to wandering thoughts about security. History here at Vercovicium museum recounted an episode, when was it, back in the nineteen thirties? A break in and the theft of that artefact, a precious deep red gemstone, which Lucius knew to be The Great Red Bloodstone of the god, Mithras. A vagrant, some wandering madman had broken into the museum, smashed the reinforced glass topping the display cabinet and made off with the valuable, unique artefact. Lucius paused and moved his hand up to his throat, feeling for something that he felt should be there, but wasn't. A leather pouch.

The silence was broken by the shriek of a night owl. Under a vast field of timeless stars, stretching from dark horizon to dark horizon, the ancient ruins of Hadrian's Wall shuddered with history to the core of every block of stone laid by those in another age. Roman legionaries, sweating, shouting, cursing, gossiping, and laughing with fellow legionaries on this dark frontier at the utmost limits of the Emperor Hadrian's realm. Where the sounds of hammer and chisel, clunking, chipping, and scraping, working the stone of the new Wall and forts had invaded the vast silence of this primeval landscape, silence had fallen now, a silence you could almost touch. Back then, the Emperor Hadrian had proclaimed it was time to consolidate. On every frontier of the Empire, from north Africa to the mighty Rhine and Danube, from Syria in the east to the wilds of northern Britain, Hadrian drew lines, permanent frontiers of stone and timber.

The lone owl hooted, breaking into Lucius' thoughts. To his left, where Macro's skeleton lay at eternal rest, he thought he heard a slight scrunch of gravel, like a light footstep, followed by a papery cough. Lucius shifted cautiously on the camp bed, another spring pinged and he turned his head to face the glass case entombing Centurion Macro, lying only a few feet away in the gloom. Surely not? An imagination running riot? Understandable really. Under a night sky of vast nothingness, Hadrian's Wall was empty. All the tourists, visitors, walkers, barking dogs, laughing chasing children had melted away as they did at the end of every day. You really are alone on the Wall at night, the infinite vastness of the sky over arching the Wall's two-thousand-year-old history and its ghosts.

Lucius moved a cautious hand to check the time on his wrist watch. The back light told him it was 2.58 am and he hadn't slept a wink. He risked a yawn and a careful stretch inside his sleeping bag to prevent cramp. This couldn't go on. He would sleep at home tomorrow night. The museum wasn't going to be broken into. This was hardly 1933 when the Great Red Bloodstone of Mithras had been stolen. He closed his eyes.

He knew he had fallen asleep briefly when his eyes shot open. That smell, familiar and yet seemingly coming from a great distance. Not the distance of space, but more of time. He sniffed. That was it, burning pine cones. He had been here before, this smell signified something, was a herald of change. This wasn't the smell of the 'here and now' but rather the smell of 'then and there.' Lucius' school days, that history lesson, the teacher, Mr MacRonald, Centurion Macro, lying just over there in his glass coffin. Lucius looked at his watch again. It was now past three o'clock in the morning, 3.04 am to be precise. He had dropped off for only a couple of minutes. There was another papery cough and slight swish of gravel being disturbed, the fine gravel on which the yellowing bones of

Macro rested, the faint dry cough from the dislocated jaw of Macro. Lucius kept very still his heart thumping in his chest. It was growing light around him, a faint glow. Something made him check his watch again. The digital read out informed him that the time was now…. what was this? His watch had stopped, the digital numbers frozen against the faint backlight. Three digits; 367 and where the pm/am letters should appear, they had been replaced with the letters A and D. Lucius' watch read 367 AD.

The scent of burning pine cones was fading, replaced now by whispers, thin, undulating but urgent. Hushed voices hurrying to tell their tale. Not a few, not a handful, not scores or even hundreds, not thousands, more tens of thousands of plaintiff ghostly voices reaching out. They weren't loud, but they were demanding to be heard. Voices of souls given one chance across the centuries, one last chance to be heard by the living; and Lucius was the living. No one common language here though. A multitude of tongues indistinguishable from one another. Lucius' brain kicked in from his world of classical studies, he could make out traces of vulgar Latin spoken in different dialects which might be Celtic, Germanic, Syrian, Arab. The ghosts from the Wall were awake and anxious to be heard.

Lucius chanced propping himself up on an elbow and looked across the museum. The camp bed protested, the springs squeaking. Dust was falling, a strange dust, more a miasma floating down and settling on everything it touched. Display cabinet glass tops became opaque, free-standing artefacts such as statues, segments of Roman column and chunks of inscribed masonry were coated in what looked like talcum powder. His sleeping bag too was coated in this fine layer of descending dust. He wiped some away with the back of his hand, unzipped the bag and swung his legs sideways until he was sitting on the edge of the camp bed which groaned a protest. He sat braced for a moment, making sure the thing wasn't about to collapse under him, and stood. Dust lay across the museum floor as far as he could see. He walked to the nearest light switch and flicked it down. After a few stuttering flashes, the fluorescent strip lights running across the ceiling, kicked in one after the other until the museum was flooded with light. Lucius turned to look behind him and in doing so he noted the absence of his footprints across the finely dusted floor. He looked up. There was no indication of where the dust was coming from, it just appeared at ceiling level and floated down. Less now since Lucius had turned on the lights. He checked his wrist watch again. It still displayed 367 AD. The screen of the wall mounted television pulsed into life with a blue glow. It was very much part of the modern museum culture of informative educational videos hoping to bring the past to life for visitors. The TV was mounted on the wall above the three carved stone hooded deities flanked by two stone altars in a secluded and darker corner of the museum. The film which had entertained and educated visitors for some years now, traced the history of Vercovicium from its initial construction to its final days. The story unfolded against the wider background of the purpose and role Hadrian's Wall played in controlling Rome's furthermost northern frontier.

Lucius walked over to the TV, the screen now alive and ready to recount the story of Vercovicium. Lucius stood with his chin cupped in his right hand, his right arm resting against his left arm folded across his chest. The familiar opening footage was accompanied by the rich, serious tones of the film's narrator. The opening title of 'Housesteads Roman Fort' lay across sweeping drone footage of the Wall's progress across the rugged, challenging landscape of Northumberland. The narrator invited the viewer into the unfolding story. He explained how Hadrian's Wall sat at the northernmost limit of the Empire, dividing the land of the Brigantes tribe in two, those to the south living under Roman rule. The dust had stopped falling now, and Lucius took a second to look back over his shoulder where the thin layer coated everything from the floor to the free-standing displays and artefact cabinets.

He turned back to the film showing the Wall marching across the rugged landscape around Vercovicium. This was drone footage reconstructing history, some might say a bird's eye view in the old parlance. A bird's eye view, perhaps an eagles' view. Lucius was carried along on the familiar footage of film as the bird's eye view arrived over Housesteads fort. Key words 'strength' and 'guardians' added weight to the narrative of Rome stamping her mark on this land, keeping the wild, unconquerable tribes to the north outside the boundaries of Roman civilisation; the tribes which the Romans called barbarians the narrator added sombrely. Lucius nodded his familiarity with the story as Housesteads fort took centre stage on the TV screen. CGI reconstructed the buildings of Housesteads from its ruins upwards. Clever stuff, the wonders of modern technology bringing the past to life with as accurate as possible reconstructions. Here on the screen Housesteads was being reborn, brick by brick, stone by stone. The bird's eye view, swept down to ground level, taking in the hollowed, pitted, and grassy expanse of the vicus lying outside the towering southern gateway of the fort. And then, by the magic hand of some technological whizz kid, buildings arose from the very ground in the shape of various civilian structures lining the main road through the vicus. Lucius had seen this footage a hundred times before as he passed through the museum going about this duties as curator, but this time something was different. He scratched at his chin and narrowed his eyes. Was this something he'd missed from previous viewings? He took a step closer to the screen and, yes, his eyes didn't deceive him. There was a ghostly figure walking up the main street of the vicus towards the south gate, a man, cloaked, his back to the viewer, the red, transverse crested helmet proclaiming him a centurion. And he limped, his left leg clearly injured or damaged. Lucius' heart skipped a beat. His mind scrabbled to recollect where the remote control for the TV was, he needed to pause, to replay this strange footage. There was no remote control. The TV was turned on automatically at the start and end of each day and off at the end of the day.

The figure walking up to the south gate disappeared from the screen. Lucius turned to Macro's glass display case now with its fine coat of powdery dust and back to the TV. The narrator was speaking again, his rich voice describing the three hundred years of Housesteads' occupation. The bird's eye view homed in on the centre of the fort, the building lying at its the heart, the headquarters building. The narrator continued. "And here at the heart of the fort, lay the praetorium and the garrison commander's house. A Roman Mediterranean style house, stone built, with heated mosaic floors, wall frescos and the finest furniture. A home fit for a Roman aristocrat with a thousand men under his command. The barracks of the ordinary soldiers bore no resemblance to the magnificent stone building standing proudly at the centre of the fort. A pattern repeated across the Empire."

Lucius took another look at his watch. 367 AD. He tapped it with his finger. No change. The film was panning in on the praetorium and the house, reconstructed, standing tall. Figures were moving, wraith like, opaque, a small group making their way into the courtyard of the commander's house. It was difficult to determine exactly how many figures there were, but Lucius narrowed his eyes and decided it was a small group, of no more than ten or twelve people. The drone view focused in on the individuals with their backs towards the camera. A cloaked man and a hooded woman led the procession as they disappeared inside a doorway. Lucius' heart caught in his throat for a couple of beats. The group stopped and a ceremony began to unfold. Lucius' mind sprinted from the starting block and raced ahead. Those two figures, despite having their backs to him, were familiar. Another glance at his watch. It was 368 AD now. Lucius' brow furrowed as he watched the screen move into close up mode something akin to a modern wedding video as the camera positioned itself directly in front of the couple. Lucius' recognised the scene; it was a wedding, in the style of ancient Rome, and the couple smiling down at him from the TV monitor were Julia and Drusus. Lucius dragged the palm of his hand down his sweating face. The story played out like a silent movie, indistinct and blurred in the telling of its tale. The couple's hands reached out and touched together, lips moved in sacred vows, the small group behind the wedding couple swayed as if in time to celebratory chants. Whoever was officiating the wedding, draped a scarf like piece of material over Drusus and Julia's joined hands and made a sign of blessing, Lucius thought, 'the sign of the Cross.' The picture was fading, becoming fuzzy. Overhead, one of the fluorescent light strips buzzed and flickered. Lucius continued to stare at the TV screen now blank. He'd seen, what..? The marriage of Julia to the Centurion Drusus? And that footage of a figure walking up through the vicus, a figure more than resembling Centurion Macro, it was Centurion Macro. How could that be? He looked at his watch. It read as normal, informing him that it was now 3.40 am. He'd stood here for some forty minutes.

The night owl shrieked again, bringing him to his senses, well almost. It wasn't until he turned around to make his way to uncertain rest on the camp bed that his attention was caught by the plain granite altar to Mithras standing waist high against the wall to his right. The weathered and worn grey stone altar was no longer that. Now carved in fine, sharp, and detailed relief it had regained the appearance of its previous life, no longer a dumb piece of blurred stone serving to excite the imagination of the present-day visitor, but a garishly painted altar, holy to and venerated by worshippers two thousand years ago. Brilliant red paint flamed out from the darker mysterious blues, greens, and rich gold shone from the radiate crown of the god Mithras slaying the Great Bull. Brown hair and yellow hats contrasted with the brilliant white of the Great Bull's body. No shallow grooves on bare stone here, but bronze letters standing bold, sharp, and angular proclaiming the devotion of the god Mithras' followers. Lucius narrowed his eyes at the trickle of blood running down the front of the brightly painted altar. He stepped nearer to the altar and took in the blood pooled on the top. A sacrifice it seemed, recent. Not a great deal of blood, a small animal then, something like a chicken. The blood felt sticky and warm. Rather ridiculously and faintly annoyed at himself for doing so, Lucius turned to glance around the museum as if expecting to see whoever had offered up the sacrifice. Nonsense. But the blood was real, the blood was warm and the blood was fresh. The museum felt different, it was different. The display cases with their glass tops covered in fine dust, glowed faintly. Lucius stepped over to the nearest display case swept an arc through the dust with the edge of his hand and peered in at the all too familiar artefacts. The artefacts he had first seen those years ago when he visited Hadrian's Wall as a teenager. He recalled great aunt Livia urging him to visit the museum instead of simply playing, climbing over the ruins of Vercovicium. In this case had lain the rusted remains of sickle blades, knife blades and a flail. Basic farm implements as familiar to us as they were to our ancestors thousands of years ago. They were now all the more familiar, having turned from flaky rusted relics into tools with brand new wooden handles sporting shiny, sharp new blades, honed, and edged, looking razor sharp. They might have been bought yesterday at the nearest local farm store. At the next display case, Lucius brushed the dust away with his hand, again sweeping an arc over the glass top. Spear heads, a couple of short sword blades a boss from a shield and a collection of bronze military buckles, every last one now in brand new pristine gleaming condition fresh from the blacksmith's forge or the bronze smith's work bench. Fifteen centuries of age stripped away before his eyes. Bronze glowed under the cabinet lights while steel glinted from new blades. Lucius moved from case to case, marvelling at the transformation of the debris and detritus of the past, crumbled and useless artefacts brought back to life, as whole and useful as the day they had had been made or crafted. He consulted his watch. It was now 4.05am. Time had moved back and forward in the museum during the night. There was a pause, so palpable you could feel it.

Lucius caught his breath, feeling that he was hemmed in a press of people, like being in a tightly packed throng of football supporters exiting a football stadium. Shoulders pressing against shoulders, feet shuffling to move with the crowd, arms pinned to your sides, the heavy breathing of those around you, hot and panting in your ears. He tried to take a step away from whatever this press was. He couldn't move, he was rooted to the spot. A panic announced itself as his chest tightened and his breath came in short wheezes. The unseen throng of humanity was pinning him to one spot on the museum floor, a thousand whispers filling his head, voices from the past, voices of the owners of the tools, weapons, pottery, and jewellery lying inside the display cases. Unseen hands of ghosts reached out to Lucius and to the items in the museum cases they had once owned. The rough and calloused hands of farmers competed with the scarred and battered hands of soldiers to retrieve what had once been theirs. Priests' hands were raised in supplication before stone altars, all now brightly painted in those garish colours so favoured by the Romans, so trashy in appearance to the modern eye. Women's fingers pointed at items of jewellery, begging the return of their treasured possessions, or at the fragments of household pottery so essential to their kitchen needs. Lucius' mind plunged into and down a long tunnel at the end of which lay the kaleidoscope world of every memory, feeling and thought he had banked in his lifetime. He had been here before. A world full of utter blackness one second and eyeball searing light the next as memories and feelings battled for his attention. Ghosts and eagles…

It all stopped, just as in that instant the dream loses its reality and you awake. Gone. Lucius took a couple of steps forward, shrugged his shoulders now he was free of the press of the ghostly throng. A moment's consideration, a gathering of thoughts. He sniffed the air. Old rags, the hot odour of unwashed bodies, musty and dry, the smell of decay, the smell of death. And then, as if someone had opened the door to a breath of fresh air, the smells disappeared. And so too was the dust. Where there had been apprehension and even fear in his heart, there was now intrigue and questioning. Lucius' watch told him it was still 3.40am. Where had 4.05am gone when it hadn't arrived yet? Time hadn't moved then.

A slight swish of gravel and a thin cough. What if…? Lucius turned to where Centurion Macro lay entombed in his glass display case. Where the fragments of foot bones lay, there were two arcs of disturbed gravel across the surface, as though booted heels had moved across the gravel. Everything else in the case was as it should be, just the strange marks in the gravel. Lucius wasn't sure what to think. A glint of steel under the museum lights caught the corner of his eye. Macro's gladius blade, suspended in its glass display case, was as smooth as a silvered mirror, razor sharp, the legend incised on the blade reading as clearly as it would have done on the day the sword left the swordsmith's workshop. A legend incised, yes, but no longer reading 'Macro Cornelius Varus Primus Pilus Legio VI Valeria Victrix.' Lucius narrowed his eyes, rubbed them, squinted in disbelief, did anything and everything to focus on the letters now running the length of the blade.

EXCALI_UR.

Only the letter B was missing, all the other letters forming the name of King Arthur's legendary sword were taken from the original engraving.

Macro Cornelius Varus Primus Pilus Legio VI Valeria Victrix.

Lucius put his hand to his forehead, his brain buzzed trying to make sense of what he was looking at. There, right there, hanging in its glass case hung Centurion Macro's gladius, apparently transformed into the legendary sword of King Arthur.

♦ ♦ ♦

Sleep came eventually to Lucius as he lay on the precarious camp bed with its protesting springs. It wasn't possible to toss and turn on the untrustworthy camp bed throughout what remained of the night. Nevertheless, Lucius' fevered brain sorted, sifted, and battled to make sense of events which had taken place that night in Housesteads museum. Once or twice he awoke and checked his watch. Dawn was on its way, and with it a day which would be crammed with questions, but before that, the night had still some more questions for the approaching day.

♦ ♦ ♦

Lucius Verus was dreaming, and in his dream he was barefoot, walking on gravel. Around him, Vercovicium was going up in flames, wild Picts ran in every direction seeking out the last remnants of the loyal Roman soldiers. Among the Picts, were members of Vercovicium's garrison who had turned traitor, along with other treacherous troops along the Wall, joining the uprising along the length of the northern frontier. Lucius Verus could not get back to the latrine. His way was blocked by a gaggle of bloodthirsty

Picts gathered by the latrine door. In the confusion spreading through Vercovicium, Lucius was forced to make his way north along the main street running through the fort. But where were his Nike trainers? He couldn't recall taking them off and leaving them in the latrine when he first coughed his way asthmatically into 367 AD and the Great Barbarian Conspiracy. Barefoot, the crunching gravel pricking at the soles of his feet, Lucius stumbled towards the granary where this dream recalled him hiding from Roman and barbarian alike. Barefoot running on gravel, his 'ouches' and yelps were lost in the din of battle, war horns, the clash of weapons and burning buildings sweeping over Vercovicium. Gasping for breath and wincing at the torture inflicted on his bare feet, Lucius reached the granary perched on its stone pillars and chose the spot where he had previously hidden, in that other life.

From his hiding place under the granary, Lucius watched in horror as scenes straight from some blood and gore movie, played out before his terrified eyes. Pairs of legs from the knees down moved back and forward as the milling soldiers battled up and down the street. The metallic clatter of weapons and shields echoed back from the surrounding buildings. A helmet clattered to the ground and rolled in a crazy half circle, coming to rest a couple of feet away from where he lay. So close, he could have reached out and touched it. He noticed with horror a smear of blood on the inside. A pair of legs crumpled downwards, bringing with them the rest of a man. He crashed heavily to the ground, rolled over in the wet gravel, and came to rest staring blankly into Lucius' face for a moment before his eyes glazed over in death. Dark arterial blood oozed from a wide gash in his neck where his jugular had been slashed open. Lucius dug his fingers into the cold, wet gravel and closed his eyes. When he opened them seconds later, nothing had changed, the severed head wore a ghastly death grin. The Cosy Kettle seemed a lifetime away.

Lucius awoke to the racket of twanging springs as the camp bed complained about its occupant moving around and tugging at a sleeping bag zip which refused to cooperate. Lucius squirmed and adjusted himself and the bag. He opened his eyes wide, rubbed the gritty sleep from them and stared at the ceiling. It was morning. How long had he slept? He checked his watch. It was now 7.55am. Images and thoughts vied for his attention. A bloody severed head staring blankly at him in death as he lay hiding under the granary, a dream, just a dream. Shit! The museum would need to open for 9.00am. Excalibur! Had that been a dream too? Had he fallen asleep and dreamt crazy stuff about the museum, its exhibits, the information film? The struggle with his sleeping bag was matching the struggle with his thoughts. Sleeping bags do tend to mummify and trap you. Finally Lucius got a grip on the sleeping bag zip and tugged at it, too fiercely, as it caught on the nylon material inside the bag.

'Shit, bugger it!' Yanking the stubborn zip furiously to undo it wasn't working. Calm your nerves, steady yourself, his fevered brain told him. Lucius took a couple of deep breaths and coaxed the zip back up before coaxing it down again. The zip cooperated and slid easily to the bottom of the bag. Lucius kicked his feet free, swung his legs clear of the camp bed and sat up. As he placed his feet on the floor, he felt something underfoot, something gritty, much like the feel of tiny sharp stones. Reaching down, he brushed the sole of his right foot with his hand and pieces of gravel dropped to the floor. It was the same with the left foot. He had been walking on gravel and here was the evidence. Lucius sat motionless, recalling last night's events, whilst feeling the soles of his feet. Events, or dreams? Evidence said events rather than dreams. Lucius turned them over in his head as he stood and made his way over to Macro's gladius in its display case. A Roman gladius turned into the stuff of legend, the sword of King Arthur himself.

Only it wasn't the sword of King Arthur now. As Lucius peered into the glass display case, the sword hung suspended, partially rusted and with the traces of the original inscription, proudly proclaiming the owner and his rank within the VI Valeria Victrix Legion. A jaw wrenching yawn reminded Lucius of just how tired he was and another look at his watch told him time was moving on apace. The night before, he had taken the precaution of squirming into his sleeping bag fully clothed and now only had to pull on his pair of socks and his Nike trainers. The camp bed would need to be folded and stowed away in the small storeroom at the back of the museum, along with the sleeping bag. Next, he would need to sweep up the scatter of gravel on the floor next to his camp bed, gravel from fifteen centuries ago. He bent down and picked up a piece of gravel, so small it was hidden between the tip of his forefinger and his thumb. He dropped it into the palm of his hand and rolled it around with the tip of his finger and decided that gravel was timeless. After all, wasn't this piece of insignificant gravel the same as any piece of gravel lying on the ground outside the museum, indistinguishable the one from the other? Mountains, boulders, rocks, stones, pebbles, gravel, grit, sand and finally, dust. Time, the master of all. Lucius brushed the preposterous bit of gravel from his palm to join the scatter on the floor. His musings about time wouldn't get the museum ready and open to the public in, how long from now? He consulted his watch. It was now 8.15am.

Lucius brushed the soles of his feet once more just to make sure no irritating of gravel remained before pulling on his socks and trainers. As he tied the laces, he thought about those trainers from his teenage years, the Nike pair he owned as a youngster. He smiled to himself as he recalled the ridiculous journeys he and those trainers had made together. One of the camp bed springs produced a loud twang as he stood, and five minutes later with the sleeping bag and camp bed back in the cupboard, Lucius took another walk around the small museum, checking every display case, stone statue, altar and finally Centurion Macro's resting place. Everything was as it should be, no reborn artefacts, no garishly painted altars, or statuary, Macro's gladius suspended in its glass case unchanged. The bones of Macro lay as dead as the day they had been laid in his glass tomb by the conservationists at the National Museum of Scotland. The gravel at the skeleton's feet lay as smooth and undisturbed as it had before the strange events of last night. Macro's lifeless, empty eye sockets stared back at Lucius, his one-time student and comrade in arms. Lucius yawned, and Centurion Macro's dislocated jaw yawned back at him. Time for work…

XVIII

A Familiar Face

The wind was quickening as Lucius made his way up from the museum to the south gateway of Housesteads fort. After a gap of a few decades, the tricks of time, as Lucius called recent events, had returned. He had given up analysing and agonising over his journey into the past with Mr MacRonald, alias, Centurion Macro. It was better to stick with 'time' as a constant, a series of numbers; how old you were, how many years you spent at university, today's date and time, the present year, the here and now. But these 'constants' depended on where you were in the world, or what religion you followed. There were areas to ponder about the nature of time travel, but to what end? Archaeologists such as himself were the closest humans got to time travel in one sense.

The brisk wind was hurrying in the new day. It blew enthusiastically from the south west, a warm autumn wind bringing the promise of an Indian summer. The dig up at the 'Chi Rho' villa, as it was now called, might progress for a few more weeks, if the weather was kind, before the excavation was concluded and the site backfilled. The gusting breeze at his back buffeted him, urging him on his way up to the fort.

Ahead of him, a figure sat in the long grass on the slope leading up to the south gate. A woman, sitting with her knees drawn up under her chin, arms clasped around her legs, eyes closed, face upturned towards the morning sun. Lucius stopped for a moment and looked more closely. An early visitor to the fort and the museum, she looked familiar. Maybe a regular visitor whom he had encountered before but could not recall at this moment? Cropped short hair, wind swept and dishevelled, an appearance reminiscent of the punk era. Was she lost?

"Hello. Hi, can I help you? Is it the museum you want?"

The woman opened her eyes and turned her face towards him. As Lucius got nearer he noticed she was wearing a cloak of some sort. Probably one of those poncho style cloaks which were very much in fashion these days. Lucius halted a few steps away from the woman.

"Hi. I'm the museum curator. Can I help you at all?"

She looked straight through him, her face and not her voice said, 'I heard you.'

"Er, that's the museum, down there. Not too grand but, well we've got plenty to give you an idea of life on the Roman frontier here at Housesteads." Lucius turned to point down the slope towards the museum. When he turned back, the woman had vanished. The brisk wind had died away and now the grass rippled, stroked by a gentle breeze. A boisterous school party was making its way up to the south gateway, the pupils' excited voices punctuated by the strict tones of a teacher trying to establish a semblance of order before the serious studies began. Paper worksheets fluttered in the breeze against clipboards. The time-honoured and mundane process for the study of things and places historical. A sharp contrast with the cries and shouts of a Roman auxiliary unit stamping its brutal iron fisted oppression on the peoples of the Caledonian wilderness. No neighing and whinnying of horses, jingle of harness, no shouted commands, or the clatter of weapons training, just the murmur of the gentle breeze, the retreating voices of the school party and the harsh, grating cries of a raven on the wing.

Lucius took a look around. Where was she, the woman sitting here just a minute ago? He shrugged his shoulders against the strange events of last night and this morning. These things happened, had happened in the world of Lucius Mabbutt; perhaps nothing stranger than the idea that the fabled sword of King Arthur hung on display in the museum behind him. Excalibur, suspended in a case of armoured glass, next to the remains of Centurion Macro Cornelius Varus, Primus Pilus of Rome's VI Valeria Victrix Legion, Father to the brotherhood of Mithras. Overhead, a raven called, like a lost soul from the past. Lucius heard it and knew, Raven to raven.

♦ ♦ ♦

The next night was uneventful. Apart from the discomfort of sleeping on the fragile camp bed, nothing else happened. Lucius' watch displayed the correct time the two occasions when he checked it. The TV remained silent, no dust descended, no gravel moved inside Macro's glass case and no gravel was stuck to the soles of Lucius' feet when dawn broke.

Lucius was up, dressed, and ready in time for the opening of the museum. The coffee in his thermos flask was still hot and he sipped at it while he ordered his thoughts for the day. The comforting sips of coffee eased an irritating cough which had decided to plague his waking hours. A quick check around the museum showed everything to be ship shape and ready for the visitors who would descend on Housesteads today.

Today was an unusual day. One of those days which just feels different. The sky was certainly that, different. It was a bruised, violet colour and cloudless. An oversized full moon hung pale above the horizon to the west. A very 'otherworldly' feel to it, the type of firmament best suited to a sci-fi tale. In the distance, down at the visitors' centre, Lucius noted a lack of cars, apart from a solitary vehicle in a sea of empty parking spaces. Well, it was autumn now and in Lucius' experience, the throng of visitors in the summer months usually slowed to a trickle by this time of year. Lucius looked at the sky again. Not a trace of cloud, just that strange ethereal violet tinge to the heavens with its pale moon. Here, the sky, whatever her mood, always dwarfed even the vastness of the Caledonian landscape, made small and insignificant the activities of humans carving out a succession of empires, cultures, religions and ways of life over the millennia, with their roads, temples, forts, cities, sacred groves, fields, towns, and cities. Dust and ashes. As was its custom here on Hadrian's Wall, the wind was gusting, as if it were trying to make a point, reminding mere mortals of the power of nature, the ebb and flow of life. That statement of power was evidenced in the timeless battle between the wind and the trees. Here, on the Wall, trees struggled against the prevailing wind. Maturing saplings would grow so high and then bend to wind's will, giving them the appearance of stunted old crones, bent double under the relentless gales. Today's gusting wind played havoc with the trees. One minute a soft breeze would offer respite and the bending trees could relax. The next second a ferocious gust would test tree roots clinging to the shallow soil. Today's wind was busy stripping the autumn leaves and bending the stooped trees over further. Lucius rubbed his hands together against the slight chill and decided to go back to the comfort of the museum. He could not afford to leave it unattended for any length of time today. The two members of staff normally running the museum had failed to show up today and hadn't contacted Lucius to say why they wouldn't be at work. Unusual for those two normally reliable members of staff. It would be a single-handed job for him today, but at least it was not too busy, given the lack of visitors. As he made his way back to the museum, Lucius sniffed at the air. A strange day so far made all the stranger by that frequent visitor, smell of burning pine cones and the sight of an eagle perched imperiously on the museum roof. Cocking its hook beaked head on one side, Hispana kept an unblinking predatory eye on Lucius as he made his way in through the museum door.

Closing the door behind him, Lucius was taken aback by the woman browsing the small selection of gifts, replica, and such like on display by the till. She had to be the owner of the solitary vehicle in the car park. It was certainly a lean day for visitors.

"Good morning. Welcome to Housesteads Roman fort museum. May I be of assistance?"

The woman was peering at the replica Roman earrings hanging from the display stand on the reception desk. She turned the price label around and took a closer look. She spoke without looking up at Lucius.

"Thirteen pounds ninety-nine pence! Is that all?" She turned her face towards Lucius. "They are beautiful. You wouldn't be able to tell them apart from the originals."

"Sorry?"

The visitor took in the curator's name badge on his lanyard. "I was just saying that these replicas in museums and historic places of interest, have come a long way in recent years, Lucius. Sorry, may I call you Lucius, mister," she took in his second name on the badge, "mister Mabutt?"

"No, Lucius is fine…er..?" He knew this face, shoulder length auburn hair, emerald, green eyes.

She reached out a hand in greeting. "Thank you, I'm Julia. Pleased to meet you." She turned to look around the museum. "Not terribly busy today, I see. Looks like I've got the entire site to myself." She laughed, and Lucius' deep memory continued to stir. With a toss of her auburn locks, Julia turned back to the replica earrings, removing them from the display stand.

"They are perfect. Look at these beauties!" Pinned against the white card were a pair of pendant earrings, the fake emerald gemstones hanging from deep red gold hooks.

"May I?" A well-manicured slender fingertip pointed at the earrings.

Lucius waved a casual hand. "Of course, be my guest."

The woman teased one of the earrings from its card backing and held it up to her right ear lobe. The well-manicured fingertip curled a wisp of stray hair back behind her ear.

"What do you think, Lucius?"

This was becoming one of the strangest conversations he had ever had in his entire life, and he had been involved in some very strange conversations in his time. A stranger, and yet he slipped with ease into this conversation about the merits of a pair of cheap, replica earrings. He studied his visitor. Her auburn hair and those emerald, green eyes, something… Lucius swallowed hard. "I think they will really suit you…Julia." He fixed her gaze with his own, trying to look deep into her mind, her soul, her past. What could he say? He could greet her again and this time tell her that they had met before, here in different time and a vastly different world. Her green eyes smiled. Was it in recognition?

"Shall I tell you why these earrings are of such interest to me, Lucius?" He nodded, yes he would like to know. "I lost an earring exactly like this, some years ago now." She held her hand up, the earring caught the light as it dangled between her thumb and forefinger. It swung imperceptibly, the tiny movements seeming to give it life. "I lost one of these earrings out there, somewhere in the fort, outside the commander's house. I was distraught. We, that is my mother and I, searched in vain for days, weeks even. All I can recall is that I must have been so young. And yet, strangely, the earrings were a gift for my fourteenth birthday, so how can I not remember that? I was fourteen years old, hardly a baby, a toddler. I can't recollect anything else about the story of the lost earring. For all I know, it might even have been in another life." She laughed at her own suggestion.

"I think that all of us at some time or another have that feeling of having lived another life," Lucius ventured. "So, these cheap replicas…"

"Exactly. Cheap and tacky they may be but, well, I can't believe my luck. I'll take these, please. May I pay by card?"

He nodded and reached for the card machine. And next? She would pay, he would pop the earrings into a paper bag along with the receipt, they would exchange parting pleasantries and Julia would walk out of the museum and out of his life…again. Before he could speak, although he didn't have the vaguest idea of what he would say, Julia tapped the contactless pad and waited for approval from the bank and they both stared at the circling circle of financial fate. To pay, or not to pay, that is the question.

"You know, I have a distinct memory, despite what I said earlier, a distinct memory of the jeweller telling my mother that the earrings had come from somewhere exotic, perhaps Egypt or even India. God knows what they cost. A darn sight more than these." She laughed.

Bank approval given, the circle complete on the card reader with a fat tick at its centre, Julia picked up the small paper bag and turned to make her way out of the museum. Lucius found himself speaking, the question formed itself without his conscious thought, or so it seemed.

"Are you alone today? I mean, did you come here by yourself?" Stupid question, he was gabbling. Julia's hand rested on the museum door handle. She turned.

"No, no I didn't. Actually my son is up at the fort, exploring the ruins. He has an insatiable appetite for history, Roman history in particular. More of a craving, an addiction even. And he tells me he is currently studying Roman Britain at school, for his GCSE History. Year ten. Project time, writing in role, you know the type of thing." Lucius nodded, yes, he knew the type of thing. "They grow so fast these days." She paused, her words hanging in the air for a few beats while the pair of them looked at each other.

"I don't suppose, I mean it's a bit of an imposition, but could you spare a few moments…?"

"Well, I am not exactly rushed off my feet." Lucius smiled at Julia. "Of course I will have a word with your son. Writing in role, eh? Something we all had to do as students at some point in our history lessons." He smiled at the fond memory of Mr MacRonald's' voice. Lucius reached into a drawer behind the shop counter and took out a bunch of keys.

"Please, after you, Julia."

"That's so kind of you, Lucius. My son will be thrilled. Thank you for your time."

With the museum door locked behind them, Lucius and Julia made their way up to the south gate of Housesteads fort, whilst behind them, Hispana looked on impassively from her perch on the museum roof.

♦ ♦ ♦

"He's up here, probably at the latrine," Julia laughed as she and Lucius made their way towards the remains of south gateway. "You know what boys are. Toilets and toilet humour. Do you have any children, Lucius?"

"Nope. Never married, never felt the need to settle down and have kids, a family."

Julia paused for breath as they walked through what had once been the enormous and imposing structure of the south gateway leading into Vercovicium. Countless thousands of souls had passed this way, from wide eyed nervous recruits joining the First Tungrian Cohort, through farmers, traders, imperial emissaries, barbarian raiders, explorers, archaeologists, and sightseers. Souls without number, including these two souls.

"I guess you're wedded to your work, Lucius. Must be a fascinating job, time consuming I would imagine."

"I moved professions, from archaeologist to museum curator. And yes, I love my work."

Julia was right. Like countless generations of visitors to Housesteads fort, especially young boys, Julia's son was exploring the delights of the latrine block at the far southeast corner of the fort.

"What's your son's name?" Lucius asked as they made their way between the timeless, dumb grey stones whispering tales from the past to those who would listen.

"He's called Drew. We named him after my husband but shortened the name. My husband, God rest him, was called Drusus. My son and I were visiting relatives up in York." Julia stopped for a second and took Lucius' arm. "Listen to me, what am I saying? You, curator, and archaeologist, why you'd call it Eboracum, I don't doubt," she said solemnly with a hint of a smile creasing the corners of her mouth as she resumed her story. She released his arm and they continued walking.

"So, as I was saying, we were visiting York for a family reunion to remember my mother. Dementia took her from us, that, and a serious lung disease, complicated by Covid. Her lungs, her breathing just, well, just gave up. She passed away in York. My mother had lost the will to live. I don't think she ever recovered from my father's death that same year."

Lucius smiled to himself in sympathy as he recalled his own mother's premature death at the hands of Covid; Covid 19, to give it its full name. The passing of time marked as ever with numbers. It's what humans do.

"Being in York, so close to Hadrian's Wall, we took the opportunity to travel up here to the Wall. Drew has never been, so.."

"But you, have, before today, I mean. Apart from the time you lost your earring, that is?"

"I've been here many times before, but not with Drew. I've certainly popped up here from York. One time I recall, I was in such a hurry, some kind of emergency. I don't know. But it's all something I feel rather than know."

"And your husband was named Drusus? That's a thoroughly Roman name."

Julia laughed. "Unlike our names, Julia and Lucius, Roman names but they sit a little easier than, Droosoos." Julia laughed at her exaggeration of the name Drusus, the face she pulled reminding Lucius of a gawping fish.

Looking ahead they could see the figure of a young lad appearing and disappearing as he clambered over the low walls one moment only to vanish behind taller remains the next.

"I take it that's him, your boy, Drew?"

"Yes, it is. He's enjoying himself, clearly."

"Most kids like the latrine block. Particularly the boys, most adults do too, I guess. I used to look forward to exploring this section of the fort when I visited here as a youngster."

Drew spotted his mother as she and Lucius approached the latrine. He waved and perched himself on a convenient block of unfinished builders' stone near the latrine entrance. Lucius had few flashbacks these days but this proved to be one of them. The block of unfinished builders' stone was that same one on which he had laid out the school worksheets and aerial photos of Housesteads to show Julia, that first time…

"It's not just a block of stone, is it, Lucius?" Julia's voice was soft but insistent. She knew too. He threw her a glance.

"Watcha, mum!" Drew waved a greeting but remained seated on the block of stone, for all the world like an Emperor observing the approach of his subjects.

"Hi, Drew. I hope you've had an enjoyable time, son. Quite some place, isn't it?" Julia swept an arm around behind her to indicate the whole of the fort and turned to Lucius. "This here is Mr Mabbutt, the curator of the museum."

"Nice to meet you, Drew. Please call me Lucius."

Drew frowned and gave Lucius a dark look. From his imperial seat he looked Lucius up and down, no welcome smile replacing the frown. He focussed on Lucius' trainers. "I don't like your trainers. In particular I don't like Nike trainers. Never have, never will."

Julia laughed. "Drew, manners please. Apologies, Lucius. That's his father speaking. Drusus never liked trainers. Had a thing about them. God knows why."

Lucius smiled. "Your mother tells me you're studying for GCSE History, Roman Britain?"

Drew looked up from Lucius' trainers and nodded.

"Well, you've come to the right place. Hadrian's Wall, and here at Vercovicium, you'll be able to find out plenty about Roman Britain. Shall we go down to the museum?"

Drew slid down from the stone block and joined his mother and Lucius as they retraced their steps back down to the museum. Drew eased up on the cool teenager act and decided that this Lucius guy, the museum curator, might just be of help for his GCSE Roman Britain topic.

"Who was Mithras then? Who built Hadrian's Wall? What was life like for the soldiers and where did they come from? What was the Great Barbarian Conspiracy?" A hurried list of quick-fire questions.

As they walked, Lucius dealt with each question in turn and felt a little touch of warmth creep into his growing conversation with Drew. Julia smiled at them both as Lucius painted an all too life like picture in answer to Drew's last question about the Great Barbarian Conspiracy of AD 367. They were at the museum door which Lucius unlocked and held open for his guests to enter. Overhead, the sky had not changed from its unearthly violet hue but the swollen moon had faded away. A glance down to the car park told him that Julia and Drew would most likely remain the only visitors today. He let the door close behind him.

"Wow! Mum, have you seen this? It's awesome." Drew stood over Centurion Macro's glass display case. Julia and Lucius joined Drew.

"A Roman centurion, complete with armour a helmet and in this case, his sword. This guy died nearly two thousand years ago. How did they find his body? Was it buried here, at Housesteads? It's kinda creepy but amazing too."

Drew turned to his mother and Lucius. "Makes you wonder what he was like, how he lived and how he died." He turned to the gladius in its case. "Love that sword." Drew made a couple of imaginary sword wielding passes followed by a final stab.

"Imagine if we could go back in time. It would be incredible to meet people from the past like this centurion." With that, Drew moved away to continue his exploration of the museum. The silence was punctuated every now and then by a gasp or a 'wow' as Drew marvelled at the displays on view.

"I'm also up here for another reason." Julia spoke whilst looking to keep track of Drew appearing and disappearing between the museum cabinets and display cases. "I think it was the recent discovery of that Roman villa beyond the frontier which clinched it for me. The so-called Christian villa with the Chi Rho mosaic. You must know the one I mean, Lucius." He nodded. "Well, ever since my husband died, I've had the urge to up sticks from my current home. To move up here to Northumberland in fact. You know, something has always tugged at me to settle in this part of the world."

"Go on."

"Can we go outside? Will it be ok to leave Drew here for..?"

"No problem." Lucius opened the museum door and they both stepped outside into bright sunshine, a clear blue sky. Julia pointed south, beyond the distant car park where her car sat alone.

"I've been thinking, doing a bit of research. There's a property not far from here. Down there, about a mile or so away." She nodded towards the land south of the Wall. "It's currently a vacant possession in need of a great deal of renovation after a fire and years of neglect. I've got money to invest since Drusus passed. The property is in right state though." She laughed. "Overgrown with weeds, complete with an old, abandoned car rusting away on the driveway, a Ford or whatever. The estate agent told me the place was once called the Cosy Kettle, a former guesthouse. I think it could be a guesthouse, a bed and breakfast, again, bit of a business venture. I've put a holding deposit down on it. What do think, Lucius? Fancy taking a look at the Cosy Kettle with me?"

♦ ♦ ♦

Epilogue

Julia apologised to Lucius with a smile as she leant across him and popped open the glove box in her car. She dropped the paper bag containing her new replica emerald earrings into the crowded mess of sweet wrappers, glasses cases, an assortment of dusters and windscreen wipes and snapped the lid shut. She adjusted the interior mirror, making sure to take a quick make up check, and turned on the ignition. A series of dashboard lights glowed briefly before she turned the key another notch and brought the engine to life. Drew was busy protesting from the rear seat he had been relegated to in order for Lucius to sit in the front.

"It's not fair," came the time worn teenage protest from the back seat.

His mother offered the time-honoured parental retort. "Who said anything about life being fair?"

Julia glanced both ways as she pulled away from the parking bay and headed for the car park exit. Cocooned as the three of them were in the comfort of Julia's car, they didn't feel the sudden bite of an icy blast bringing the threat of a hailstorm. It was only the sudden misting of the car windows which told of the change in temperature in the outside world. They were about to turn left onto the B6318 when a car coming from their right, indicated to turn into the car park. Close enough now for Julia and Lucius to see the face of the driver, both of them spoke in the same instant, their voices drowned as the dark heavens erupted and a thunderous onslaught of hailstones rattled across the car roof and bounced off the bonnet onto the road which swiftly turned from black tarmac to a slushy stream of melting hailstones. In the grey of the sudden storm surrounding the two vehicles as they passed each other, Julia broke the deadlock.

"Did you see that face, Lucius?" Thunder cracked and hail rattled furiously as if wanting to break into the car. The tick, tick of the car indicator struggled to be heard above the din of hailstones hammering on the car roof.

"What's going on?" Drew piped up, "and where the hell did that lot come from?" He wiped his hand across the misted side window to peer out.

Lucius nodded an acknowledgement to Julia's question. What they had both seen at the wheel of the other car was a red bearded man, his face a mass of swirling blue tattoos, his ice grey eyes as cold as the hailstones beating down. It was a face Julia knew, and Lucius had glimpsed in another life. They stared at each other, the moment broken as Julia slammed her car into first gear, swung left out onto the main road soon reaching a speed which had Lucius reaching for the grab handle above the door.

"Julia, slow down, we need to stop, please. We have to turn around and get back to the car park. I didn't like the look of that guy. Something…I don't know.." A life and death struggle to save a Roman girl called Julia.

Julia's face was grim, her hands gripping the steering wheel. She shook her head and spoke without taking her eyes off the road. "Go back? I don't think so, Lucius. Do you know who that was.? No, you wouldn't. But I for one am not going to fall into his hands again, ever."

The wipers swished furiously as they battled to clear the icy film from the windscreen. Out of reach of their efforts, the ice from the hail was drifting along the lower edge of the windscreen and into the corners where the wipers ended their sweep. Lucius' heart matched the frantic rhythm of the wipers.

Behind them, Housesteads, perched on the edge of the beetling escarpment of Whin Sill Crags, was covered in an icy blanket of hailstones. The empty fort sitting in the empty landscape shivered, as it had done for fifteen centuries; shivered sometimes, scorched at others. The heavy hand of those centuries had levelled the fort to its foundations but Housesteads had survived its journey through time, despite the best efforts of man and nature to destroy it. It was living stone.

As Julia and Lucius continued to speed off in the direction of the Cosy Kettle, the red bearded man pulled up in the empty car park. His pale grey eyes peered through the subsiding hailstorm up to where Housesteads fort stood. Perfect cover for what he had in mind. He smiled at his careful preparation and at the cover offered by the storm, and as he smiled, the swirling tattoos distorted across his face and around his pale grey eyes. In his car boot was all the necessary equipment to deal with the security of Housesteads museum and its armoured glass case containing the legendary sword Excalibur. Once free, the sword could be returned to the land of the Picts, the land we call Caledonia.

The End

A Final Word

I thoroughly enjoyed writing this trilogy, 'Ghosts and Eagles.' It was never intended as any kind of history lesson, even less so, an in-depth informative study of Hadrian's Wall. There is much I have changed or adapted to facilitate the narrative of this historical fantasy. Some parts are historically correct, but in other parts I have followed the author's necessity to change, adapt, shorten, or extend time and reader credulity in order to make the story work, poetic licence is a fiction writer's gift. I had two motives in writing this trilogy. I wanted to fill a perceived gap in the market for Young Adult historical fantasy, a gap left by the likes of Rosemary Sutcliff and Henry Treece, simply good old-fashioned characters in a fairly traditional story with no messages or political agenda. A bit o' fun. My four decades as an English teacher taught me that most of my pupils preferred classic tales told in a traditional way, and I hope I have achieved that aim in this trilogy.

I enjoyed my journey writing this trilogy and I hope you, the reader, enjoyed travelling with me. Please remember to leave a review, I'd love to know what you thought of my efforts.

'Time' to go now.

♦ ♦ ♦

Printed in Great Britain
by Amazon